RUN YOU DOWN

Julia Dahl

First published in the UK in 2019
by Faber & Faber Limited
Bloomsbury House,
74–77 Great Russell Street,
London WC1B 3DA

First published in the United States in 2015
by Minotaur Books
an imprint of Macmillan
St Martin's Press
175 Fifth Avenue
New York NY 10010

Printed and bound by CPI Group (UK) Ltd, Croydon CR0 4YY

A CIP record for this book
is available from the British Library

ISBN 978–0–571–34778–0

10 9 8 7 6 5 4 3 2 1

This book is dedicated to my husband, Joel Bukiewicz
— the bravest man I know.

PART 1

CHAPTER ONE

AVIVA

Florida was not as I imagined. There was no ocean where your father lived, that was the first thing. This had not occurred to me; in Florida but no beach for fifty miles? Brian pointed out the swimming pools, and yes, they seemed to be everywhere. It's so much better than the beach, he said. The water is clean and you don't get sand all over. Your father was very good at a sport called water polo, which was why he looked the way he did. Wide, smooth chest, strong shoulders, bronzed skin, and blond-tipped hair. He was the most beautiful thing I had ever seen. All he did was smile. I had never seen a man's body until the afternoon your father took his shirt off and we jumped into the fountain in Washington Square Park. The men and boys in Borough Park were always covered in black clothing. They were skinny or fat and had bad posture, arms too long for their bodies. Untrimmed fingernails, bony wrists, and stiff little hairs growing out of their faces. They were always so serious—at least around me—and they seemed so frightened of the world outside Brooklyn.

Your father was not frightened of the world. Brian came to New York City to participate in a summer exchange program at NYU. He was taking a class called The Bible as Literature, and as part of the program he worked at a YMCA in the Village. He taught swimming and was horrified when he learned I couldn't swim. You have to learn! he said, as serious as I had ever seen him. But I avoided it. I tried to explain, when he told me the pool was better than the ocean, that going to the ocean wasn't about going in the water, it was about witnessing the water. The waves that never stop coming. The wind and the sand and the salt in the air that leaves your skin stiff and your hair in knots. I loved the long showers I took after going to the beach. I loved that I had to wash it off. But the first time I took your father to Coney Island, he remarked about the garbage. What could I say? He did not see it as I did. He wanted to. He said, Aviva, tell me what it means to you. But how could I? There were no words I could think of to make him see.

To get to Florida, we took the bus from Port Authority. Brian bought me a duffel bag at the NYU student store, but I brought almost nothing with me. Just some cheap new clothes that showed my body, and a photograph of me and your namesake, my sister Rivka, the summer before she died. The ride south was thirty-two hours of sticky floors and sneezing strangers and body odor and anticipation. At a truck stop in Virginia there was food on a conveyor belt. Heaping meals of greasy brown and yellow and white that glowed beneath heat lamps. In North Carolina we put quarters into televisions attached to hard plastic chairs and watched a game show while we waited for a transfer. There was vomit in the sink of the rest stop in Georgia. Bloody menstrual pads overflowing the courtesy bins in the bathroom stalls. Door latches broken, coffee burnt, half-dressed women, dead-eyed men, inconsolable children, and everywhere fluorescent bulbs blinking and buzzing overhead. It was all ugliness and sorrow—exactly as I'd been warned the goyish world would be. I touched as little as I could manage and ate almost nothing.

On the way, Brian and I talked about what I would "do" in Florida. You can totally find a job, he said. At the mall. Or TCBY—whatever that was. I nodded because I didn't care. I just wanted out of Brooklyn. And your father, well, he wanted me.

It was raining when we finally arrived in Orlando. Your father's roommate, I don't remember his name, picked us up at the bus station and brought us to Brian's room at the university. We climbed together onto the top bunk of his bed and slept for almost an entire day.

Your father was wonderful, of course. Supportive and loving even as it all fell apart. He used to say I deserved a little rebellion—a little bad behavior. He said it was good for me after almost twenty years with no choices. You have to learn what you like, he said. You have to learn what makes you happy. Rum and Coke made me happy.

My bare legs exposed to the world made me happy. Rock music turned up loud so I could sing along and not even hear my voice made me happy. Eyeliner made me happy. And red nail polish. And smoking pot. I called it "doing pot" then, which made your father laugh. Let's do some pot, Brian, I'd say. Let's do some pot and fuck. "Fuck" was a word I learned from a girl at the Coney Island house who'd fled a *shidduch* and had a job selling sex toys at a store on West Fourth Street in Manhattan. She was the one who told me to go to the Strand and buy a book called *Our Bodies, Ourselves* to learn all the things about my body that I didn't know—and there was a lot. Your father didn't like it when I said fuck. He said making love. But that didn't sound right to me. Frum girls learn about sex in secret. In shards of stories that don't fit together into anything that involves love. We're not supposed to know about sex until we get engaged, and then they send us to a class before the wedding where an old woman tells us how to make a baby.

Brian and I lived in his dorm room. No one could tell by looking that I wasn't a student, and it was the beginning of the school year so people seemed to expect new faces. While he went to classes, I slept late and walked around the campus. Some frum girls go to college, but they live at home until they marry. Even in July, we wear long sleeves and stockings. Everything from our neck to our toes is covered all the time. The boys call it body armor. But the girls in Florida wore bikini tops to class. They drove little cars with figurines and photographs and beads hanging from the rearview mirrors. They drove with ease. Careless, with bare feet, applying lip gloss at stoplights. Their arms out the window, fingers flicking cigarettes, hands tapping the side of the car to the beat of the music that was always playing. That's Madonna, your father would tell me. Or the Eagles. Or Bon Jovi. The names meant nothing to me, but the music, and everything else about the girls, made me want to jump in their windows—made me want to jump in their skin. I studied how they dressed and did my best to imitate it. I loved the feeling of the sun on my arms. The sensation of breeze between my legs beneath a short skirt. I wore very little. Why not? And the *boys*. Tan and smiling all the time. Tall, with smooth shaved faces, bare necks, and hairstyles nearly as diverse as the girls: bleached blond spikes and wild black waves, bangs falling in their eyes so they had to brush them aside with a jerk of the head. Their hair told me a story about who they were. If you were lucky enough to live in a world where you could use your body as an expression of yourself, wouldn't you? I had the idea that I could tell what they were like inside by the way they appeared: that one must be goofy, that one timid, that one angry. They noticed me when I walked alone, and after just a few days I stopped looking away when they stared. I imagined that because so many of them looked athletic and cheerful like Brian that they were like Brian. I was wrong.

At the end of September, a boy started talking to me

while I was drinking a Coke outside the gym. Girls played tennis there, and I liked to watch them. In Borough Park, girls are taught that physical maturity is a provocation. As we grow, we grow ashamed of our bodies. We dislike the parts of ourselves that make us different from the boys. We hide those parts as best we can. Not these girls. They were so confident, so wild and at ease inside their bodies—throwing themselves after the ball, slapping each other's hands, shrieking and laughing, always laughing.

"Do you play?" asked the boy. He was wearing a tank top and holding the strap of his backpack so I could see the wisps of light brown hair peeking from beneath his armpit.

"Me?" I asked. I shook my head.

"I'm Chris," he said.

"I'm Aviva," I said.

"Aviva," he said. "That's pretty." He had perfect white teeth and blond hair that was longer in the front than in the back. He almost glowed in the sunlight. "Is this your first year?"

I nodded.

"I'm a junior," he said, sitting down on the bench next to me. "It's a pretty cool place. What hall do you live in?"

I didn't remember the name. In fact, I hadn't been entirely clear there was an official name for the building where your father had a room. So I told the truth.

"I do not go to school here. I am just staying for a while with my boyfriend."

"Your boyfriend," he said, drawing out the word. "And where is he now?"

"In class," I said.

"He just leaves you alone all day?" He leaned toward me and I caught a faint whiff of his sweat. But it didn't make me want to lean back—it made me want to lean closer. "If I were your boyfriend I wouldn't leave you alone for other guys to come hit on."

"If you were my boyfriend?" I said, dumbly. He was so forward. I remember I was shocked, although I hated myself for it. It was very important to me that other people saw me as brave. I'd escaped Brooklyn, hadn't I? But bravery is no substitute for experience, and at that point I could count on two hands the conversations I'd had with boys I wasn't related to. Your father and I started talking because we were both in the religion aisle of the bookstore. We had probably been standing within five feet of each other for half an hour before he said hello. Navigating a conversation with a boy like this, a boy who was flirting with me for no other reason than that he liked the way I looked—that was advanced non-frum behavior. And back then I was only a beginner.

"I'm just saying," he said, knocking his shoulder into mine. It was sweaty hot and our skin stuck together for an instant. His eyes were a kind of golden green, and he focused on nothing but me. I could kiss him and Brian would never know.

"Where are you from?" he asked.

I blushed. He knows, I thought. Next he'll say, You're one of *those* girls, and walk away laughing. Now I know that he could no sooner have imagined the world I came from than he could have imagined life on the moon.

"I'm from New York," I said.

"Your accent is sexy."

Your father was the first person to tell me I spoke English with an accent. My first language was Yiddish; we spoke Yiddish at home and Yiddish in school. According to your father, my voice was also lower than most girls. Just like this boy in the tank top, he'd called it sexy.

"You should come to El Cinco tonight," said Chris. "It's two-for-one margaritas."

"Okay." I didn't know what a margarita was.

"Bring your boyfriend," he said, standing up, grinning. Grinning the whole time. "Or maybe don't."

I told your father I met someone near the tennis courts who said there was a good time at El Cinco tonight.

"See? You're already making friends," he said. "I knew people would love you as soon as they got to know you."

He told some of his friends to meet us at the restaurant, and we all sat around a table with margaritas coming and going and chips and salsa for free. The music was loud and everyone had to scream over it. People were dancing by the bar and after two margaritas—they tasted like Slurpees from the 7-Eleven—I got up and said I wanted to dance. Your father held my waist as we walked through the crowd. We danced and I drank another margarita. I waved my arms in the air and felt my shirt lift up, exposing the skin of my belly. I twisted my hips and kissed your father, right there in front of everyone. He pulled me close and whispered in my ear that he loved me. I love you, Aviva, he said. I love you, too, I said.

I had to go to the bathroom, but there was a line. I stood for a minute and as soon as I stopped moving, I knew I'd had too much to drink. I closed my eyes and felt sick to my stomach, so I slid down the wall and sat on the floor. The girls around me didn't say a word. I put my head between my legs. Everything was spinning and lopsided. And then a hand grabbed mine.

"Aviva!" It was Chris. He pulled me up. "Uh-oh, too many margaritas! Where's your boyfriend? Come on, come here, you just need some water." He pulled me into the men's bathroom, which had no line. I went straight to the toilet, and up came the lime-flavored drinks and salsa chunks. I threw up twice. Chris held my hair. When I was done he gave me a wet paper towel to wipe my mouth.

"Feel better?" he asked. I nodded, but I didn't really feel better. Where was Brian? Chris reached for my hands and pulled me up and close to him, locking an arm around my waist. He kissed my neck, and in one motion slid the strap of my bra and tank top down my shoulder, letting my left breast fall out. He grabbed it and squeezed my nipple. I tried to squirm out of his arm but he held me tight.

"No," I said.

"No?" he said, grinning, his cold hand kneading my breast like dough, pulling at it. He pushed me against the wall and put his mouth on mine, shoving his tongue between my lips. I twisted my head sideways and he moved his lips to my neck. "What's the matter?" he said. And then he grabbed my hair and turned me around so my face was pressed against the greasy tile wall. I teetered on my high-heeled shoes and he righted me. He pressed one hand against the back of my head, and with the other he pulled my waist toward him and put his hand under my skirt, his clumsy fingers pushed aside my underwear, which, like everything else I was wearing that night, was new, still a kind of costume. Six months before I wore underwear my mother bought me. Big, thick "full-coverage" cotton underwear with tight elastic hugging the tops of my thighs and a waist at my belly button. I thought: If I was wearing my old underwear it would be harder for him to get in. I thought: I've brought this on myself. He shoved his hand up. I felt his fingernails scratch me and that's when I thought of you. It was the moment I admitted you were inside me. I had allowed myself to ignore the fact that I hadn't had my period in two months, but I could not let this boy hurt you. He took his hand off my head to open his pants and I struck him in the face with my elbow. He stopped smiling and stumbled backward and I ran to the door. It was a little latch lock, a flimsy nothing. Why didn't Brian break in? I got it open with shaking fingers and burst into the hallway.

One of the girls was still in line for the bathroom. We looked at each other and she pointed to my chest.

"Pull your shirt up," she said.

I ran through the loud music to the front door and out of the bar. People were drinking beer from cans and smoking cigarettes on the patio. A different song was playing over speakers hidden in palm trees above our heads. I found a chair and sat down but stood back up immediately because it hurt to sit. I wondered if I was bleeding. I didn't know how to get back to Brian's room, but I couldn't go back inside to bring him out to me. I was scared Chris would see me, and I was scared to try to walk home alone, and I was scared that if I told Brian what happened he would blame me. I stood on the patio shivering in the heat for a long time. People just moved around me. Finally, your father came outside.

"Aviva, are you okay? What happened?" He reached up to smooth my hair and I flinched.

"I got sick," I said. "I fell. Can we go home now?"

"Of course," he said.

When we got back to his room I climbed into bed in my clothes. I slept until noon the next day and woke to find Brian studying at his desk. He asked how I was feeling and I told him I was going to have a baby. When he asked me to marry him an hour later, I said yes.

CHAPTER TWO

REBEKAH

Every night I go to bed telling myself that I will call her tomorrow. And every morning I wake up knowing that I won't. It's been almost two months and I can still hear the gunshot in my ear. The doctor said the ringing would go away, but apparently not yet. I went back to the *Trib* two weeks after I came home from the hospital. My job is different, though, at least for now; instead of rushing from scene to scene, I'm in the office for the late rewrite shift. It's supposed to be a step up because it means the editors think that in addition to being able to gather information, I can figure out what information is important enough to include in the article, and actually write the article myself. I come in at 2:00 P.M. and stay until 10:00 P.M. I sit at an old computer in one of several semicircles of old computers that make up the newsroom. Stringers, my former compatriots, call in their notes about dead bicyclists and celebrity nightclub shenanigans and corrupt hospital CEOs and police shootings, and I turn them into column inches. I also "rewrite" stories from other, often dubious, news sources. The British tabloids are the worst. They're almost never right in the end, but we always print their stuff anyway—with "allegedly" and "reportedly" sprinkled throughout.

When I'm not at work, I sleep. Tony, the guy I was dating for a couple months, is out of the picture. I didn't exactly mean to stop returning his texts, but I never really want to go out—or have anyone come visit—so it felt pointless to keep things going. He came over one last time at the end of February and said he really liked me but that it was clear I wasn't ready to be involved in something. He was right.

In early March, my roommate Iris starts bugging me to go to the psychiatrists-in-training at Columbia.

"They charge on a sliding scale," she tells me, looking all interested. We're sitting on the couch—which is basically the only place I see her anymore. It's Saturday evening and we've been arguing because she's meeting some people we know for margaritas and Mexican food, but I'm not going.

"It'll be like fifty bucks," she says. "I'll pay half."

"You're not paying for my shrink," I say.

"I'll pay for your margaritas if you come tonight."

"I don't feel like it, okay?"

Iris closes her laptop and gets up.

"You know you're not acting right," she says.

She says that a lot these days.

The next week, Iris makes me an appointment and I agree by not canceling it. She takes a morning off work and we ride the A train to 168th Street together. The magazines in the waiting room are several weeks old, which, for some reason, pisses me off.

"I can't believe I let you drag me here," I say.

Iris rolls her eyes. "Don't be a bitch about this, please? Living with you has gotten *hard*. It's obvious you're depressed. Just face it, please, and let's move on."

"I don't have depression, Iris, I have anxiety."

"Well, I've done the online tests and you are *definitely* depressed. I checked every box. Lack of energy, lack of interest in things that you once enjoyed, excessive sleeping, irritability. Come on. You weren't like this last year. You gotta get your shit together."

A woman calls my name before I can retort. Not that I had a retort. Even sighing seems like a lot of effort. I stand up and approach the woman, who looks just a few years older than me.

"I'm Anna," she says. I shake her hand. "It's nice to meet you. Follow me?"

We walk down a wide hallway and into a tiny room with two chairs and a small table with a lamp, a clock, and a box of Kleenex on it. There's a framed poster of a field of flowers on the wall. She sits and I sit across from her.

"What can I help you with?" she asks.

I run my hand over my head. It's become a tic. Touching the soft, sharp fuzz where my long hair used to be grounds me in what happened, reminds me it was real. "My roommate thinks I'm depressed."

"What do you think?"

I shrug. "She sort of dragged me here."

"Why do you think she did that?"

"Because she's worried about me."

Anna remains unfazed. She is schooled, I suppose, in humoring people.

"What do you think makes her worried?"

"I've been sleeping a lot."

"What is a lot?"

"Basically, if I'm not at work, I'm asleep."

"What kind of work do you do?"

"I'm a reporter," I say, and somewhere, below all the heavy blackness inside me, a tiny light flicks on when I do. I love saying I'm a reporter. It makes me feel strong. "I work for the *Trib*."

"Difficult work, I imagine," she says.

I almost laugh. "Sometimes, yeah. Mostly I'm in the office right now, though."

"Is the amount of sleep you're getting now unusual for you?"

"I guess."

"Why do you think you're sleeping so much?"

"I guess because I'm depressed."

She nods. "Is depression something you've dealt with before?"

"Not really. It's always been anxiety with me."

"Have you ever been treated for anxiety?"

"Oh yeah," I say. "I was in therapy most of college.

And I still take medication."

She asks me for names and dosages. I give them.

"And are you seeing anyone for therapy now?"

I shake my head.

"So how are you getting these medications prescribed to you?"

"My regular doctor, at home," I say.

"Where is home?"

"Orlando."

"And when was the last time you saw this doctor?"

"Um, last year. Like, May, maybe."

"And this has worked for you until recently."

"Pretty much."

"Has something happened, some life event, a stressor in the past few months that might have triggered something?"

Again, I almost laugh.

"Yeah," I say. "Definitely some stressors." I tell her about Rivka Mendelssohn's naked body, and Saul, and my mother suddenly surfacing after twenty-two years. Moving my mouth is hard. I haven't spoken this many words in a row in weeks.

"It's not unusual for a symptom like anxiety to morph into or remanifest as depression. Or vice versa. I'd like to prescribe you a medication that is specifically indicated for people experiencing both depression and anxiety." She explains the dose and the side effects (sleep disturbance, loss of libido, headaches—basically what I'm already experiencing) and walks me out to the waiting room to make me an appointment to come back in a month.

"Call me if you have any questions," she says, handing me a card. "It was very nice to meet you, Rebekah."

I let Iris fill the prescription that night, because, why not? The shrinks and their prescriptions were the net that caught me in college when the lies and contradictions and despairs of my motherless childhood nearly felled me. Two weeks later, Saul calls and I pick up the phone. He asks to take me to lunch and I agree to meet him.

The Kosher Kitchen is a narrow storefront on Atlantic Avenue between a halal meat market and an old botanica selling dusty Blessed Virgin candles. The proximity of this threesome makes me smile, genuinely, for the first time in weeks. The Jewish restaurant next to the Muslim butcher next to the Christian reliquary. I love New York.

Saul is at the counter when I get there. A couple is sitting at one of the tables: he with a beard and the black coat-and-pants uniform, she in a glossy auburn wig. Another young man is working on a laptop. Every male in the restaurant, including the black barista, is wearing a yarmulke. I hop onto the stool next to Saul.

"It's still so cold," I say, unzipping my winter coat.

"The people on the television say it's going to get warm soon," Saul says.

"Not soon enough," I say. "It's almost April, for Christ's sake." Twenty-two years in Florida and it never occurred to me until recently how much sunshine was a part of my life. The cold makes me feel smaller and less consequential. My reactions are slower. Even if I weren't depressed I'd hate going outside.

"It must be difficult adjusting to the weather," says Saul.

"It is," I say. "I guess eventually I'll get used to it."

"Do you think you'll stay here, long term?"

"That's the plan," I say. "There's nothing in Florida. I mean, even where there's something there's nothing. Not compared to New York."

The menu is written on the wall in chalk. We both order tea and decide to split a smoked fish platter with bagel chips.

"I've never been to a kosher restaurant before," I say.

"This one is new."

"How have you been?" I haven't seen Saul since right after I got out of the hospital. Since he told me my mother wanted to get in touch.

"Not bad," he says. "What about you?"

I shrug. "Just work, mostly. I'm feeling a little better, I guess. My ear still rings."

"It'll go away eventually," he says.

"That's what I hear," I say. And then: "Oh, ha. I didn't mean . . ."

Saul smiles.

"I haven't called Aviva," I say. "But maybe you already know that."

"She sent me a text message about a month ago, asking

if I'd passed along her message," he says.

"What did you tell her?"

"What could I tell her? I tried to call her back, but she didn't pick up, so I just sent a text saying that I'd given you the message and that you said you'd call."

The counter man sets out our tea.

"I haven't seen your name in the newspaper lately," Saul says.

"Yeah. I'm mostly doing rewrite. It pays a little more."

"So no more reporting?"

"I'll go back. I'm just . . . I don't know, taking a break."

"Well," he says, "if you're interested, I have a possible lead for you."

"A lead?"

"I've been doing a little freelance private investigative work."

"Really?"

"It sounds more exciting than it is," he says. "Mostly parents trying to track down kids who have gone off the *derech*." He pronounces this last word I've never heard of as "der-eck."

"The what?"

"Off the derech means off the path. Jews who've left the fold. Your mother, for example. And the people you met at the Coney Island house. They're all OTD, as they say. Anyway, I got a call from a man in Roseville. It's a little town about an hour north of the city. In Rockland County. A lot of *Haredi* live up there."

"Haredi?"

"'Haredi' is another way of referring to the ultra-Orthodox."

"Okay," I say. "Is 'Haredi' the same as 'Hasidic'?"

"No," he says. "Hasidism is a specific branch within the larger Haredi community." He smiles at me. "Perhaps you should do some reading on this."

I look down at my tea. He's right.

He continues. "The man called me because his wife died somewhat mysteriously a few weeks ago. He said that her family didn't want any fuss—apparently they're worried it may have been a suicide—but he thinks it was something else."

"Something else?"

Saul raises his eyebrows. "He didn't say specifically. He said she was upset in the days before she died, but he's convinced she wouldn't have killed herself. They have a young child. And he is very unhappy with the police in the town."

"He wants you to investigate?"

"No," says Saul. "He said he doesn't think anything will get done unless someone from outside puts pressure on the police and the community. He called hoping I might pass the information along to you."

"Really?"

"Your work on the Rivka Mendelssohn case did not go unnoticed, Rebekah."

I'm not sure what to say. I guess I didn't think it went

unnoticed, but it definitely didn't occur to me that exposing a murderer and a cover-up inside the cloistered world of Borough Park might *recommend* me to members of the larger Haredi community.

"What's his wife's name?"

"Pessie," he says. "Pessie Goldin."

My shift at the *Trib* is always hectic for the first few hours when we're scrambling to get copy in for the morning deadline. But things slow down after about six, and I Google Pessie Goldin. A newspaper obituary is the third and only relevant link. It says that Pessie Goldin, twenty-two, was buried in Roseville on March 5 and that she is survived by her husband, Levi, twenty-eight, and their infant son, Chaim. There is no mention of cause of death. Pessie's son, like me, will grow up without his biological mother. But unlike me, there's no chance his mother will suddenly appear when he's twenty-three years old. When I think this I realize how insane it is that I haven't called her back. It hits me hard: I want to meet Aviva.

Her phone number is in a note application on my phone. No name, just the ten digits. It is time to call. The newsroom is mostly empty. I dial, and it goes automatically to a generic voice mail announcement. I don't leave a message, and the shock of my immediate fail is so palpable that I laugh out loud. The absurdity—the agony!—of anticlimax. Fine, I think: if I can't solve Aviva's riddle, I'll try to solve Pessie's.

I call the number Saul gave me for Levi Goldin. He answers after the third ring.

"Hello?" He sounds out of breath.

"Hi," I say. "My name is Rebekah Roberts. Saul Katz gave me your number." Levi doesn't say anything but I can hear a baby whining in the background. "Thanks for . . . taking my call. Saul told me a little about your wife's death—I'm really sorry."

"Thank you," says Levi.

"Saul said you were interested in talking?"

"Now is not a good time," he says. He shushes the child, whispering something in a language I don't understand. Yiddish, I assume. "Can we meet tomorrow morning in Manhattan?"

"Sure," I say.

"There is a diner on the West Side," he says. "Frank's. On Forty-ninth. Ten o'clock?"

"We'll be there," I say.

CHAPTER THREE

AVIVA

In Brooklyn, my future was always set: I would marry before I was twenty and have babies until I could not have more. That is what my mother did. That is what my aunts did, and that is what my cousins and friends from school wanted to do. We would support our husbands in their endeavors. Their endeavors would either be studying Torah, which was spiritually preferable but financially unstable, or working elsewhere within the community—teaching at yeshiva, property management, shopkeeping, imports. My father ran a taxi company. He and several of his cousins in Israel were the owners. The cousins put in all the money and my father put in all the labor. He worked very hard and made the business a success. There were nine of us, counting my sister Rivka (which I always do), and we were always fed and clothed. If my mother needed something—a stroller, or a washing machine—someone from the community would provide.

There were times that I thought I could live that life, but for the most part, from as far back as I can remember, I wanted to live another kind of life. I didn't know what kind, exactly, and of course I didn't talk about it. After Rivka died, I stopped loving Hashem. There was no good reason to kill her like that, to have nature attack her with such force. To sting her to death? Outrageous! I decided as I watched them lower my sister's body into a hole in the ground that I would never do anything again *for* Hashem. I would never praise him, and I would certainly never live my life in his honor. I did not tell anyone how I felt for a long time. And when I finally did, I was ready to go.

It sounds ridiculous to say it now, but I did not consider the possibility that I might get pregnant once your father and I began having sex. I assumed you had to do something special—something only married people knew to do—to actually make a baby. I didn't associate the domestic burden of a child with the physical pleasure of our sweaty afternoons in Coney Island. But when I told your father, he felt differently. He said we should have been more careful.

The first weeks I didn't feel much. Your father immediately took the burden of preparing for your arrival onto himself, and I let myself be pulled along. First to the doctor to get a test, and then to his parents. He had told me his family was close. Brian and his older brother, Charles. The Roberts boys and Mom and Dad. Mom a school nurse and church choirmaster; Dad working in an office for Walt Disney. I was prepared to face them as if they were my parents. But their anger lasted what seemed like mere seconds, and then there was joy: a baby! And all was forgiven when your father said we were getting married.

But I did not want to get married. Men in Brooklyn change when they marry. My cousin Pesach's husband was a nice boy when they got engaged. He took her out to restaurants and they talked about traveling together. But when they got married she said he became nervous and strict with her. She said he was consumed by the fear that she might shame him in some way, by dressing inappropriately or saying something that would offend someone. And when a year passed and she wasn't pregnant, he grew even more frantic, and the fear turned him cold. Pesach told me they had problems having sex. She said it hurt when he tried to put his penis in her.

"Did you go to the doctor?" I asked her. I was seventeen then.

"I did, but he said there is nothing wrong." She lowered her voice. "He said the problem is in my head."

I could not see your father becoming like Pesach's husband, but I also could not see running a thousand miles from home just to end up in exactly the same life—married with a baby by twenty—as if I'd stayed. It was just too crushing. I'm sorry, Rebekah, but that is the way it felt. I managed to postpone the wedding until after you were born, and then your father postponed it because he started to see what was happening.

Your grandparents moved us into the bedroom in their basement once I began showing. Brian went to classes during the day and I took walks and cleaned the house. It was easy, wiping and washing and vacuuming. I had done it for my mother most of my life, and it made your grandmother very happy. We did not get along well, she and I. I was not the good Christian girl she imagined her oldest boy would marry, and I did not know how to talk to her about where I came from. When we talked, it was about you. She told me she had been hormonal through both her pregnancies and that she understood it must be difficult for me to be so far away from my family. They invited me to church every Sunday but I did not go.

Once you came, my mind began to turn against me. You were beautiful, with milky blue eyes and tiny ears that curled at the top just like your father's. But I knew I could not take care of you. I knew it the moment I first saw you, all swaddled tight by the nurses, your eyes barely open. I knew there was no way I could be trusted to keep you alive. I fell backward into that feeling of helplessness and your father basically kept us both alive for the first few weeks. He changed your diapers and woke me when you needed to feed. My breasts were enormous. I had half-waking nightmares that they would smother you to death. My mother gave birth to five more after me, but I never saw her breast-feed. I believe she did, but in private. Exposing her breasts to the family—even the girls—would have been considered unacceptably immodest in our home. I heard your father whisper to his brother that I hadn't smiled since giving birth. I suppose he thought I should be joyful, but to smile felt as impossible as to fly. Sadness pulled at the corners of my mouth, and exhaustion coated my skin like a liquid iron cape.

After a month, he introduced the idea of a baptism.

"I will not have my child marked by your God!" I screamed at him.

I was sitting up in bed and he was standing across the room we shared, holding you. He turned you away from my voice.

"Aviva," he said, patiently, always patiently, "please, be reasonable. She is my daughter, too. You know this is important to me."

I should have known. From the very beginning I'd pretended that your father's support for my rejection of my religious upbringing meant that he was also moving away from his faith. But I hadn't really been listening to him. He had supported my rejection of the suffocating, sexist daily rituals that my community insisted were the only path to God. He had not, I realized, supported rejecting God. He was not Jewish—which is part of what drew me to him—but that did not mean he did not live his life according to how he believed God wanted him to. It was just a different God and a different way. I cried and cried and he asked me to please tell him what he could do. But what could he do? He was a religious man and religious men are all the same: they turn to God for answers they cannot come up with themselves. They trust God, but the only thing I trusted was me.

He relented for a while, and one day, when we were driving back from one of your doctor's appointments, he made a detour past a building. A shul.

"It's Reform," he said. "I thought maybe you could see what it was like. Maybe it's just different enough to feel . . . okay?"

When we got home I went to bed and dreamt I was in the shul in Roseville, where we buried Rivka. I held you out to my mother but she did not extend her arms.

"Her name is Rebekah," I said.

"No," she said. She shook her head. There were other women all around her. My aunts and sisters and cousins. They all shook their heads. "No."

"Yes, Mommy," I said. I pushed your little body into her chest, but her hands were clasped tightly at her waist. I let go and you fell. Your screams shook the shul. I looked up and all the men were above, in the women's balcony, reciting the mourner's kaddish.

Yit'gadal v'yit'kadash sh'mei raba

I waved my arms and tried to cry out; I felt the scream coming up strong from my stomach, then turning to dust in my mouth. Nothing but a whistle against the howl of their prayers, growing louder and louder. The women joining in.

b'al'ma di v'ra khir'utei

"*Niddah*," said my mother, her face ugly with disgust. "You have not been to the *mikveh*."

It's true, I thought. I have not been to the mikveh.

I looked down and you were no longer on the ground. I was not wearing shoes. I looked up and there was Rivka. Eleven years old forever. Puffy red hair, perpetually chapped lips, the thin scar on the underside of her chin from when she tumbled down the steps in front of our apartment building as a toddler. Her eyes swollen shut.

"Rebekah is dead," said my mother.

I woke up sweating, the sheets around me damp. Sunlight everywhere. Always sunlight. I had to find a mikveh.

The next day was Friday and I put on a long skirt and borrowed your grandmother's bicycle to ride to the shul. I rode a circle around the parking lot. One entire wall was glass windows. When the sun went down, I went inside. Fewer than half the seats were occupied. Men and women sat together. Some of the men's heads were uncovered. A woman wearing coral-colored lipstick and a sleeveless dress handed me a paper program. It was all in English. It was all wrong. I sat in the back, soaked in the sadness I still could not shake. I wanted to ask about the mikveh. I wondered if the matron would allow me to bathe. The service began with music coming from somewhere I could not see. The rabbi was clean-shaven and wore a white satin *kippah* on his head. He was very tan, and he spoke about something that had appeared in *TIME* magazine. Everyone sang together. It was over in less than an hour. People walked up the plush carpeted center aisle, some wearing flip-flops, and out into the hall where there were tables set with food and wine.

There were happy moments in my childhood, and many of them involved eating. But I felt nothing when I looked at the bountiful Shabbos meal that evening. I had come for one reason. I saw the woman with the lipstick and approached her.

"Excuse me," I said, trying my best to seem pleasant. "Could you tell me where is the mikveh?"

"I'm sorry?" said the woman, smiling. She, like many of the people I met in Florida, spoke with an accent from the South.

"The mikveh," I repeated.

"I'm sorry," she said again. She was ten or fifteen years older than I was, with a deep tan and athletic arms. Her toenails were exposed and painted a shade similar to her lipstick. "The what?"

"Mikveh?" I did not know how else to say it.

"I'm so sorry, hon, I don't know what that is. Just one sec . . ." She raised her hand and caught the attention of the rabbi, flagging him over.

"Oh no," I said, horrified. "That's fine . . ."

But it was too late, there he was.

"What's your name, sweetie?" asked the woman.

"Aviva," I said.

"What a beautiful name," she said. "I'm Estelle. This is Rabbi Siegel. Rabbi, Aviva had a question I couldn't answer."

"Welcome to Temple Beth Israel, Aviva," he said, and reached his hand to shake mine. I was so shocked I stepped back. He and Estelle both smiled weakly, indulging my strangeness. "What can I do for you?"

I must have looked as helpless as I felt, because Estelle spoke first.

"She asked about the mik . . . What was it?"

"The mikveh," I whispered. It was everything I could do not to run.

"The . . . ? Oh!" The rabbi rubbed the place on his jaw where a beard should have been. He wore a white robe, and at his neck I could see the knot of a tie with pink flamingos embroidered on it. Pink! Was this a joke?

"I'm sorry, we don't one have. I actually don't know any temples in the area that do. But let me make a few calls. Have you recently moved to Orlando?"

It was enough.

"Thank you," I said and ran out of the building. I rode home in the dark and with each pump of my bicycle pedals I became more upset. Who were these people? They couldn't possibly think that what they were practicing in that big airy room was Judaism. I told your father I had to go back the next day. He looked concerned. I did not sleep that night. There was so much to tell them, and it was so important. I rode there before dawn. The air was already steamy. I forgot my shoes. I waited more than an hour in the parking lot before a car pulled in. It was not the rabbi, but an older man. I ran to his car.

"Where is the rebbe?" I asked him.

"Rabbi Siegel? He's in about nine."

"I need to talk to the rebbe."

"Okay," said the man, rolling up his window, gathering a bag, taking his time getting out. "Like I said, he'll be here . . ."

"It is *very important* that I speak with him," I said, starting to breathe more quickly. "Please!"

"Look," said the man, "you need to calm down. You can wait . . ."

"I have been waiting!"

He put his hand out to touch my shoulder.

"What are you doing!" I screamed, frightening him. He stepped back.

I froze. What was I doing? "What are you doing!" I screamed again, this time at myself. I slapped my hand to my head. Hard.

"Miss . . ." said the man, but I was already running. I grabbed the bicycle and tripped. The metal edge of the left pedal skidded along the skin on my right shin, tearing it open, drawing blood. But I hopped and hopped and finally got on and got away.

The next time I went to Temple Beth Israel they called your father. The time after that, they called the police.

CHAPTER FOUR

REBEKAH

Frank's Diner is on the corner of Forty-ninth Street and the West Side Highway. It's a 24–7 joint, with mustard-colored pleather booths lining both windowed walls and a full bar with a mirror backsplash. A man in work boots and paint-splattered jeans is sitting at the counter with a beer and the *Trib* in front of him. A couple, both men, one wearing dramatic eye makeup, whisper across a table along the back wall. Saul and I choose a booth by the west-facing window looking out at the *Intrepid* docked in the Hudson. It was so cold this winter there were ice floes in the river. One of the *Trib* photogs snapped a shot of an eagle on one, and it ran with a story about the record-breaking temperatures. The ice is gone now, and with the heat cranking in the diner and the sun shining outside I can almost imagine what it might be like when the weather finally gets warmer.

I asked Saul to come with me because I figured Levi would be more comfortable talking to me with another man present. Other than Saul, all of my sources in the Haredi world have been female. I'm not sure if that's because men are actually more reluctant to speak to outsiders, or if they're just unpracticed in interacting with women they aren't married to. Maybe a little of both.

I see a man in Hasidic dress coming up the block, his head bowed against the wind off the water, one hand pressed down on his tall black hat, sidecurls blown horizontal behind his head. When he comes through the door he looks around expectantly. I wave and Saul stands. They shake hands. I know enough not to extend mine for a greeting. Levi is a good-looking man. Short, with eyes so dark they almost appear black, and a full beard covering half his face. He sits down next to Saul and the waiter comes over with a menu.

"Just tea, please," says Levi, taking a Kleenex from his pocket. He blows his nose.

"Thank you for meeting us," I say. "I'm sorry about your wife."

Levi nods. "Thank you," he says. He puts his Kleenex back in his pocket and looks at me. "What do you need to know?"

"Well, Saul said you had some questions about Pessie's death."

"I have lots of questions. Although I seem to be the only one."

"What do you mean?"

"My wife should not be dead," he says. "She was twenty-two years old. She was a mother. Her family seems to think it was . . ." He shakes his head. "I do not understand them."

I open my notebook. "Can you tell me how she died?"

"That is what I am trying to find out."

I'm not making myself clear. "I mean . . ."

"Our son, Chaim, was scheduled to go to the doctor for a checkup. A woman from the office called me at work and said that they had missed the appointment. I called Pessie, but she did not answer her phone. I thought something had happened, perhaps with her father. He has diabetes and Pessie's mother often calls her to help with his insulin. But when I got home . . ." He pauses. "I could hear Chaim crying from outside the front door. When I got inside I saw he was strapped into his car seat, just sitting there on the floor in his dirty diaper. Pessie would never have left him like that. I heard the water running in the bathroom. The door was closed. She was in the bathtub."

Levi rubs his hand across his face. I look at Saul, who raises his eyebrows as if to say, your move. What's my next question? To me, dying in a bathtub conjures up images of slit writs, or maybe an overdose. Should I ask if he saw blood? Or vomit? Or spilled pills? I decide to wait.

"I called 911," he continues. "And Pessie's mother. She called the *chevra kadisha*." I must look like I don't understand him, because he translates. "The burial society." Ah. "The Roseville officer arrived first. He was very professional. He asked me if I had touched her, and when I said no he took some photographs. But when Pessie's family and the chevra kadisha arrived . . ." Levi purses his lips, like he's trying to press back whatever emotion is threatening to pop out. "There was an argument about who would take the body, and when Pessie's mother learned the officer had taken photographs she became hysterical. She insisted Pessie be taken immediately to the funeral home."

It's a story I've heard before. The story that got me nearly killed in January was about a dead Hasidic woman whose body was never autopsied. Ultra-Orthodox Jews adhere, well, religiously, to a law that states the dead are to be buried within twenty-four hours of their death. Their bodies are not to be disturbed, and female bodies are definitely not to be disturbed by non-Jewish men like whoever this Roseville officer was. Women prepare the bodies of other women for burial in this world; men do the same for men. Their bodies are cleaned and prayed over and watched until their coffin is covered in dirt in a Jewish cemetery. Meaning, in some cases, no autopsy. No collection of DNA from fingernails or mouths or vaginas; no forensic examination of wounds or internal organs; no toxicology report. The last case I covered was an obvious murder: a woman found dumped in a scrap pile. The fact that her body wasn't autopsied was completely outrageous. But her husband had enough money and power to pull strings most people couldn't—or wouldn't. I imagine that circumventing an autopsy is easier in a town like Roseville where the police department is probably small and poorly funded. And it occurs me that this practice is more insidious when a death like Pessie's occurs. A body in a scrap pile is obviously a murder. No one gets like that without help. But a woman in her own bathtub? That's when you really need someone asking questions.

"Why was her mother so insistent?" I ask.

"Fraidy is a very . . . conservative woman," says Levi. It seems like he wanted to use a harsher word to describe his mother-in-law, but demurred. "They seem to believe that Pessie . . . well, I think they are afraid she committed suicide."

The waiter comes and sets down Levi's tea. He pushes it aside.

"What do you think made them think that?" I ask once the waiter is out of earshot.

"Pessie had a very hard time after Chaim was born. She felt very overwhelmed. Chaim did not take to her easily, and I believe she was ashamed, which drove her into despair. She went to the rebbe, of course, but I suggested she see a psychologist when speaking with the rebbe didn't seem to help. I came to this country from Israel. We do not have so much of a stigma about these sorts of issues. Pessie was hesitant, but after a few weeks taking the medication, she felt much, much better. She insisted we keep the fact that she was taking antidepressants from her family. She said they would not understand."

"But Pessie would never have taken her own life. I suppose you hear that a lot. But I have never been more certain of anything. She was very religious and she would never have sinned against Hashem in such a way. And she would not have left Chaim without his mother. I am certain."

I look at Saul, who is looking at his coffee. His only son committed suicide last year. But Levi probably doesn't know that.

"Truthfully, I do not believe her parents actually think Pessie . . . did this. But they are so afraid of the shame—the speculation and the gossip about their family, and how difficult it would make shidduch for her younger sisters and brothers—that they would rather not know what happened to her than risk the possibility of confirming it was suicide. Or related to drugs they would not want people knowing she had been taking. Now, they can say it was a tragic accident. That she fell in the shower."

"What do you think happened?" I ask.

"I have no way of knowing that."

"Right," I say, "but you suspect . . . what?"

"I suspect someone killed her."

"Have you been in touch with the Roseville police?"

"I gave a statement to the first officer. I told him that Pessie always folded her clothing and put on a robe before taking a shower. She did not drop her clothes in a pile on the floor. I told him nothing appeared to be stolen. I told him she would never have left Chaim in his car seat in the living room while she bathed. And I told him that the front door was unlocked when I came home."

"What did the officer say?"

"He took notes."

"Have you heard from him since?"

"No," says Levi.

"Did you reach out again? Like, to follow up?"

"I called once but did not receive a call back. I assumed that if they had information, or needed information, they would contact me. It is their job, after all." Levi sighs. "It has been a very difficult time. I did not wish to remain in the house where she died, and Chaim and I have had to move in with Pessie's brother."

"Have you shared your suspicions with anyone else?"

Levi shakes his head. "I do not wish to contribute to the rumors."

"There are rumors?"

"Of course. Everyone is always talking. Pessie was engaged to another young man, a neighbor from Brooklyn, before she and I met. Her parents would not let her tell me. They were afraid I would not marry her if I knew."

"Would you have?"

"I am not an unreasonable man," he says. "But it was wrong to keep Samuel a secret from me."

"Samuel?"

"That was his name. Pessie finally told me about him after she became pregnant. She said they were engaged very young, when she was just seventeen."

"Did she say what happened?"

"She said that he was a nice boy, but that he wanted to live a more modern life. He left the community, and talking about it seemed to embarrass her, so I did not probe further. I felt happy she trusted me enough to tell me. I thought perhaps it meant our marriage was growing stronger."

"Did you ever meet him?"

Levi shakes his head. "We did not speak of him often."

"Do you know his last name?"

"No," he says. "I know it probably seems strange to you, but I did not feel I needed to know so much about him. He was not a part of her life anymore. I do not believe it is healthy to dwell on the past. Which is why I am taking Chaim home to Israel. I do not want my son to grow up around people who believe his mother did something so sinful as take her own life." I look at Saul. We've never talked about his son's suicide—I learned from someone else—but I can't imagine it feels good to have someone else proclaim your dead child a sinner. Saul doesn't flinch, though, and Levi continues. "But before I leave I want to make an effort to clear my wife's name. I do not know why the Roseville police are uninterested in Pessie's death. And I do not know why her community seems to have already forgotten her."

I nod and scribble *I do not know why r police uninterested p's death; her comm seems already forgot her* into my notebook.

"Will you write about this?" he asks.

"I'd like to," I say. "I have to talk to my editor."

"I know a lot of people think that your stories about

what happened to Rivka Mendelssohn were bad for the community, but I disagree. I believe in justice. If a Jew commits a crime he must pay for it, like anyone else."

"Do you think a Jew did this?" I ask.

"I have no idea. I hope not. But that is not a concern for me. Pessie's family and the rest of the community in Roseville are afraid of any negative publicity. They believe the goyim will use it to destroy us. I am more concerned with what causes this publicity. If we are the cause because our actions are unjust, we have brought that pain onto ourselves."

I look at Saul and see that he is nodding. I know that he agrees; he's said as much to me before. It's why he joined the police department, and it's part of why he had to leave. But Saul no longer wears the black hat. I wonder, looking at Levi's thick beard, what else about the world he lives in does he disagree with? How much does he have to believe to remain in the fold? Is the costume just a habit? What will he teach his son?

"Thank you for reaching out," I say. "I'm going to call the Roseville police as soon as I get to the office."

"I will be interested to hear what they have to say."

"One last thing," I say. "Do you happen to have a photograph of Pessie?"

"A photograph?"

"Yes, just a snapshot. You could e-mail or text it to me."

"Yes," he says, to my enormous relief. I've been at the

Trib long enough to know that they won't even consider running a story about Pessie's death unless we have a photo of her. But no one teaches you how to ask people for photographs of their dead loved ones. It's so outrageously invasive, especially when you have to ask just days, or even hours, after a death. The only way to do it is to step out of your human ideas about decency and become a reporter-bot.

Before Levi leaves, I double-check the spelling of his name and his age, and the same for Pessie. I ask for their wedding date, and Chaim's birthday. The first six months I worked for the *Trib* I made a lot of mistakes. I trusted people I shouldn't have and avoided asking questions I should have. Because my job was basically to run from place to place gathering information, and then call it back to someone in the office who wrote it into an article, I felt little ownership over the stories I worked on. If I didn't catch a last name, I figured someone else would be able to find it. If I forgot to ask an age, or an exact date, oh well. But that carelessness, I think now, is corrosive. And as I have lain in bed, night after night, trying to find the courage to call my mother back, one of the things I have asked myself is, what will she think of me? Which meant I had to ask, what do I think of me? I've always considered myself ballsy, an essential ingredient for a reporter. But no one has ever accused me of being careful, and I know now that I can't be a good reporter—I can't really be good at anything—if I don't get serious. In college, journalism was my major, but now it's my life. It's the only thing I'm certain of: I am a reporter. One day, perhaps, I will be a journalist.

After Levi leaves, the waiter brings the check and I pull it toward me; it's barely six dollars. Saul is looking out the window.

"Are you okay?"

"Yes," he says. "Why do you ask?"

"Well, that thing Levi said about suicide . . ." I trail off.

"Being shameful?"

I nod.

"I think about my son every day," he says. "In some ways, suicide is a perfectly rational response to great pain. If you do not believe in God and you feel that the people in your life will be more hurt by your continued presence . . ." He looks back toward the river. "I think a person can come to a place in his mind where he thinks he is doing something positive. Something almost kind."

"I wonder if that's what Pessie did?"

"Anything is possible," he says. "And of course her husband would probably feel a great deal of guilt."

"He could be in denial."

"Yes."

I wait for Saul to say more, but he is finished with this topic. "I think it's worth asking about at least," I say.

"I agree."

I slip a ten-dollar bill into the black pouch and motion for the waiter.

"I called Aviva yesterday," I say while we wait for change.

"That's wonderful" says Saul, unable to suppress a slight smile. "What made you decide to call?"

I shrug. "I guess I was thinking about Pessie. I don't know. Now that I know she's alive I don't want her to, like, die in a bathtub before I get to meet her."

"What did she have to say?"

"It went straight to voice mail."

"Oh," he says. "I'm sure she'll call you back."

"I didn't leave a message," I say. "I might try her again tonight."

When I get in to the newsroom, I ask the library to do a backgrounder on Pessie Goldin, and then I look up the Roseville Police Department. The Web site is a single page located inside the larger Town of Roseville site. There is a portrait of Chief John Gregory—a white man with a ruddy red face and graying hair who looks fifty-ish—and a short statement about the department's commitment to preserving public safety. I call the phone number and ask for the chief.

"May I say who's calling?" asks the woman who answers the phone.

"My name is Rebekah Roberts," I say. "I'm a reporter for the *New York Tribune*."

She puts me on hold, and after about a minute of soprano sax, Chief Gregory comes on the line.

"Chief Gregory," he says.

"Hi, Chief Gregory," I say. "My name is Rebekah Roberts and I'm a reporter for the *New York Tribune*."

"What can I do for you, Rebekah?"

"I'm working on an article about a woman who was found dead in Roseville last month. Pessie Goldin?" I wait. He says nothing. "Are you familiar with this case?"

"What can I help you with?"

"Well," I say, "I'm wondering if there has been any investigation into her death. Her husband believes she may have been murdered."

"Does he, now?"

"He does," I say. "He told me that he found her in her bathtub, and that her son was left alone in his car seat. I know she was buried without an autopsy but . . ."

"Did he tell you she had been taking antidepressants?"

I shouldn't be surprised that he asks this, but it pisses me off nonetheless. I remember that right after I started taking pills for my anxiety, Iris and I happened to be up late watching *Law & Order: SVU*—as college girls will do—and the episode centered around a woman who was raped, and who had been undergoing treatment for depression. The defense attorney was like, she takes antidepressants, clearly, she's unstable. The jury didn't convict. I was like, shit, if I'm ever the victim of a crime they could use the fact that I take pills to completely undermine my credibility. We both agreed this was total bullshit.

"He did," I say.

"Well, then."

"Are you saying that you didn't investigate her death because she was taking a kind of medication about thirty million Americans take?"

"Now you're putting words in my mouth."

"I'm sorry," I say. "*Are* you looking into her death?"

"I'm not going to comment on that."

Well, then.

"Okay," I say. "Thank you for your time."

I slap down the phone and let out a groan. I suppose I should be happy that I at least got a "no comment" for the story; getting anyone on the record at the New York City Police Department is practically impossible. At least in a small town like Roseville the chief picks up the phone when you call. Even if he is a douche bag.

I put Pessie's story aside for the time it takes to pound out the articles the city desk wants for tomorrow: a rewrite of a British tabloid story about Jude Law; a fire at a pizzeria on the Coney Island boardwalk; baby gorillas at the Bronx Zoo. At three thirty, I get a text from Levi with a photograph of him and Pessie, presumably on their wedding day. The text that follows says: *pessie and levi, 2/3/10.* Levi is standing and Pessie is sitting. He wears a double-breasted black coat and an enormous fur hat shaped like a cake box. Pessie is in white, lace collar to her chin, puffy shoulders. Neither is smiling, although they don't look unhappy, exactly. Pessie has light hair, not blond, but not quite brown, either. Her eyes are gray-blue and she appears very young. A few months ago, I would have laughed at this portrait. I would have joked that it looked like it was taken in 1910—even 1810—not 2010.

I would have made fun of Levi's "ringlets," as I derisively called sidecurls. Ringlets like Shirley Temple had. Ha! Did he sleep in curlers? Did he hold them steady with hairspray? I would have rolled my eyes and felt a mix of pity and scorn for Pessie and Levi in their stupid costumes. Now I still feel pity—for the dead woman, her grieving husband, her motherless child—but the scorn is gone. Inside those outfits, I know now, are human beings, just like me.

An hour later, the library e-mails Pessie's backgrounder, with possible addresses for her kin in Roseville, Brooklyn, and Lakewood, New Jersey. Levi said that Pessie's mother was named Fraidy, and there is a listing for Shmuli and Fraidy Rosen. I call the number and a woman answers.

"Hi," I say, "my name is Rebekah Roberts. I'm a reporter for the *New York Tribune*."

Silence.

"I'm trying to reach Pessie Goldin's family."

"What do you want?"

"I, um, I'm very sorry to hear about Pessie. I met her husband, Levi, earlier today and I am working on a story about her death . . ."

"I have nothing to say," says the woman, and hangs up the phone.

Perhaps someday I will get used to being hung up on, or having a door slammed in my face, or being run off a front lawn, or shouted out of a business. But I'm not there yet. Shame creeps like fog up my cheeks and squeezes my heart. If my daughter died in a bathtub, would I want to talk to a stranger about it? Probably not. But what if that stranger wanted to help? And is that what I'm doing, helping? It's hard to feel like it sometimes. Sometimes I just feel like a predator.

Just before the 5:00 P.M. deadline I e-mail a draft of Pessie's story to Larry Dunn, the *Trib*'s lead police reporter and, since the Rivka Mendelssohn story, a kind of mentor for me at the paper. After I press send, I call him at the Shack.

"Rebekah!" he says when he picks up. "How are you?"

"Good, thanks," I say. "How are you?"

"Oh, the same. Working on the NYU jumper." The night before last, a sophomore fell, jumped, or was pushed off the ledge of her fourteenth-floor dorm balcony and landed on the sidewalk along Sixth Avenue. The cops found a lot of weed in her room, and a little coke, so the paper is calling it "The Dorm Drug Den Death," though it is unclear whether she was a heavy user, a dealer, or if the stuff had been planted.

"Do you have a minute? I just e-mailed you a story."

"Hold on. Let me check."

"It came from a source in the ultra . . . Haredi world."

"Oh God," says Larry, "you're not done with those people?"

It's not a terrible question. "Not yet," I say. "There's a man in Roseville, up north of here. His wife is originally from Brooklyn and she died sort of mysteriously.

He found her in the bathtub with the baby screaming in the other room."

"When was this?"

"She was buried March fifth."

"That's almost a month ago."

"I know," I say.

"What do the police say?"

"The chief was a douche. He was like, did you know she was taking antidepressants?"

"One of those," he says.

"Yeah . . ."

"Gimme a second," he says. "I'm reading."

I wait.

"Do you think this is another pressure-from-the-community thing?" he asks.

"I don't know. The husband said her parents are worried she killed herself and are, like, ignoring it. But he definitely wants an investigation."

"Bathtubs are tough," says Larry.

"What do you mean?"

"Even with an autopsy it's hard to prove how someone died if they're found in water."

"Oh," I say.

"I'm not saying you shouldn't look into it, I'm just thinking out loud."

"Okay."

"Do you have a photo?"

"Yes," I say. "A wedding portrait."

"Good, gotta have a photo. Have you talked to the parents?"

"I think the mom hung up on me."

"Ah. Okay, well I guess this works for me. I'll send it to Mike for tomorrow." Mike is the city desk editor. He hired me and used to tell me where to run when I was on the streets. Now that we're in the office together, we rarely talk. I think he's better with people over the phone than in person.

"Cool," I say. "If I get anything from the parents, I should e-mail him?"

"Yup," he says. "You ready to make more enemies in the black hat world?"

Ready as I'll ever be.

CHAPTER FIVE

AVIVA

I left your grandparents' house late one night while everyone was sleeping. I kissed your face and held you, your tiny body zipped up in pajamas with sheep on them, a bit sweaty, and deep in sleep. Your eyelids fluttered and you blew a little bubble of spit as I said good-bye. I felt my heart contract, as if someone were squeezing the blood out, when I set you back into your crib. I wore a backpack and soft shoes and I walked out the sliding glass door in the kitchen. I took a bus from Orlando to Jacksonville and north to Ocean City, Maryland. My cousin Gitty was there—or at least I hoped she was. Gitty left Brooklyn a few years before I did. When I was fifteen, I asked her mother, my tante Leah, if she ever wrote to Gitty, and she said no. I asked why not, and she said that she had four other daughters who were good Jewish girls and would make good Jewish wives, and she had no time to waste on a girl like Gitty. That was how she said it, "A girl like Gitty." I didn't need to ask what that meant.

"She sends letters to her sisters, trying to poison their minds," she said. "I throw them away."

When I asked where the letters came from, she shooed me out of the room. Tante Leah and Feter Izzy lived on the second floor of a house halfway up the block from ours. The mail came late in the day on our street. Sometimes I saw the lady from the post office pushing her bag as I walked home from school. I had a key to their apartment, so one day I let myself into the first floor where the mailboxes were. I went back every day, and after about a week, I found a letter from Gitty. I took it home and that night I wrote to her telling her what I'd done. I told her I missed her and that I hoped I could visit her. I sent the letter to the return address in Atlantic City, New Jersey. Gitty wrote me back and told me that she was very happy and that she was living with some nice people in a house near the ocean and working selling sunglasses and t-shirts in a little store along the boardwalk. She said she went to the movies sometimes and was saving her money for driving lessons. We wrote to each other every week for almost three years. And then, right after I met your father, she stopped writing. I sent four letters that went unanswered. A fifth came back marked *return to sender.* I asked Tante Leah if she'd heard from Gitty, and she said no. About two weeks before I left for Florida, Gitty sent me a letter from Ocean City. *I'm still alive,* she wrote. *New job, new city. Come visit!* I sent a letter telling her my plans. I wrote again after you were born. I asked her to send me her phone number. I said I really needed to talk. But I never heard back.

I had saved almost five hundred dollars from money your grandparents gave me for cleaning. The bus ticket cost one hundred. It was the middle of the night when I arrived at the bus station in Ocean City. I had barely slept. Every time I shut my eyes I saw you. Your swirl of fine red hair. Your upturned nose. The tiny, sharp fingernails I had to file down every day. I saw your chubby legs, kicking, always kicking. I saw your smile as I changed your diaper. And your blue eyes, wide open, astounded by everything you saw. You were so beautiful. I looked for Gitty's name in the phone book attached to a booth outside the station, but she wasn't listed. I had the address from the year-old letter and I asked the man behind the thick glass if he knew how I could get there. He said it wasn't far and that I could walk. I waited at the station until dawn and then I started walking. I could smell the ocean but I couldn't see it. Seagulls circled overhead like vultures, squawking. The streets were quiet. Little houses with little squares of grass in the front. I could feel I'd caught a cold on the bus. I sneezed and sneezed and I didn't have any Kleenex so I wiped my nose on my sleeve. The address on Gitty's last letter was a house separated into apartments. There were metal lawn chairs and green Astroturf on the front porch. It was barely eight o'clock, but I felt feverish and desperately wanted someplace to curl up, so I rang the bottom bell. No one answered. I rang the other two. Nothing. I tried the doorknob and it was open. *Hello?*

I said. It smelled like cigarette smoke and urine inside. I stepped into a room covered in thin carpet, with old food and beer cans strewn about. A girl was asleep on one of two sofas. There was a dog in the corner, which frightened me. It wasn't big, but I had never spent the night in a home with a dog. No *Chassidish* family has a pet. They are not kosher. But I felt so weak I would have slept in a room with a tiger. I sat down on the sofa opposite the girl, pulled my feet up beneath me, wrapped my arms around my backpack, and fell asleep.

It must have been hours later when I woke up. The girl on the sofa across from me was still there, but she'd changed positions. I heard voices and dishes, and a shirtless man sat down next to me and turned on the television. He bent forward, revealing a white back spotted with moles. More moles than I had ever seen. Moles with hair poking out of them. I stood up.

"Is Gitty Rosenbaum here?"

"Who?" he said, barely looking up. He was probably my age now. Forty-ish. I remember there was gray in his week-old beard.

"Gitty," I said again.

"I have no idea," he said. "Ask one of the girls."

I walked past him into a tiny kitchen. He called after me: "And while you're at it, ask which one of 'em is letting that dog piss all over the place. That dog is gonna be gone next time I come here."

I kept walking down a hallway and found two girls

in a bedroom. I asked them if Gitty lived here and they looked at me blankly.

"Ask Sandra," said one. "She's been here a while."

I knocked on the bedroom door across the hall and someone said to come in. The room was black, thick curtains drawn against the sun. I squinted into the darkness and made out a figure in the bed. I asked if Gitty Rosenbaum was here and a female voice said Gitty hadn't lived there in months. I asked if she had any idea where she was and she said, "I think she's in her car."

"Her car?" I said.

"She was parked behind the 7-Eleven on Third," said the girl, flopping over to face me. She wasn't much older than me and she had a black eye. I asked her what kind of car and she said a Honda. And then she flopped back over.

I slept that night and the next in a motel room that cost twenty-nine dollars plus tax. I ate what I could buy at the 7-Eleven while I waited for Gitty. On the third day, she appeared in her Honda. She was skinny, and her dark hair was streaked with blond, but I knew her. I called her name and she stopped and turned. And then she screamed. We both did. She ran to me and we hugged and laughed until we were out of breath. But that excitement didn't last very long. We bought hot tea and sat on the curb outside. I told her my story and she told me hers. She had been living in the Honda since May. It wasn't so bad, she said, but I knew she didn't mean it. She had deep puffy circles under her eyes, and a cold sore on her mouth. She smelled bad. I asked why she wasn't living at the house I'd been to anymore, and she said she left because you can't stay there if you don't work.

"Don't you want to work?" I asked.

Gitty shook her head and looked away from me. "It is not good work," she said. And she wouldn't say any more.

We both looked for jobs while we stayed together in the motel. After four days, we were down to fifty dollars. On the fifth day I got a job at a Goodwill store making four dollars an hour sorting through donated clothes, but they only needed me from noon to five. And, I learned at the end of my first shift, it would take ten days for my paperwork to go through, which meant I wouldn't get paid until then. So Gitty and I slept in the car. The hardest part was finding a place to take a shower and go to the bathroom. Gitty had a bottle she peed in at night, but I couldn't bring myself to use it. I usually held it in until dawn when we could drive to a McDonald's. I asked Gitty if she'd ever gone to shul to ask for help and she shook her head.

"This is not Brooklyn," she said.

Gitty had changed almost entirely since I'd known her. When we were children, our families went to the same bungalow colony in the Catskills and Gitty and I shared a bed. She had a pretty singing voice and she practiced songs in our room. Girls are not supposed to sing in front of boys, but Gitty liked to show off. She was always getting into trouble for singing. Sometimes she made up new words for the songs—inserting impressions of people we knew, making everyone laugh. Tante Leah and my mother told Gitty she talked too much. But now, Gitty didn't say much of anything. And she never sang. Or smiled. When she did talk, she didn't talk about anything that mattered. She never once mentioned her family.

I tried not to think about you, Rebekah, but it was impossible. Almost every day I said to Gitty, "I wonder what Rebekah is doing right now?" I imagined you in your stroller on the way to the park with the baseball field at dusk. I imagined your father smiling and cooing at you as he lifted you out of your seat and set you on his chest, your head, still a little unsteady on your neck, wobbling as you tried to look all around you at once. Gitty did not want to imagine with me, but I have played the game of imagining where you are every day since I left. I have told you all my stories. I have asked for your advice. I have carried you everywhere, Rebekah. Always.

After I started at Goodwill, Gitty told me she was spending the afternoons looking for work, but she was bringing men into the car for money. They left their smell. We showered at night by the beach, where there were nozzles for people to rinse off after a day in the sand. And then one night a police car drove into the parking lot behind the Rent-A-Center and saw me peeing beside the car. I spent that night and all the next day and night in a cell with seven other women. One was naked except for a bed sheet. Gitty didn't come to get me, and when I got out, I called home to Brooklyn. My brother Eli answered the telephone, and at first I didn't recognize his voice. I had been gone for fifteen months and he had become a man.

"Aviva?" he said. "It's Eli."

"Eli!" I cried.

"Aviva, please come home," he said. "Mommy is dead, Aviva. And we have a new brother."

CHAPTER SIX

REBEKAH

When I wake up, Iris has already left for work. I open my laptop and find Pessie's story six headlines down inside the News section.

ROSEVILLE MAN ACCUSES COPS, COMMUNITY OF IGNORING WIFE'S MYSTERIOUS DEATH

By Rebekah Roberts

The family of an upstate mother whose body was found in her bathtub is accusing local police of ignoring her mysterious death.

"I have no doubt that Pessie was killed," says Levi Goldin, 28, of Roseville.

"I do not know why the Roseville police are uninterested in Pessie's death. And I do not know why her community seems to have already forgotten her."

Goldin told the *Tribune* that on the day of her death, his wife was supposed to take their son to the doctor but did not show up and stopped answering her phone. When he got home he found his wife in the bathtub and the child screaming, strapped into his car seat in the living room.

Pessie was born in Brooklyn but her family moved to Rockland County when she was a child.

Roseville police chief John Gregory declined to comment on the case.

I click into Facebook and see that I have a message from someone named Dov Lowenstein.

Hi! I'm SO glad you are trying to find out what happened to Pessie! We grew up together and she was the nicest girl in the world. No WAY she killed herself. Thank you thank you thank you!

I click into Dov's Facebook page and see that he has more than a thousand "friends." His profile picture depicts him in short shorts, waving an Israeli flag at some kind of parade. I write back immediately.

Thanks for reaching out! I'd love to interview you about Pessie. Do you have time to chat today?

Moments later, a message pops up.

I'll be in Brooklyn tonight speaking at a

chulent on Ocean Pkway. Wanna come? We can talk after.

He includes a link to a Facebook event page. Fifty people have already RSVPed saying they will attend. According to the invitation, the event begins at 10:00 P.M. and is BYOB.

I Google "chulent" and discover that it's a traditional Jewish stew made with beans and potatoes and onions and meat that takes twelve hours to cook. It is also the word used to describe, as the Web site NeoHasid puts it, "a drop-in lounge for folks that have traveled (or strayed) from the Chasidic world, whether in spirit, mind or body, along with their allies and friends."

I message Dov back saying I'll be there, then I send Iris a text asking if she'll come with me. While I wait to hear from her, I click back to the event invite. It appears to be sponsored by a group called OTDinNYC. I click onto their Facebook page, which is open, and see that there are 978 people in the group. A long post in the "About" section lays out the rules of the group, which include refraining from personal attacks and "outing" people who have joined with fake names ("Mikveh Mouse" and "Shtetl Gretel"). The administrator is a woman named Chasi Herzog. She describes the group as a place for off-the-derech and OTD-curious to share, connect, question, and find support and advice. The most recent post is from someone named Ben Silver who asks: "Do you still plan on marrying

Jewish?" He posted less than twenty minutes ago and there are already nineteen comments. Further down, a woman named Shimra Reich posted, "If you had a dollar for every person you've had sex with, what could you buy?" There are more than a hundred comments. One person named Yisrael Greenberg wrote: "A Ferrari!" sparking a series of comments about STDs and whether oral sex counted. Another, named Hindy Levin, wrote: "A cup of coffee—and not at Starbucks!" Her post was met with approving remarks about honesty, sexual repression in the Haredi world, and invitations to fill her wallet, so to speak. There is a post saying "Like this status if you were thrown out of yeshiva!" There are 235 likes and fifty-eight comments recounting skirmishes over skirt-length, smuggled magazines, OTD siblings, and insufficiently pious parents.

Iris texts back saying that she's up for the chulent. I tell her I'll try to leave work early and meet her at home, then we'll go together. I turn on the shower and undress. For the first few days and weeks after I lost all my hair, I was surprised every time I dipped my head back into the stream of water. I felt the hair that wasn't there. I'm getting used to it now. Iris encourages me to "play up the look" with big earrings and more makeup, but there's something interesting about being, well, less pretty than I have been most of my life. I feel like it's making me stronger; like that little happiness I'd get when I looked in the mirror before all this was a false, or at least a shallow, psychological bump. And now that I don't have it, I have to find something else, something more substantial, to look for in my reflection.

Ten minutes before I have to leave for my shift I try Aviva again. Again, her number goes straight to voice mail: *This mailbox is full. The user is not accepting new messages.* This time, the automated message pisses me off.

"Really, Aviva?" I actually say out loud to the empty apartment. "You're gonna play me like that? Clean out your fucking in-box."

It's a slow news day, so once I plunk out my assigned stories (Staten Island state representative's son arrested for domestic assault; another crane incident at the luxury condo going up on Fifty-seventh Street; gang-related shooting on the B31 bus in Brooklyn) I Google Dov Lowenstein. Dov, I discover, is a plaintiff in a lawsuit against a group called New Hope, an organization of unlicensed "therapists" who purport to turn gay Jews into straight Jews. The *Trib* actually did a story about the lawsuit last year when it was filed. Dov is quoted as saying that the people running the group are frauds who prey on Jewish parents desperate to "fix" their gay children.

Mike lets me leave early when I tell him I'm going to interview a source on the Pessie Goldin story. I get home at nine and Iris asks me what she should wear.

"If the girls are frum they'll probably be in long skirts and long sleeves and stockings," I say.

"From?"

"Frum. F-r-u-m. It means, like, observant."

"Rocking the lingo," she says, "I like it."

"Anyway, I don't think it matters. Clearly they're liberal. I mean, it says BYOB."

"BYOB! Really? This could be awesome. Are pants okay? I think I'll wear pants."

"I'm wearing jeans."

"Cool. How about we get a six-pack? I'll bring a big bag and if it's weird, I'll just keep it," says Iris. I agree this is a good plan.

We leave the house at nine thirty and take the F train to Avenue I. It's a little warmer tonight than it has been in weeks and it feels nice not to have to rush from one place to the next. I even left my hat at home. The address on Ocean Parkway, it turns out, is a synagogue.

"It's in a church?" whispers Iris. We're standing across the street.

"It's a synagogue," I say.

"I know," says Iris, still whispering. "I just meant, you know, a house of worship. I wouldn't have guessed they'd let them do that."

"I don't think they can hear you," I say.

"Come on," she says. "Isn't that strange?"

"I read about two in *The New York Times*. One was in somebody's home. One was in a community center basement in Manhattan. A synagogue is kind of a community center, so . . ."

The ornate stone building is probably at least a hundred years old. Two sets of steps come together in the front, and on them linger about a dozen people. One man is very fat, with an enormous beard and wild brown hair. A Jew-fro, I've heard it called. He is wearing a yellow hooded sweatshirt with a Hawaiian scene silk-screened on it, and talking to two girls about my age. Both girls are dressed in long skirts and flat shoes, their hair covered with scarves. But the skirts aren't plain black like the ones most of the women I saw in Borough Park wore; one is denim, and one is a crinkled, fiery red-and-orange fabric. Little rebellions, I think.

Iris and I walk toward the threesome and Jew-fro greets us.

"We tend to start late," he says, with a smile. "Welcome. There's food and drink inside."

Iris and I say thank you and continue inside the iron gates and up the stairs to the entrance. People are smoking and drinking from plastic cups and chatting with each other. I spot two black-hatted men. We walk into the foyer, an elegant, if worn, mosaic-tiled rotunda with a dome rising fifty feet into the sky. I look up and see a stained glass window. It's too dark to tell whether the image is abstract or depicts some sort of scene. At my dad's church they had a stained glass window called the Christ window. It wasn't a terribly artful illustration—just white Jesus in a white robe with his hands out, a halo above his head—but I remember that when the sun lit the blues and yellows and pinks on the mornings when I used to go to Sunday school I couldn't help but be a little bit mesmerized by it. Iris and I follow the noise down the hallway from the foyer to a multipurpose room big enough for a wedding or a concert. Plastic and aluminum folding chairs line the walls. There is a buffet set on tables along one side of the vast space. I see beer and wine. We set down our six-pack and Iris opens one for each of us with the flamingo bottle opener on her key chain (a hold-over from college). There are probably twenty people in the room. Most of the men wear some kind of covering on their head. Many have black yarmulkes, and several wear sidecurls and black pants. But more than one wears a knit beanie, or a baseball cap. One has a hat that says COMME DES FUCKDOWN. I alert Iris and she loves it.

The buffet is mostly canned or bagged—chips, nuts, salsa, Oreos, a plastic barrel of Cheez puffs—but everyone seems to have chipped in. There is white wine in a box, several varieties of juice and punch, and a half-empty jug of Smirnoff. We drink our beers and look around. It's mostly men inside, and everyone appears engaged in conversations that don't lend themselves to interruption, so we walk back out to the front steps. We aren't leaning against the railing a minute when a woman approaches us.

"Are you here to see Dov?" she asks.

"Yes," I say. "Are you?"

The woman nods. She is wearing a wig and a navy blue turtleneck. She is probably in her late thirties. "You know him from Facebook?"

"Sort of."

"I do not agree with everything he says, but I think he is doing a good thing."

I nod.

"You are frum?"

"No," I say.

"But you are Jewish?"

I hate this question. Before I moved to Brooklyn, I don't think anyone had ever asked me if I was Jewish. Now I feel like I get asked every other day, and my answer is more complicated than they assume, or, frankly, want to hear about. Fortunately, Iris jumps in.

"I'm not," she says. "But she is."

"Are you from Brooklyn?"

"No," I say. "We're from Florida."

"Florida! Miami? I have cousins in Miami."

"Orlando."

"Are you married?"

Iris opens her mouth, but doesn't say anything. She's shocked, I can tell, that we've been asked this personal question by a total stranger ten seconds after meeting.

"No," I say.

"Do you have a boyfriend?"

I look at Iris, who speaks, finally, and without any of her usual grace: "Uh-huh."

"Why not get married?"

"We've only been dating a little while."

"Do you want children?"

Iris shrugs. "Someday."

"I had my first son when I was nineteen," she says.

Iris looks at me. She knows I had an abortion when I was nineteen. She smiles and puts her hand on my arm. "Well," she says to the woman, "I hope that worked out for you. Rebekah, I need to go to the bathroom." She pulls me back into the rotunda.

"Sorry," she says once we're inside. "I just hate that shit. What is she, your mom?"

"Maybe," I say, which makes her laugh. "I don't think she was trying to make us feel bad. At least you have a boyfriend."

"Whatever," says Iris. "I smelled weed out there. Let's find that person. I bet they don't ask why we're not married."

The weed, it turns out, is being smoked at the bottom of the stairs by two young men, one in sidecurls and black pants, one beardless, with his button-down shirt open, revealing chest hair. He has a small New York Yankees yarmulke clipped to his hair. Iris approaches first, smiling.

"Got any to share?" she says.

The man in the sidecurls, who is more a boy than a man, freezes. His friend seems momentarily stunned by our presence as well, but recovers quickly, taking the joint from his friend's hand and passing it to Iris.

"Hello there," he says, obviously thrilled. "I haven't seen you before."

Iris takes a pull from the joint and passes it to me. I decline. I feel like I need to be sober for this. She offers her hand to shake. "I'm Iris. This is Rebekah." Both men look at her hand. Chest hair shakes, sidecurls does not.

"Are you from Williamsburg?" asks chest hair.

"Gowanus," says Iris, taking a second puff.

"Are you married?"

"Jesus Christ," says Iris. She hands the joint back. Chest hair giggles (poor man doesn't know what he's gotten himself into) but before she can lay into him, we hear a commotion at the front gate.

"Is that him?" says sidecurls, straining to see over the half-dozen people who are crowded around a livery cab at the curb. Chest hair seems more interested in Iris than whoever has arrived, so sidecurls abandons him and joins the group escorting a man I assume is Dov Lowenstein up the stairs and into the synagogue.

"Do you know him?" I ask.

"From Facebook. I've read about him. Everyone hates him, but I don't know. I wanted to see for myself."

"Why do they hate him?" asks Iris.

"Because he calls the Chassidim a cult."

"He does?"

"Yes, of course. Don't you know? I understand he had a bad time. But he is hoping for a big payday."

"We should go in," I say.

"One more smoke?" says chest hair. He loves Iris.

I take her hand. "We're good," I say. "Thanks."

We follow the rest of the smokers and stragglers into the multipurpose room. Iris grabs two more beers from our six-pack and we find two folding chairs along the edge of the room. As we wait, I blurt out: "I called my mom."

"Excuse me?" she says, almost spitting out her beer.

"She didn't pick up," I say. "I tried twice. Straight to voice mail."

She stares at me, her eyes glassy.

"You're high," I say.

"I know!" she says. "Wow."

If she wasn't high, Iris would probably have questions, but she's just sort of staring at me, shaking her head. At the front of the room, Dov has taken off his jacket. He is wearing a white t-shirt with a rainbow Star of David on it, and his head is uncovered. He has very light hair, so light his eyebrows blend into his pale face. People start sitting down, but everyone is still talking. Finally, the boy with the sidecurls from outside, who is sitting in the front row, stands up and yells "Quiet!"

Dov steps forward to the standing mic at the front of the room. He opens a spiral notebook and sets it on the table beside him. "My name is Dovi Lowenstein," he says, leaning forward. "But you probably know that." The crowd murmurs a light laugh. "Let me ask you a question. How many of you know somebody who is gay?"

Iris and I raise our hands. I look around and about half the room does the same.

"Okay, put your hands down. Now, how many of you know somebody who is gay and Chassidish?" About the same number raise their hands.

"Yes," says Dov. "You see. Yes. Now how many of you know Chassidim who are gay and married?"

Fewer hands this time, but Dov's point is made.

"Yes, you see?" he says. "This is what I am talking about. Why would a gay man marry a woman? Why! Because he has no choice. His parents tell him to marry and so he marries. Or she marries. What else can he do? If he does not want to lose everything he has to pretend. He has to keep who he really is a secret." He pauses and picks up his notebook, looks at what he's written, remembers, continues. "Now, how many of you know someone who went to New Hope?"

About a fifth of the room raises a hand.

"And are they still gay?"

"Yes!" shouts a man at the back. Everyone turns around.

"My friend!" says Dov, gesturing to the man. "Was it you?" The man, who appears, like Dov, to be in his mid-twenties, nods. He is wearing jeans and a hooded sweatshirt with BROOKLYN written across it. I don't see a yarmulke. "How old were you?"

"Sixteen," says the man.

Dov says something to the man in Yiddish. The man says something back and the room becomes agitated, people whisper to each other, shift broadly in their seats.

"What did he say?" asks Iris.

"I don't know," I say.

"We will talk later," says Dov to the man. "But see?

See?" He is trying to bring the crowd's attention back to the front of the room. "And that is why I said it is a cult. Not Judaism. No. But the way we grew up. You know. In Williamsburg and Monsey and Roseville. It is a cult because you cannot get out without being damaged. You cannot get out without losing your family. It is a cult because you are isolated and insulated. The problem isn't the religion. Judaism is a beautiful thing. Community is a beautiful thing. The problem is that the people who are born into it *have no choice.* And the cult, it is not about Hashem. It is about fear. Everybody thinks their neighbor is spying on them! Your parents, maybe, your sisters and brothers, they believe what the rebbe tells them. If the rebbe says send your son to this place, they have doctors, they will make him well. What do they do?"

Under their breaths, people respond. In the row behind me, the woman who asked us if we were married whispers, "You send him."

"Yes! You send him! Because the rebbe knows best. But they are not doctors! They are frauds! Everyone knows this. Everyone outside. But your parents, and your brothers and sisters, they do not know this. Because they are in a cult! They may be wonderful people. They may be kind and they may mean well. But they are in a cult! Their minds have been abducted by the wrong priorities. Their priorities are appearances. And if you make a different choice—if you dare to choose something else—pack your bags!"

Dov is a riveting presence. I've never seen someone speak so viscerally from the heart. His remarks seem both prepared and completely spontaneous; eloquent and clunky. He gestures wildly, waving his arms as he tells stories, his voice up and down—practically shrieking at points, then mumbling and making little jokes with his friends who are gathered at the side of the room. Like so many of the ultra-Orthodox I've met, he has an accent, and for the first time it strikes me as quite beautiful. Iris's mouth is slightly open; she looks hypnotized. Dov talks for the next forty minutes. He says he was born in Brooklyn and moved to Roseville when he was a child. He says he was never sexually attracted to girls and at age fifteen his sister caught him kissing another Haredi boy. When his mother confronted him he told her he was gay. He said he found the word on the Internet when he rode his bike to the public library and looked up "boys who want to kiss boys." (Everyone laughs at this.) A year later, his parents sent him to New Hope, and when he ran away from the program, they cut him off and he lived on the street and with friends and people he met on Facebook. I wonder if he ever stayed at the Coney Island house. He says he started speaking out when one of the boys he knew from New Hope committed suicide. And then, he says, he was approached by the lawyers. He stops speaking abruptly.

"I have been talking a long time. Thank you for coming. If you would like to get more information about the lawsuit you can talk to me."

He steps back from the mic and the room fills with applause. The front two rows are on their feet. Dov suddenly looks shy. He smiles and puts his head down, then grabs a friend from the front row and drags him to the buffet table.

People stop clapping and immediately start talking.

"Did you know about any of that?" Iris asks.

"I knew gay people weren't accepted. But, I mean, they're barely accepted at my dad's church."

"I've read about gay conversion therapy," says Iris. "There have definitely been articles about it. You know Brice's sister is gay." Brice is the nice young man that Iris has been dating for a few months. I don't really get the attraction—he doesn't seem terribly interesting. He works in men's fashion, which is one strike against him in my book. And he has highlights, which is two. Iris hasn't brought him around much. But I guess I haven't been very fun lately.

"I didn't know," I say. "You never told me."

"You never asked."

True. "So did she go through gay conversion therapy?"

"No, but he said her girlfriend did. She's from Utah and her family was Mormon. Anyway, in California, I think they actually outlawed it. Or maybe they tried to."

"They should," I say.

Iris nods. "That guy was amazing," she says. Dov is surrounded by people; everyone seems to have a question or a story to share. "Are you gonna talk to him?"

"Yeah," I say, "but it looks like it might be a wait."

"So we wait. I'm getting another beer. I have cotton-mouth. I'm calling in sick tomorrow."

Iris goes to the buffet, and I lean against a covered piano in the corner of the room, watching. It's almost midnight on a weekday, but the event shows no sign of slowing down. A group of young men in black hats brings in a case of beer. Three frum girls are bent over an iPhone, laughing. A teenage boy in Borough Park black is challenging a man maybe ten years his senior to explain why, if it's okay to be gay, it isn't okay to be a heroin addict or a prostitute or a murderer?

"If there are no rules, where do you stop?" he asks.

After about twenty minutes, I see an opening and approach Dov by the buffet table.

"Hi," I say, "I'm Rebekah. From the *Trib*."

"Rebekah!" he says, opening his arms for a hug. I oblige. "Thank you for coming." He looks to his friends and says, "This is the reporter I was telling you about. She found out who killed Rivka Mendelssohn. She's writing about Pessie."

Dov's friends nod and say hello.

"Do you have time to talk?" I ask.

"Of course," he says. "Let me finish here. There is a diner nearby. Can we meet there in half an hour?"

"Sure," I say. Dov gives me directions and Iris and I step out of the noisy, overheated synagogue and into the nearly still late night. Ocean Parkway is a four-lane highway with wide pedestrian and bicycle promenades leading to the beach at Coney Island on either side. It's a mix of residential and commercial here. Big prewar apartment buildings next to doctors' offices and day care centers, many with Hebrew lettering on the signs. We pass a Haredi man sitting alone on a bench, talking on his cell phone. He turns away from us as we pass.

"You seem a lot better," Iris says as we walk. "Do you think the medication is helping?"

"I guess it must be," I say. And then: "Thanks. For, you know. Taking care of me. I know I've been a pain in the ass. I just . . ." Just what? Just everything.

"It's okay," she says. "So you called your mom."

"Yeah. I can't help but think she, like, sees my number and is purposely ignoring me."

"That's dumb. She's the one that called you."

"And now she's disappeared again."

"You're the most ridiculous pessimist I know. She probably forgot to pay her bill or something."

"Maybe."

"Have you told your dad she called?"

"No," I say. "I thought I'd wait until I actually talk to her."

Dov and his friend Frannie get to the diner about twenty minutes after we do.

Frannie tells us she was also frum, but grew up in Baltimore. She and Dov met through Facebook, and now they're roommates, along with four other people, in a house near Poughkeepsie. The rent is cheap, and none of them like the big city. Dov says that they've both applied to the community college there, but won't hear whether they've been accepted until the summer.

"Pessie's sister Rachel told me that Pessie had a bad reaction to her medication, passed out, and drowned," says Dov. "But when I asked what medication she wouldn't tell me."

"Her husband said she'd been on antidepressants since after the baby was born," I say. "But you can't, like, OD on those."

Dov shakes his head. "You know that, and I know that, but Pessie's family probably thinks Prozac is the same thing as, like, OxyContin. They probably heard 'antidepressants' and assumed she wanted to kill herself. She still has sisters and brothers who need to get married and a suicide in the family would make shidduch much more difficult."

"What's that?" asks Iris.

"Shidduch is the matchmaking process," says Frannie. "And every little thing matters."

Dov nods. "And who wants to tell people their sister committed suicide? Blaming it on the goyish medication they don't know anything about is easier. But none of it makes any sense."

"What do you think happened?" I ask.

"I really don't know," he says.

"But you don't think it was suicide."

Dov wipes his hand across his face. "I don't. She just . . . wasn't the type. Some of us don't fit in from the start, but Pessie did. She was a happy kid. Kind of a goof, you know? Her mother was a great cook and she sold food for holidays and stuff. There were always people in and out of her house. And I think she was one of eleven or twelve. . . ."

"Twelve kids?" gawks Iris. "Holy shit." I kick her under the table.

Dov nods. "In a house like that, there just aren't enough adults to keep an eye on everybody. It can be easy to get into trouble. Her older brother went OTD back in, like, the nineties. I think he got into drugs."

"A lot of people do," says Frannie.

I've heard this before. Iris and I take the fact that we can dabble in drinking and drugs and casual sex, or take the occasional "sick day" from work, without really having to worry that one indulgence will lead to too many. We've had years to learn self-control and moderation in a world full of temptation and moral relativity. Not Dov and Pessie. Like the boy at the chulent asked: If there are no rules, how do you know where to stop?

"It caused her parents a lot of heartache and I know that upset Pessie. She used to say that she thought it was very selfish of her brother to leave like he did. But it was easy for her to say that. She was pious. She really believed that all the rules and rituals were important."

Dov pauses. "I haven't seen her in a few years, though. Since before she got married. If you can find him, you should talk to Sam Kagan. He probably knew her better than anyone."

Iris and I look at each other. Kagan. That's Aviva's last name.

"Sam Kagan?" I ask.

"They were engaged at one point. We all grew up together in Borough Park and our families moved to Roseville around the same time. His family and Pessie's lived a couple streets away from each other. There was a lot of turmoil in his family; his mom died in childbirth and his father never remarried. One of the sisters was OTD, too. Boys and girls aren't supposed to hang out, especially if they're not related, but no one noticed they'd become best friends. By the time they were sixteen, the families were discussing marriage. They got engaged, but there were big problems: he had been abused." Dov shakes his head. "Monsters like that are very good at finding the boys who are different."

"It's really hard to be gay and frum," says Frannie. She has been slumped low in her seat picking at a Greek salad while Dov has been talking. "The number one thing we are supposed to do is to make a big family. When you are gay you are shamed because you are gay. But also you are shamed because you betray Hashem by not marrying and making more Jews."

Dov nods. "Sam loved her, I think. But not the way she loved him. She would have married him even knowing he was gay. She probably thought she could fix him. It was a while before she agreed to consider another match. And Sam's been in a lot of trouble since he left. We haven't spoken in years. His family sent him to New Hope, too. I found him on Facebook when the lawsuit was first getting started and asked if he wanted to talk about joining. He was, like, fuck lawsuits, I've got a gun."

Dov purses his lips for effect, then sighs.

"I'm glad you're looking into this, Rebekah," he says. "I think what you did writing about Rivka Mendelssohn was very brave. And very important. A lot of people don't agree. I'm sure you've read the blogs. People can be such assholes online when they know they're anonymous. Believe me, I know. I've been getting death threats for, like, years. But maybe it takes someone outside the community to really investigate the bad things that are happening. I don't know how Pessie died, but I don't think she killed herself. And if all she was taking was Prozac, it doesn't make sense she OD'd. But if that's what her family is saying I doubt anyone in the community is going to do anything about it. They just want everyone to go back to normal and pretend no one has problems that can't be solved by prayer.

"But prayer doesn't make you straight," he continues. "That's why I'm in this lawsuit. And prayer doesn't do police work. Her sister says she had a reaction to her pills, but how could anybody know? There was no autopsy."

Dov wipes his mouth with his napkin and sets it on top of his plate.

"Do you know if Sam has a sister named Aviva?" I ask, feeling my face flush.

"Yeah," he says. "I think that was the one who went OTD. She was a lot older than us, though. I never met her."

"Do you know where she lives now?" asks Iris.

Dov shakes his head. "No idea."

It's after three when we leave the diner. Dov and I exchange phone numbers and he promises to call or text if he hears anything about Pessie or Sam.

In the livery cab home, Iris asks about the blogs Dov mentioned.

"Have you read any of them?"

"No," I say. And I don't want to, I think. Dov said he'd received death threats. And he said it with a kind of conciliatory tone—like I might have, too.

"Are you gonna look Sam up on Facebook?"

"I guess," I say. My lips feel swollen, buzzing with the anxiety shooting up from my stomach. "If he's OTD and she is, too, maybe they're close."

"Maybe he knows where she is."

"Maybe," I say. "Or maybe she bailed on him, too."

We get out in front of our building on Third Avenue. The F train rumbles above us. Across the street, a sanitation truck idles. One of the men who collect steel in grocery carts and push it to the scrapyard on Smith Street rolls by, his cart empty.

As soon as we get upstairs, I open my laptop and

Google myself. The first page of results is all stories from the *Trib,* but halfway through the second page there is a post on a Web site called FarFrum.com with the headline "Who Is Rebekah Roberts?" The author—whose name is simply "Administrator"—links to my articles about Rivka Mendelssohn and writes:

> *You've by now read all about the murder of Rivka Mendelssohn. We at FarFrum applaud the reporter who apparently risked her own life to get justice for Rivka—but* WHO IS REBEKAH ROBERTS? *A quick Google search reveals she is from Orlando and is a graduate of the University of Florida's school of journalism. Is she a Jew? And what do you think of her reporting on the charedi? We suspect there are some unhappy heebs out there. . . .*

There are thirty-three comments. The first is from username "davenDan":

> *this woman has blood on her hands. the goyim will use this to hurt us. she should be stopped before she brings death to us all.*

Username "Ruthie718" posted beneath davenDan:

> *she is not jewish. no jew would do this.*

Below that is "Heblow":

Slut. I heard she fucked a cop to get her story.

Further down, username "Bodymore666" posted:

just like you chassidish puppet-bitches to hate on someone speaking the truth instead of actual MURDERERS! no wonder everyone wants to kill you all.

There are multiple blog posts on multiple sites with hundreds of comments, all devoted to me. The comment threads routinely devolve into personal spats and general complaints. Some people say that I should be thanked for exposing the ugliness in their secretive community. They post about how my stories, and the recent sex abuse trials and the New Hope lawsuit, are bringing attention to problems they want solved. Most, however, post that I probably have ulterior and sinister motives and should not be trusted.

"I can't believe we didn't know about this," says Iris. "Does it freak you out?"

It does. It freaks me out so much I don't really know what to say. I feel stuck to the sofa, like my body is made of hot, wet sand. They see right through me, I think. They see I've just stumbled into all of this. They see I'm just a little girl looking for her mommy.

"I'm surprised you haven't gotten, like, hate mail or something," says Iris. "Oh God, do you think they know where we live?"

"Anybody can find out where anybody lives," I say.

"Okay, I can't think about this anymore," she says, standing up. "You should close your computer and go to bed." She looks down at me and offers her hand. I should take it.

"I'll go in in a minute."

She doesn't protest.

"Thanks for coming with me," I say.

"You're welcome," she says.

She uses the toilet and I hear the sink running.

"Good night," I call, when she comes out.

"Good night," she calls back.

After she closes her bedroom door I turn on the TV. NY1 says it'll be warmer tomorrow—if you can call forty-five warm. The computer is still open on my lap. I close my eyes and take ten deep breaths. My old therapist recommending breathing to "soothe" myself and return to reality. Usually, whatever ease the breathing brings is short-lived—a few seconds of relief from the pain in my intestines or the weight pressing down on my chest or the crackling heat in my face that makes it hard to see. But I can almost never do the one thing that would really help: refocus my attention away from the disaster my mind is racing toward. When I started at the *Trib*, one of he reporters warned me not to read the comments on any of my stories, which of course meant I had to do it. In college people rarely commented on our student newspaper articles. The residents of New York City, however, do comment. And most of the time, they are vicious, racist, homophobic, Islamophobic, sexist haters, and the "dialogue" usually devolves into ranting about Obama. The people posting on FarFrum and the other blogs seem split into a similar ratio of reasonable to crazy. There is, however, a legitimate question buried in the responses, and it's that question that is making my anxiety come alive: what do *I* think of what I am doing? Have I seriously considered the fact that exposing Jews to scrutiny from the gentile world is a potentially dangerous thing? That for, oh, all of civilization, pretty much every generation has persecuted or slaughtered the wandering chosen people? Have I internalized the number six million? Can I defend the fact that I am reporting on the darkest corners of this community, writing about their deaths, not their festivals or small businesses or artistic endeavors? I didn't ask this question when I was reporting about Rivka Mendelssohn, but now I have to. And, even though the terror has me practically bolted to the futon, I know the answer is yes. In college, one of my professors did a lecture on the theories of journalism's "role" in society. One of those theories was called the "wandering spotlight"—the idea that the light of scrutiny spins, resting on people in power and instances of injustice. And you never know when it might land on you. In January, I landed on Borough Park.

Now, it looks like I've landed on Roseville.

I click into Facebook and search for Sam Kagan. More than a dozen profiles pop up, but one catches my eye immediately. The photo is of a young man holding one of those AK-47-looking rifles. His head is shaved and he is wearing a white "wife-beater" tank top. Facebook says he is "in" Cairo, New York—which according to the Google map is about sixty miles north of Roseville—and "from" Brooklyn. The page is set to private, which means I can't see any of his friends or what he's posted, so I click the profile picture to get a closer look. When this photo was taken, Sam was thin, with knotty, defined muscles, and strawberry-blond hair. The only thing that might tip you off that he is Jewish is his slightly long nose, a nose very much like mine. The photo was taken on September 14, 2008, by someone named Ryan Hall.

I click the message button and begin typing.

Hi Sam. I'm a reporter with the New York Tribune working on a story about Pessie Goldin. I know it sounds crazy, but I think it's possible that you and I are related! Shoot me a message if you get this—I'd love to chat.

Sam's page doesn't list any family, so I click on Ryan Hall, whose page is also set to private. His profile picture is a faraway shot of a male in a canoe on a lake. Ryan, according to Facebook, is "from" Greenville, N.Y.

I decide to message him, too:

> *Hi Ryan, I'm a reporter for the New York Tribune and I'm trying to get in touch with Sam Kagan. Any chance you could pass my info along to him? Feel free to message me back. . . Thanks!*

I send an e-mail to the *Trib*'s library asking for a background search on Sam Kagan and Ryan Hall. I add that they likely live—or lived—upstate. And then I go back to Facebook and do what I have done several times over the past five years: I search for Aviva Kagan. But none of the Aviva Kagans that come up match. They are too young or too old. Probably, I know, she married, and has a new last name. Or maybe she never joined Facebook. I pick up my phone and scroll to the number I've been told is hers. I know it by heart now. I will die with this phone number planted, roots deep, in my brain. Maybe it is all I will ever know of her. I press CREATE NEW CONTACT and enter just a first name: Mom.

CHAPTER SEVEN

AVIVA

When I returned to Borough Park my mother had been dead for almost half a year. She was forty-seven and Sammy was breach. Something went wrong during the delivery—no one ever told me what, exactly. She never got to hold her ninth child. Eli and his new wife were already living in the apartment above my mother and father, so they took the baby. My father was not equipped to care for an infant. My sister Diny was engaged, and my two teenage brothers were studying in Israel. Only Sara, who was eight, and Chasi, who was twelve, still needed looking after, and Chasi could mostly look after Sara.

I took the bus from Ocean City to Philadelphia and then to Manhattan. Eli came to meet me at the house in Coney Island where I'd spent nights with your father. I tried to hug him when I answered the door but he stepped back. He was furious that I was wearing pants. He lectured me for a long time. He said making shidduch for Diny had been nearly impossible because of me. He said her fiancé had no sense and that we would have to support them because his family was poor and that Diny's job at the grocery would barely pay their rent. He said the only way for my sisters, and now little baby Sam, to avoid the same fate was for me to move away and marry as quickly as possible.

I think of it now, and I see that Eli was still practically a boy then, just twenty-two years old. But he was also a man with a pregnant wife, a dead mother, and an infant brother to raise. He told me that after I called he'd hoped I would come home and help him take care of the family.

"But I see now I was mistaken," he said. "You disrespect me the moment you see me. You disrespect Hashem."

I looked down at my hands in my lap, at my pants, and tears began to form in my eyes. He had no idea what the past year and a half had been like for me, and he had no desire to know. He just wanted me to help him make his life easier. I asked if he had told my sisters that I telephoned. He had not.

"How do I know what kind of ideas you are going to give them, Aviva? How can I let them see you?"

I remember thinking, I should be very angry at the way he is treating me. I wish now I had shouted back, *Let* me?! Let me see *my* family? The outrage rose inside me, but it was not a rocket like it had been before. I was so tired, Rebekah. So much had gone so wrong. I had failed at creating a life away from Borough Park. This, it seemed in that moment, was what mattered. What I really thought about his stupid hat and beard or my sisters' shidduch or dressing *tznius* didn't matter if I could not survive without them. And when I think back now, I know it did not matter to Eli, either. Now I know he did not expect me to believe everything we did was meaningful. He did not believe it all himself, but he couldn't tell me that. He couldn't tell anybody. That was part of how it worked.

I asked him what I had to do. He said I should stay by Coney Island until he made some calls.

"Can I see the baby?" I asked.

Eli said he would be in touch. The next day, he called and asked me to come watch Sammy while his wife, Penina, prepared my family's apartment for Shabbos dinner with Diny's fiancé's parents. I borrowed a skirt and stockings from one of the girls staying by the house and took the subway to Borough Park. It was noon, and the streets were full of people shopping and running errands before sundown. I felt like I was watching them from far away. It was so familiar—the sound of men and women speaking in Yiddish, the train rattling above New Utrecht Avenue, the Hebrew lettering in the store windows—but it was as if I wasn't really there. I was almost surprised when a woman ran into me with her stroller. I felt as though she should have been able to pop me like a soap bubble and keep walking home. You do not matter, Aviva, I told myself. This all goes on without you.

Eli met me at the end of our block and secreted me up the back staircase to the third-floor apartment. For as long as I can remember, the apartment was used as temporary housing for family visiting from Israel. My father's cousin Ezra stayed there by his wife and their twin sons for several years when he and my father were starting their business. After that, my mother's cousin Yankel stayed for a year while he worked for a company that exported Torah scrolls. Now, the apartment was my brother Eli's. Penina greeted me with a shy smile. She was nineteen years old, and eight months pregnant, padding around in wool socks. Penina and I had been in the same school, but she was a year behind me and I did not know her well. She was cooking chicken soup and the apartment smelled wonderful. She took me into the bedroom where Sammy lay in the same white crib all the children in our family had slept in. He was just a little bigger than you were when I left and I felt that same squeeze in my heart when I looked at him. Could I start again, I wondered. Could I take care of little Sammy? Could I give him what I could not give you? Eli left and Penina went downstairs and I spent the day with Sammy. He had more hair than you did, and his was lighter. He had a pink birthmark on his left shoulder blade in the shape of a smile. I fed him and held him and sang to him all afternoon. In Florida, I read you the books your father and your grandparents said were "classics," books about bunnies and moons, but there were no baby books in Eli and Penina's apartment. I told Sammy about you, and I asked him if he thought it would be better for him if I stayed in Brooklyn or went away. What is better, I asked him, a sister who is absent, or a sister who is a problem? Because even then, I knew that if I stayed I would never be able to do what Eli wanted. Not for long, anyway. What kind of man will you become? I asked Sammy. Will you be pious? Will you be afraid? Will you be wise? I remember thinking that I did not want him to become like Eli and my father if he didn't want to, but I didn't want to spoil him for this world, either, if that was how he wished to live.

I was not invited to Shabbos dinner, and Eli insisted on telling my father that I was home himself. I stayed in the apartment and helped Penina put Sammy down while Eli went downstairs after the girls had gone to bed. He returned an hour later with my father. My father is a big man. Broad shouldered and tall, but he had shrunk significantly in the time I was away. He looked older. He had dusty brown circles beneath his eyes and his beard was whiter and unkempt without my mother's attention. Neither of us said a word. I didn't run to him and he did not reach for me. I had missed my mother's death, and he had missed his first grandchild's birth. The gap between us was enormous, and I knew immediately that it was unbridgeable. Or rather, that it would never be bridged. Penina went to the kitchen to bring tea. I sat on the sofa and my father sat in the armchair with Eli standing beside him. They both looked at me as if they expected me to begin speaking.

"Diny is engaged," I said.

My father nodded.

"When is the wedding?"

"The wedding is in the spring," said my father.

"I would like to help," I said. Diny would need to shop for a *sheitel* and a dress and new clothing for her married life. We would need to reserve a hall, send invitations, select a caterer and decorations, create a seating chart. My brothers and uncles and aunts and cousins would fly in from Israel and we would need to arrange for their stays. I wondered: had the family come for Mommy's funeral? She did not live to see any of her daughters married. But I would make sure that Diny's wedding was beautiful, just how she would like it.

"I do not think that is a good idea, Aviva," said my father. "I think it is better if Penina helps Diny make preparations. Your tante Leah has offered as well."

I did not object because I knew he was not going to change his mind. He spoke without emotion in his voice, but I could see he was struggling. He did not look me in the eyes. I wanted to ask him about my mother. Did she know I loved her? Did she know I had not imagined for a moment that when I said good-bye that late August morning, when I told her I was going to Crown Heights to buy new shoes, that I would never see her again. I knew it would be a long time. Years, perhaps. But what is a few years when you are eighteen and wild with ideas? What is a few years in a world suddenly a billion years old? If man came from monkeys, maybe I would live to be one thousand. Maybe we all would. I hadn't written because

I assumed they would throw my letters away, like Tante Leah threw Gitty's away. I had not even known Mommy was pregnant again.

When Penina came back into the living room, my father rose. I did the same.

"I am very tired," he said. "We will talk more tomorrow."

I had not expected to be welcomed home with a celebration, but I had also not expected the coldness. My father was never a cruel man. He was strict, but loving. He told us stories around the dinner table. He fished with us in the Catskills. On Purim, he helped us create our costumes—assisting my mother with face-painting and hairdos and hat-making. He walked us to parties up and down the streets, smiling, stopping to chat with whomever we encountered along the way. When Rivka died, he cried more tears than my mother. He held her swollen eleven-year-old body and shook. I wished I could have told him that I named you for her. Two years later, Diny named her first daughter Rivka.

After my father went downstairs, I began to cry. Eli was unsympathetic. He said that gossip about where I'd been and what I planned to do would upstage Diny's day of joy. I did not ask what Diny thought because I was afraid she might agree with Eli and my father. And anyway, it did not matter what she thought. She would go along with what they wanted.

"Why did you ask me to come home?" I wailed.

"Because you can still find your way back to Hashem," said Eli. "But not here. Tatty and I think it is best if you go Israel to live with Feter Schlomo and Tante Golda. They have a new baby and you can help care for her. They have offered to arrange shidduch. Finding a match will be easier there."

I shouldn't have been surprised, Rebekah, but I was. In one hour they had determined I would not be allowed to rejoin my family. My father made the decision without even looking at me.

"Is it so easy for you to send your sister away?" I asked Eli, tears falling down my face.

"You already left!" shouted Eli. The boom of his voice startled Penina. She put her hand on her protruding belly, as if to shelter the child inside. "You thought nothing of us! We *searched* for you, Aviva! We thought you were dead! And when we found out you had run off with a goy . . ." He was so enraged he could scarcely speak. He was spitting into his thin copper beard. "You killed Mommy, Aviva."

"Eli!" whispered Penina. But her protest was weak. She only wanted calm. And Eli barely heard his wife.

"She *loved* you! And that meant nothing to you. But you question why we do not welcome you back? You are a selfish girl. You are dangerous to this family."

I stared at him, my mind knocking like a pinball between anger and despair and longing, hitting each feeling with a force that shook me. I held my head in my hands, but I couldn't stop it. I sat back down on the sofa and rocked myself. Forward, forward, forward. Eli and Penina exchanged a look. A look like the look the rabbi in Orlando exchanged with the woman who didn't know the mikveh. In their faces I saw that my physical reaction to their decision to send me to live five thousand miles away told them they'd done the right thing. I was dangerous; I was to be managed. I grabbed my hair and rocked harder. A long stream of clear liquid hung from my nose, swaying as I moved. I saw it and didn't care. I liked it. Let him see my sadness pouring out of me.

"Wipe your face, Aviva," said Eli, not a trace of pity in his voice.

But I felt like I needed my hands to hold my mind still. Penina took a napkin from the table.

"Here," she said, leaning over me, her belly bumping my shoulder. When I did not take the napkin, she scooped up the stream herself and wiped my face for me as if I were a baby. And I did feel helpless then, Rebekah. I would not have agreed to go to Israel and live with Schlomo and Golda and their spoiled children if I thought I had a better choice. I knew I could never go back to Florida. I had proved to your father the only thing that would keep him from taking me back, which was that I was an unfit mother. And I knew I would not survive the winter in a car with Gitty. I know now that there were other choices, but I couldn't see them then. And truthfully, when I resigned myself to their plan, I felt a slight relief.

I would do what they told me to do. I would go back to following the rules and the rules would make it possible to live. I would make no decisions. I would be like a train on a track. Turns and stops and the destination all set by someone else.

Eli and Penina went to bed and I fell asleep in my clothing, curled up on the sofa. I woke up to Sammy's quiet crying at three o'clock. I had a headache and my eyes were red and swollen. I splashed hot water on my face in the bathroom and tied one of Penina's scarves around my hair. There were half a dozen subway tokens among the loose change in a dish by the front door. I took two and stepped out of the apartment into the darkness. It was September, my favorite month in New York. The air still almost warm in the middle of the night. At first I was just walking, making loops in the neighborhood toward the shuttered stores on New Utrecht Avenue. And then I turned south, back toward Coney Island.

CHAPTER EIGHT

REBEKAH

I wake up around noon, and when I open my computer I see that the library has e-mailed me with attachments on Sam Kagan and Ryan Hall. I start with Sam. He was born, like me, in 1989. The search lists addresses in Roseville, New Paltz, and Cairo, New York. Could the Roseville address be where my grandparents live? Are they still alive? There are three possible phone numbers listed. Without even getting out of bed, I try the first number, which corresponds to the Roseville address. A woman answers the phone.

"Hello?"

Aviva? "Hi," I say, stumbling. "Is this Aviva?"

"Aviva?" says the woman. "Who is this?"

"I'm sorry," I say, throwing the covers off. "My name is Rebekah Roberts. I'm trying to reach Sam Kagan."

"Sam has not lived here in years."

"Oh," I say. "Can I ask who am I speaking to?"

"Please do not call this number again."

"I'm sorry," I say, but it is too late. She has hung up. "Fuck!" I know better than to call a possible source without ready questions and a plan to keep her talking. But

I'm not thinking like a professional, I'm thinking like a desperate orphan. Fail.

I go back to my laptop and dial the second number listed for Sam. Before I press SEND, I take a deep breath. Another. In and out. I will take control of the conversation. I will speak slowly. I will introduce myself as a reporter first, and then ask if he is related to Aviva. But the number goes to voice mail: "This is Sam. Leave a message."

"Hi," I say. "My name is Rebekah Roberts. I sent you a message on Facebook. Um, if you can, give me a call." I leave my number and then hang up. My face is hot. My lips itch. The Kagans are real people. With addresses and phone numbers. With voices and attitudes. They are so close.

The last number I dial corresponds to the Cairo address. A woman answers.

"Hi," I say. "I'm trying to reach Sam Kagan."

"Sam? He doesn't live here anymore. Did you try his cell?"

"I left a message," I say.

"Okay," she says.

"So, this might sound like a kind of random question, but you don't know a girl named Pessie Goldin, do you?"

"Sure," says the woman. "I mean, not well or anything. She used to hang out with Sam and Ryan sometimes."

"Did you know she died recently?"

"Pessie? Really?"

"Yeah," I say. "I'm actually a reporter for the *New York Tribune* working on some articles about her. I've heard she and Sam were close."

"They grew up together," she says. "What happened? When did she die?"

"Early this month," I say. "That's what I'm writing about. It's kind of a mystery. Her husband found her in her bathtub, but he thinks she might have, like, been killed."

"Jesus. I can't believe I didn't hear about it. If you're looking for Sam you should talk to Ryan."

"Do you have his number?"

"Yeah," she says, and gives it to me.

"Do you mind if I ask your name?"

"Kaitlyn," she says. "With a K."

"And your last name?"

"Morris. Am I gonna be in the paper?"

"I'm not sure," I say. She seems okay with this. "Is this the best number to reach you at? In case I have any more questions?"

She gives me her cell number. "I'll text Ryan and Sam and let them know you want to talk."

After we hang up, I click into the search attachments for Ryan Hall. The library found two addresses: one is the Cairo address where Kaitlyn picked up the phone; one is about fifteen miles away, in a town called Greenville. I call the phone number listed for the Greenville address, but it just rings and rings.

I go into the kitchen to make coffee and while it's brewing my phone rings. It's a blocked number, which I assume is the city desk.

"Hi, it's Rebekah," I say.

"Rebekah Roberts?" It's not the city desk.

"Yes."

"My name is Nechemaya Burstein. Levi Goldin gave me your phone number. Are you still reporting on the death of Pessie Goldin?"

"I am."

"Good," he says. "I have some information I would like to share with you. I realize it is a lot to ask, but might you be able to travel to Roseville tomorrow to meet in person?"

"I might," I say, thinking, maybe Saul will loan me his car. "Were you a friend of Pessie's?"

"I did not know her particularly well. But I believe her death may have been part of a larger plot."

"A plot?"

"I do not wish to say more over the telephone, if you do not mind."

"Okay," I say. "Let me get back to you in a couple hours. Is that all right?"

"Yes," he says, and gives me his phone number,

When we hang up I Google Nechemaya Burstein. He is, apparently, a member of the Rockland County Chevra Kadisha, which is a Jewish burial society. His name pops up in a 2012 article in *The Journal News* about two men from Roseville traveling to Israel to attend a conference on Jewish burial rites.

"As our community grows, so do our responsibilities," he is quoted as saying. "This conference is an opportunity to improve our response to those in need."

The group's Web site doesn't say much—just that they are members of the National Association of Chevra Kadisha and affiliated with three funeral homes, two of which are in Roseville. I encountered a Jewish burial group once before when the NYPD allowed their members to snag Rivka Mendelssohn's naked body from a pile of scrap along the Gowanus Canal. At the time, those black-hatted men did not strike me as the kind who would reach out to a secular female reporter with a tip. But maybe it's different upstate.

Iris finally comes out of her bedroom about twelve thirty. She's got her hair in a ponytail and is carrying a yoga mat.

"I figure if I'm bailing on work I should do something semi-productive," she says, opening the refrigerator. She picks up a carton of orange juice and shakes it, then pours some into a glass that had been sitting upside down on the drying rack in our sink.

"You are a better woman than I." I haven't done any sort of physical exercise, other than walking to and from the subway, since getting out of the hospital in January. I know enough to know that I should; that exercise is almost as good for depression and anxiety as, well, antidepressants and antianxiety pills, but going to the gym—or yoga or Zumba or spinning or whatever Iris does—feels really, like, optimistic. Like, look at me, I'm so *healthy*. Fuck that.

"You working your shift?" she asks.

"Yeah," I say.

"Brice is coming over tonight. I was thinking maybe we could all get drinks together or something. Are you done at ten?"

"Should be," I say.

"Cool. I'd love us to hang out a little more."

"Yeah?"

"You'd like him if you got to know him," Iris says. "It's stupid that you judge him by the way he looks."

"I don't," I say.

"Yes, you do," she says. "I love you, but sometimes you're kind of a reverse snob. Just because he likes nice clothes and products doesn't make him an asshole."

"I never said he was an asshole."

"He told me he loves me the other night," she says, sitting on the sofa.

"The other night? You didn't tell me!"

"I'm telling you now," she says.

"Did you say it back?"

Iris nods.

"Is this a good thing?"

"I'm really happy," she says. "It just feels fast."

"They say when you know, you know," I say.

"He mentioned getting married."

"Are you serious?" Pop, there goes the pilot light in my stomach.

Iris nods.

"*How* long have you been dating?"

"Four months, but three exclusively," she says. "But

it's . . . intense. He really knows what he wants. Ford offered him a job managing models in Asia. . . ."

"Asia?!"

"He's not gonna take it," she says. "He doesn't want to leave New York yet."

Yet.

"But his career is good," she continues. "And he wants a big family."

"How old is he?"

"Twenty-eight."

Iris wants me to say something encouraging, which is what a real friend would do. A real friend would be thrilled for her. A real friend would feel elation, not dread.

"What are you telling me, exactly?"

She hesitates, unsure herself, it seems. "I guess I'm telling you that . . . he might be the one."

"The one? Do we really believe in that?"

"I do," she says. "You know that."

"Do I, like, need to look for a new roommate?"

"No," she says, sounding slightly irritated. "I mean, maybe, eventually. But . . . I'm trying to tell you something happy. And kind of scary. Like, what if this is the guy I'm gonna have babies with?"

"And I'm being selfish."

"A little."

I exhale and lean forward to hug her. "I'm sorry," I say. "I'm *happy* for you."

What I don't say is that I worry I may have forgotten

what happiness feels like. I'm not a zombie like I was a couple weeks ago, but what she's going through—*falling in love* . . . I can't even fathom such a thing.

"Thanks," she says, getting up. I can tell I've hurt her. I can tell that the way I reacted has made a mark, maybe even a permanent one, on our friendship. I am ashamed and afraid at the same time. But I don't know what to do.

"I'm sorry, Iris," I say again.

"It's okay," she says. But I can tell she's shut me out. She rinses her glass and grabs her keys.

"So, I'll see you tonight?" I ask.

"Sure," she says. "We'll be here."

After Iris leaves, I stay curled on the couch for a few minutes, trying to think my way out of the pain in my stomach. You haven't lost your best friend over one selfish reaction, I tell myself. You haven't.

Ten minutes later, I send Iris a text that says "I love you" and then I call Saul and tell him about Nechemaya.

"He wants to meet in Roseville," I say. "Any chance I could borrow your car?"

"Sure," he says. "You're in luck. I'm staking out a nightclub in Greenwich Village but there's a bench on the sidewalk outside. The Doom Room. Do you know it?"

"The *Doom Room*? No. What are you doing there?"

"My client thinks her husband is seeing a dominatrix," Saul says, chuckling.

"It sounds like we've switched jobs." I staked out a fetish place in Queens last year when we got a tip that a local politician was into S&M. The *Trib* paid day rates to keep a photog and a reporter sitting outside for almost a week, around the clock, to get that story. But none of us saw him coming or going. I don't miss that kind of work at all, but I know that I have to prove myself capable of coming up with headlines on my own if I have any hope of getting a staff job—and thus some freedom—at the *Trib* or anywhere else. Coming up with headlines means having sources, which are basically impossible to cultivate sitting at a desk rewriting copy. I've been hiding in that office since Aviva called. It's time to get out.

"I went to a chulent last night," I say. "And I met a guy who knew Pessie. Listen to this: the Sam she was engaged to is Sam *Kagan*. Aviva's brother. I found a number for him in Roseville and when I called the woman said he hadn't been there in years. I asked for Aviva, too, and the woman got all upset. She definitely knew her."

"How old is this Sam?"

"The readout I got from the library at the *Trib* says he's my age, almost exactly."

"You know," says Saul, "I believe Aviva's mother died in childbirth while she was in Florida . . ."

"What? Wait, how long have you known that?"

"I guess I'm just remembering," says Saul. "I wonder if Sam is that child?"

My mother is motherless. "I can't believe you didn't tell me this before."

"I'm sorry," he says. "I'm just . . ."

“We need to talk,” I say. “It’s time.”

Saul takes a moment to answer. “Okay. I will be in the Village starting at about nine tonight. Why don’t you come join me?”

Right before I leave for my shift, I call Larry at the Shack and inform him I have a meeting tomorrow with a member of the Roseville burial society about the Pessie story. He says I can put in for my day rate and get paid for mileage.

“If I stay overnight, do you think I can get reimbursed?” I ask. “I’ve got a couple leads on addresses related to the ex-fiancé.”

“Okay,” says Larry. “Run ’em down. Just one night, though. And make sure the room’s cheap. Less than one-fifty. I can swing that.”

On the subway to Manhattan, instead of listening to a WNYC podcast to pass the forty-five-minute ride, I do something I haven’t done in months: I think about a story. When a woman dies, the first suspect is always the husband. But if Levi Goldin killed his wife he wouldn’t be begging a reporter to pay attention to her death, so I feel safe assuming he’s not the perp. It sounds as though Sam was the one that dumped Pessie, so jilted lover doesn’t fit, either. Unless she had another ex-fiancé, or lover, which Levi isn’t likely to know about. Her family probably wouldn’t know either—though even if they did I can’t imagine they’d tell me. So far, Sam seems like the best possible source for information on what was happening in Pessie's life. Sam and maybe this Nechemaya. The fact that Nechemaya called me is, frankly, a huge coup. If he didn't hate me, I'd call Tony and brag: Scoop's got a scoop. I wonder if he'd even want to hear from me again. He probably thinks I dumped him because I got bored or hooked up with someone else. He doesn't know that I've never had a relationship that lasted more than four months. He doesn't know that the only time I didn't run when I felt like I might be in danger of falling in love was when I was pregnant in college and imagining that my boyfriend and I would make up for where my dad and Aviva went wrong. He doesn't know that that boyfriend was also sleeping with two other people, and that Iris was the one who took me to Planned Parenthood. He doesn't know that I haven't been able to make myself come since we broke up. He's probably with somebody else by now, anyway.

Shit. Iris.

I call her but the call goes to voice mail. Maybe she has her phone on silent for yoga.

"Hey," I say, "I'm really sorry but Saul says he has some stuff to tell me about my mom, and I think I should hear it before I head upstate tomorrow. Get this: apparently her mom died in childbirth, like, while she was still with my dad. And Saul thinks Sam might be that kid. I doubt I'll be too late. Maybe you guys can wait up? I'm meeting him right after work. Okay. Did you get my text? I love you. I'm really happy for you. Okay. Bye."

When I get into the office I call Nechemaya and tell him I can meet him tomorrow.

"Thank you," he says. "There is a Starbucks in the Target just off the Thruway. Can we meet at eight thirty?" Saul always used to ask me to meet him at Starbucks. So did a former Haredi woman I met a few months ago. What's with Starbucks?

"Sure," I say.

I walk over to the editors' desk at the center of the newsroom and fill Mike in on my plans tomorrow. There have been two arrests in Drug Dorm Den, and a small plane just went down on Long Island, so he's not terribly interested in my little maybe-murder upstate. I start to walk back to my desk when he stops me.

"Wait," he says. "Does this mean you have a car now? We need somebody in Nassau County tonight to door-knock when we get an ID on the plane vics. I'd rather have you on that than this . . . other thing."

"It's a friend's," I say. "He can't loan it to me until tomorrow."

"Oh." And he's done with me.

I leave work at ten and get on the F train to West Fourth Street. Saul is sitting inside his car, which is parked in front of what I assume is The Doom Room. It looks like your standard downtown club—blacked-out windows, no sign—except that there isn't a velvet rope or bouncer outside. I knock on the passenger-side window and Saul unlocks the door.

"How's it going?" I ask.

"Oh fine."

"Anything happening?"

"I've been here two days and haven't seen him or the woman who the wife thinks he's seeing."

"How does the wife know what she looks like?"

"She found a photograph in his e-mail," he says.

"How long are you going to keep waiting?"

"As long as she wants, I suppose. Or until I get a better client. She is paying well. By the day. And a bonus if I find them together."

"How would you find them together?"

"I would have to follow him inside."

"Exciting."

Saul shrugs.

"So," I say, "Aviva's mother died in childbirth?"

"Yes," says Saul. "That is what I was told."

"But you decided not to tell me."

"It's not that I decided not to."

"You just didn't."

Saul looks out the window. "What do you want to know?"

"Everything. Anything. How did you meet? What was she like?" I didn't ask Saul these simple questions when we first met in January. I'm not sure if it was because there didn't seem to be time, or if because, even now, the possible answers terrify me. The devil I know—the runaway mother I've had nightmares about meeting in strange, perilous circumstances—is still less frightening than the unknown truth. I don't know how the truth will hurt me, but I'm pretty sure it will. I've been practicing for the pain as long as I can remember. Closing my eyes at night and imagining the worst and how it will feel when I encounter it. I felt a lot of fear lying in that little bed in Orlando: My heart raced as I discovered her happy, beautiful, raising a different, better daughter. It raced as I imagined her fat and unthinking in Brooklyn, surrounded by a dozen screaming children and a husband she hates. And it raced when she was a crack whore, or a surfer, or a nurse, or long dead and buried without a headstone. I wonder how many hours I lost letting my mind spiral into those stories, that dread? Here I am, I think. About to learn the truth.

"I knew her casually in the neighborhood," says Saul. "Two of my younger sisters went to school with her and sometimes she would come to our apartment to play, or for Shabbos dinner. She was just a child then. Maybe eight years old when I was eighteen. I remember my mother complimenting her table manners. She used to ask my little sisters why they didn't have table manners like Aviva Kagan."

"Table manners?"

"It was very important to my mother that my sisters marry well."

"Make shidduch," I say, parroting Dov.

"Yes." Saul looks at me with a half smile. I think he might be as nervous as I am. "My mother felt that anything less than perfect manners might stand in their way. I don't remember Aviva being especially polite or impolite—I wasn't really paying attention. But my mother used to say her name to my sisters all the time. It struck me as strange because I always had the sense that she was a bit of a troublemaker. She behaved one way when adults were present and another way when she thought they weren't. She talked about movies she said she'd seen, or books she said she'd read—none of which would have been allowed by the rebbe, or her parents, probably. And she told stories about people she said she knew, people she'd met in her father's taxicabs."

"You think she was lying?"

"I did then," says Saul. "I told my mother I didn't think she was a good influence. But my mother didn't believe me. She was terrified my sisters would not make good matches, and she was always trying to fix them in some little way. My sisters were timid and not terribly creative, but my mother constantly imagined them into trouble. She could believe no good of them."

That sounds like a terrible way to grow up. "Did she believe good of you?"

"Oh yes," he says. "She was very different toward her sons. We could do no wrong. I married when I was nineteen years old and we moved to Lakewood, New Jersey, for a time before coming back to Brooklyn. I did not see your mother again until about ten years later."

"Did she remember you from before?"

Saul nods. "We met again at the house in Coney Island. I was separating from my wife and helping Menachem Goldberg renovate. Menachem was in his fifties and a widower. He and his late wife had emigrated from Ukraine through Israel in the 1950s. When his wife died of cancer, he renounced his faith, and his children shunned him. He bought a rundown house to live in and he invited people to stay because he did not like to be alone. There was a woman from the community named Tova Horowitz who had been holding meetings in apartments around the city for people to come and question. She asked if she could have the meetings at the house and Menachem said yes. Aviva came for a meeting.

"I remember she didn't seem fearful that night. Most of the people who came were paranoid. They were certain their brother or father had followed them there, or that someone else in the group was a spy sent by their family. But not Aviva. She stayed all night. She had a notepad with her and she had written pages and pages of questions. Menachem and Tova and I had different perspectives, but they all validated what had been dawning on her, which was that much of what was deemed sacred in her life meant nothing to her."

I have been to the Coney Island house, and as Saul speaks I picture my mother in the same small living room-kitchen-dining room I'd stood in in January. It was full of people then, but seemed a lonely place.

"When was the last time you saw her?"

"Soon after she came back from Florida," he says. "Again, at the Coney Island house."

"And?"

"She was not there long. I was hoping we would talk but . . ." Saul clears his throat. He looks out the window and shifts in his seat. "Her mother had died while she was away and her family was very angry."

"Did she say anything about me?"

"We really didn't get much of a chance to talk," says Saul. "She came and left very quickly. And then she went to Israel. I heard from someone that she was back in New York, but that was probably ten years ago. Apparently, she was at the Coney Island house, but not for long."

And there it is. A rough sketch of twenty-three years in the life of Aviva Kagan. Coming and going. Was she always running from something? Or to it?

"When did you start communicating with my dad?"

"He made a trip to Brooklyn looking for your mother a few months after I'd seen her."

"Did you tell him she'd gone to Israel?"

"Your father always seemed like a nice man, and he clearly loved your mother, but I felt that if she left him, she must have had a good reason. I didn't think it was my place to tell him where she had gone."

"Did he tell you about me?"

"Yes."

"And that didn't make a difference?"

Saul hesitates. "At the time, it did not," he says. "I'm

sorry. I would make a different decision now."

"But you kept in touch."

"Your father sent me a card every year on Pesach, and I sent him one on Easter."

"That's cute," I say.

Saul looks at me disapprovingly. My dad doesn't like sarcasm either. "I don't have any other religious friends who are not Jewish," he says. "And I don't think he had friends who were not Christian."

"And when you heard she'd come back to New York you didn't reach out."

Saul confirms my statement with silence. My eyes start to burn and I look up, sniffing back the tears that are gathering. If Saul had just told my dad what he knew . . . what? At least we would have known she wasn't dead. My dad actually went to Israel once when I was in elementary school. He took his youth group to Bethlehem and the Galilee and brought back a bottle of water from the Jordan River that his church has been using to baptize people with ever since. A day trip to search for his baby mama wouldn't have been on the official itinerary, but might he have made an attempt? It almost makes me laugh, thinking of my dad hunting Aviva in the Holy Land. How poetic.

"Did he keep asking you?"

"No," says Saul. "He never asked me after the first time."

"Because he assumed you'd tell him if you knew."

Again, Saul's silence is a yes. I blink and blink but there is no holding back the tears now. And why should I hold them back? I haven't cried about my mother in years. I thought I'd outlived the sadness, but really I've just learned to live with it sitting quietly inside me, tainting everything. Gotta get it out, I think. Gotta get it out.

"I'm sorry, Rebekah," Saul says finally.

"It's okay," I say, wiping my nose. "You didn't owe us anything."

CHAPTER NINE

AVIVA

I got back to the house in Coney Island before the sun broke the horizon. The front door was open and I smelled brewing coffee inside. I walked toward the back of the house and there was Saul Katz in the kitchen, wearing a blue police uniform and reading a newspaper spread across the counter. His black belt and boots shined. He'd cut his hair short and lost weight since I'd seen him last, and he seemed to stand up straighter. He didn't hear me come in, and I stood in the doorway watching him for a few seconds. He was probably thirty or thirty-one years old then. Ten years older than me. The girl I borrowed the skirt from had told me that Saul recently left his wife and child and been shunned by his family and hers. But he was a success. He was up early, preparing to go to work protecting the city. Why was I incapable of such a thing? Was it because I was a woman? Or was it because I was weak?

"Saul," I said finally.

He looked up, and when our eyes met we both smiled. I couldn't help it. I was so happy to see a man who knew me and did not hate me.

"Aviva!" he exclaimed, leaning forward, looking me up and down.

"It's nice to see you," I said. And I remember that I meant it. I'll never forget how his eyes shone. They twinkled just like your father's did when I told him I would come live with him in Florida. I had been so powerful then. The way Saul looked at me in that pre-daylight kitchen made me feel powerful again. But by then, I sensed it wouldn't last.

"And you!" he said. "Where have you been?"

"Florida," I said.

He shook his head, amused. "You went with Brian."

I nodded. "And after a while I stayed with my cousin Gitty," I said. "In Maryland."

"You are well? Where is Brian?"

"Brian is in Florida," I said, leaving out the information he was really asking for. "You are a policeman now?"

Saul smiled again and patted the NYPD patch on his shoulder. "I am. I work in Crown Heights."

"Do you like it?"

"I love it," he said. "I meet so many people."

"You look very happy," I said.

"Thank you," he said. But he could not say the same thing about me. "I am so sorry about your mother, Aviva. Is that why you returned?"

I shook my head. "I only just learned that she died," I said. "If I had known I would have come back sooner." What I did not say, but what he probably knew, was that it was my fault. I left no way for them to contact me. No one knew I planned to leave because at the time it had seemed very important to keep our "Florida adventure" a secret. To speak of it, I foolishly imagined, might bring bad luck.

"Do you need a place to stay?" he asked. "There is room."

"I am moving to Israel," I said.

"Oh," he said. "Soon?"

I nodded. "Eli and my father do not want me here for Diny's wedding."

"Why Israel?"

"I am to live with family."

Saul looked puzzled. "What will you do there?"

"What else? Find a husband." My voice was flat. All the anger and loss I felt screaming at Eli had fossilized inside me as I walked through the night.

"Is that what you want?"

I didn't answer him.

"Aviva," he said. "You have friends here. You have choices."

I stared at him, blinking, hearing the words but not thinking that they applied to me. It was actually a good feeling, the hardness. If I could hold on to it, I thought, I could keep steady.

"Will you stay here today at least? There is a kugel in the refrigerator. And two empty beds. You can't have slept. I will be home in the afternoon. We can talk."

I nodded.

"Good," he said. "We've missed you. Your spirit and your questions. There are more of us, Aviva. I think you could help the new ones. You could tell them about your experience. Good or bad. It makes no difference. Just that window into another life, that it can't kill you."

I did not say anything. I did not say, *But Saul, it almost killed me.*

"Go upstairs. Take a shower if you like. There are linens in the bathroom. Rest."

After Saul left, I went upstairs. There were four bedrooms in the house, each not much bigger than a closet, all along a narrow hallway. The summer before we left for Florida, your father and I slept together in the room closest to the bathroom. The one with the window that looked over the little concrete backyard. We slept together on a single bed, never exactly comfortable, but so happy to be exactly where we were: together, naked, free. Intoxicated not just by each other but the circumstance, the fact that the long afternoons and sleepless nights seemed to be for nothing but our pleasure. Since I had last been there, the room had been transformed from a flop pad to a true bedroom. Three black-and-white framed photographs hung in a row on the wall across from the neatly made bed: one of the Brooklyn Bridge, one of a placid lake scene—upstate, probably—and one of three old men on the Coney Island boardwalk, standing with their backs to the camera, looking out onto the ocean. There was a small table with a lamp atop it and a fresh coat of pale blue paint on the walls. Everything was clean—even the thin carpet. I closed the door and took off my coat and shoes and then lay down. The morning sun was just beginning to come through the window as I closed my eyes.

I awoke in the early afternoon and used the toilet, avoiding my face in the bathroom mirror. I stood in the hallway and listened, but the house seemed empty. I lay down again and closed my eyes again, looking deep into the darkness for more sleep, more escape. Perhaps I could sleep through the next week, the next year. Perhaps I could sleep until I was dead. It was dark again when Saul knocked on the door.

"Aviva," he whispered, gently pushing the door open.

"Mmm," I murmured. I'd had an orgasm in my sleep—my dream a frenzy of seeking relief for the deep ache that crawled and scratched inside me, begging to be satisfied. It was a blur of men and women, lined up somewhere, and me grabbing ahold of whoever didn't push me away, groping, grinding against them like an animal in heat. The relief, when it finally came, was waves of warm. And then Saul's voice.

"Aviva," he said. "Would you like some dinner?"

"Saul," I said, my face still against the pillow. I wanted him more than I had ever wanted anything. I needed to keep that warm feeling for just a little longer. It didn't matter that it would be gone in minutes. Minutes was all I needed; all I deserved. I reached out my arm and he took my hand and sat down on the bed. "Lie here," I said. "Touch me." I felt his body tense, and I turned over beneath the covers to look up at him. By the time our eyes met, he had consented. He leaned forward and kissed me. It was the kiss I remember most. He was as hungry as I was. He lay down beside me, his uniform belt pressing against my stomach. I pulled off my sweater and I heard him gasp quietly. I had complete control over him. He would do anything I wanted at this moment. He didn't waste time asking me this and that like your father did at first ("can I touch you here?"), he just tossed back the blanket and climbed on top of me. We kissed and kissed and he held my face in his hands. "I don't have a condom," he breathed into my ear. "I want to, but we can't." I looked at him. We huffed in unison, both red-faced, exhilarated. "What?" I said, lost, barely listening. "I know, but we can't," he said again. I closed my eyes to his protest, smiling, falling back into the swell of the moment, arching my back to unhook my bra. "Just kiss me," I said. "Kiss me more." We kissed and I wiggled out of my skirt. I was naked and I felt as safe as I had ever felt. I knew nothing could go wrong. "Please," he said. But I couldn't hear him. I pulled down his zipper. He loved me, I thought. How could he not? "Please," I said. And that was all it took. We both kept our eyes open, each experiencing the other for those few minutes as everything we had ever wanted. Ecstatic, and alone. Afterward, he lay beside me, his hand resting on my ribcage. I turned my head toward him and, mercifully, he did not smile. A smile, I thought, would ruin it. This was serious.

It was dark in the room, and neither of us had anywhere to go, so we fell asleep together. It was long after dinnertime when I woke up. I slipped out of the bed to go to the bathroom. I hadn't planned to leave, but it quickly became the best choice, for both of us. If my family did not want me in Brooklyn, I would leave. Brooklyn meant less than nothing to me. I had been to Israel three times to visit family and my impression was that it was both much the same and completely different. I needed some completely different. Saul did not need me. Saul was just fine. I dressed as he slept, watching him for signs he was hearing me. He didn't move—what if he had moved?—and then I was outside, with a subway token back to Borough Park in my pocket.

Eli drove me to the airport. I dressed tznius. I brought very little from Florida, so it was easy to pull on Penina's cast-off stockings and a shapeless sweater and long skirt and pretend that it was simply practical. Half a day later I was at Ben Gurion, carrying a suitcase toward a taxi stand.

One year later, I agreed to marry a man named Etan Shiloh. He was twenty-nine years old and his family lived in the Old City. The wedding was small. Etan was a good husband to me. I tolerated his humorlessness and he learned to manage my moods. We were married for nearly ten years before he found my birth control pills. And then, just like that, it was over. I was sent back to Brooklyn.

PART 2

CHAPTER TEN

REBEKAH

Iris and Brice don't wait up for me. And if I want to get to Roseville by eight thirty—right in the middle of rush hour—I figure I have to leave at six thirty, before they're likely to wake up. I leave a note:

Hey lovebirds ☺ Got a meeting with a Jew upstate this morning. Then headed to try to find my uncle (??) Might stay over . . . will call. Drinks soon?? xoxo

It's been months since I've driven a car—my old Honda died before the New Year—and driving in New York City is more than a little hairy. It takes almost an hour to get through the Battery Tunnel, up the West Side and over the George Washington Bridge, during which time I am nearly sideswiped by a livery driver and a delivery truck, and end up the product of some serious taxi-driver rage when I accidentally "block the box" near Chelsea Piers. I follow the directions on my Google Maps up the Palisades and then north on the Thruway. The sky is white and the trees lining the road are still winter bare. On WNYC, Brian Lehrer is interviewing the parks commissioner about post-Sandy progress at city beaches. Iris and

I didn't make it to the beach last summer; we were still getting acclimated, I guess, and there is something almost unbelievable to begin with about the idea that the original concrete jungle even has beaches. But listening to this man talk enthusiastically about the Rockaway Beach Boardwalk, and the new Brooklyn waterfront's pop-up pool makes the prospect of spring—and even better, summer—seem almost real. I wonder if the sadness I've been stuck in has something to do with the weather. Does Seasonal Affective Disorder even exist in Florida?

After about twenty minutes on the Thruway, I see signs for Roseville. It occurs to me, as I pull into the vast lot outside of the Target-anchored shopping center, that escaping strip malls like this has been an unexpected perk of leaving Florida. I guess when they first got built somebody imagined that because all the stores are connected by a walkway, the Panera Bread and the Rite Aid and the Foot Locker and the Pier 1 might simulate a kind of neighborhood. But now that I've moved to New York City, I understand that a real neighborhood is one that can't be planned, but that grows like a field of wildflowers from whatever blows in and has the fortitude to survive.

The Starbucks is just inside the automatic glass doors of the Target, across from rows of red shopping carts. Nechemaya, or a man I assume to be Nechemaya because he is the only person I see wearing the ultra-Orthodox uniform, is sitting alone at a two-top with a venti-sized paper cup in front of him, typing intently on his smartphone.

"Mr. Burstein?" I say

He looks up. "Rebekah? Hello, yes. Thank you for coming." He pushes back his chair and stands up.

I hate not shaking hands with people I meet; it feels like our interaction is incomplete, somehow. But I guess if I'm going to report in the Haredi world I better get used to it. "I'm gonna grab some coffee real quick," I say. "You good?"

He nods. I wait in line behind a woman in a pink tracksuit talking on the phone to someone with whom she disagrees, and in front of a man with a gray ponytail and John Lennon–style eyeglasses carrying a shopping basket full of recycled toilet paper. At the counter, as I mix in milk, I watch Nechemaya. He takes a manila folder out of the black bag at his feet and places it in front of him on the table. With his left hand, he cups the lower half of his face and smooths his beard.

I sit down and he puts his hands over the folder. I take out my notebook.

"I do not wish to have my name in the newspaper," he says. "I am not coming to you because I wish to bring attention to myself."

"Okay," I say. "I won't publish anything you tell me now. But can we discuss the possibility again in the future?"

Nechemaya nods. His face is very round, and his beard, though several inches in length, is thin enough that the pale skin beneath it shows through. The beard is not an attractive addition to his face, but I suppose its aesthetic qualities don't enter into his decision to wear it.

"I have some information I hope you will follow up on. After Pessie Goldin was buried, the man and woman who live in the apartment above hers contacted me. They told me that the day Pessie died the wife saw a strange vehicle—a pickup truck—parked across the street from their building."

"What do you mean by 'strange'?"

"I mean unfamiliar," he says. "It was not a vehicle they had seen before. She said several neighbors saw the truck, too, but she was the only one who thought to write down the license plate number. She gave it to me and I gave it to the police, as well as contact information for the woman who saw the vehicle. About two weeks later, I learned the police had not contacted the woman or, as far as she knew, any neighbors, for an interview. I called and I was told that they could not discuss the case."

"You talked to Chief Gregory?"

"Yes. I consulted with the other members of chevra kadisha, and the Roseville *shomrim,* and we decided to take the information to Pessie's family. Myself and another member sat down with her father and mother last week, but they did not wish to pursue it further. They did not want more scrutiny on the family. They have four children younger than Pessie who still need to make shidduch. There are rumors that Pessie was taking drugs."

"Drugs? You mean medication?"

"Medication?"

"Levi told me Pessie had been taking antidepressants."

"That may have been what they were referring to. Truthfully, I do not know if they actually believe she had been involved in drugs or if they are just afraid of the rumors. They said Pessie was gone and there was nothing that would bring her back. But when I saw that Levi had spoken out about his suspicions, I contacted him and he gave me your phone number." He pushes the folder toward me. "I gave this information to the Roseville police chief. Now I am giving it to you."

I open the folder and inside find a single piece of lined yellow legal paper, torn in half. On it is written, in what I assume is Nechemaya's hand, *New York LCG6732.*

"The neighbors said the truck was blue and white. They could not provide a make or model."

"Did they see anyone get in or out?"

"No. She said she had been in the back of the apartment and only happened to walk by the front window as the truck was leaving."

"Would she be willing to talk to me? I don't necessarily have to use her name. I could just refer to her as a neighbor."

"Possibly," says Nechemaya.

"I'd also like to talk to some people who knew Pessie. I know it sounds a little crass, but the more the readers know about her the more they will care , and the more they care, the more likely it is that the newspaper will let me keep covering the story. I tried calling her parents, but the woman who answered the phone hung up on me. Do you know any of her friends?"

"I don't, but I will make some phone calls. And I believe the neighbors knew her fairly well. I will ask if they are available for an interview."

"Great," I say. "I can even do it over the phone if that's better for them."

Nechemaya nods. I fold the piece of paper and put it into my notebook.

"Why do you think the police chief never followed up on this?"

Nechemaya draws a shallow breath and flares his nostrils. "It is not like Brooklyn here in Rockland County. These people still think they can make us leave." He shifts in his chair, agitated. "This chief . . . I have heard him say in council meetings that he does not work for us because we do not pay taxes."

"You don't pay taxes?"

"Of course we pay taxes!" he says, a little too loudly. "Everyone pays taxes. But people are ignorant and it is easy to believe stories about us. We look different. Our children do not attend their schools. We do not mix with them so they assume we are bad."

"You said on the phone that you thought Pessie's death might be part of some kind of plot. What makes you think that?"

"There have been several instances of vandalism, and two of our young men were attacked along the road."

"Attacked?"

"Bottles were thrown at them by a passing car as they

walked. Again, we reported the incident and nothing was done."

"When was this?"

"January. The boys did not get a good look at the vehicle, or the occupants, so the chief said there was nothing he could do. The vandalism was at one of our yeshivas. Someone spraypainted a swastika and the words 'go home.' In Catskill, a woman attacked two Chassidish men at a grocery store. She spat on them and yelled slurs."

"And you think this might be related to Pessie's death?"

"How can we know if there is no investigation!" The woman sipping a Frappuccino next to us looks over. She rolls her eyes and shakes her head at me as if we share some similar understanding about how ridiculous people dressed like Nechemaya are. How unlike her and me. How downright *weird*. They cast themselves as "other" so it's easy to see them as such. But easy is lazy. I meet the woman's eyes with an expression like, *what?* You got a problem?

"I'm going to give this license plate number to my editor," I say. "But I'd also like to go to the Roseville police with it. Is that okay?"

"Of course," he says. "Perhaps they will take action now that the newspaper is involved."

"We'll see."

After Nechemaya leaves, I call Larry and fill him in on what I've learned.

"It's interesting, I'll give you that, but what's the story?"

"What do you mean?"

"What can you write for tomorrow? Your guy isn't on the record, and we can't print a license plate number."

"Right."

"I'll see if I can get somebody at the Shack to run the plate, but so far you don't have anything new on the record. Weren't you going to try to run down the ex-fiancé?"

"I'm on it," I say. "I've got a couple possible addresses and that's where I'm headed."

"Good. Go at the cops with the plate. If you're up there, maybe stop in instead of calling. Makes it harder for them to blow you off."

The Roseville police headquarters is inside a single-story brick building with one American flag and one black-and-white POW flag waving out front. The town clerk, the courthouse, the post office, and the cops all appear to share space. I park across the street in a low-rent strip mall whose anchor is a stationery and medical supply store displaying sun-bleached Hallmark cards, a portable toilet, and a FedEx sign in the window. A sticker on the door says WE ACCEPT MEDICAID. The smaller storefronts on either side are vacant. Leaning against the window in one is a FOR RENT sign with Hebrew lettering and a phone number. The other's window is soaped over. Three doors down is a wig shop, and next to that a store that sells Judaica and has a "*sofer*" present, whatever that means. The restaurant at the end of the strip is called The Grille. A neon sign indicates that they serve Heineken.

There are very few cars in the lot and none of the stores look like they're thriving.

The door marked ROSEVILLE POLICE is on the far side of the long municipal building. A bell announces my entry into the waiting area. Above a bench of metal chairs is a bulletin board with a faded "This Is Your Brain on Drugs" poster, and a AAA warning against texting and driving tacked to it. On the opposite wall are six framed photographs of Roseville police chiefs from 1930 to the present. Chief Gregory, unsmiling and thick-necked, has been in his position since 2000.

In the bullpen behind the reception desk are two women. Both are overweight, but the younger one is certifiably obese. She wears an enormous wool poncho over her jeans, and waddles around on sneakers worn down sideways by her weight. I'd guess she's twenty-five. The other woman is probably twice that. Both are bottle-blond. The younger one is on the phone and on the move, squeezing around the desks and office equipment like she's looking for something.

"I told you we don't have it," she says, clearly exasperated. "It's civil. We don't keep the civil files. You have to call the town clerk."

"Is that Friedman again?" asks the older woman, who is eating a pastry while standing in front of a printer spitting white paper.

"That's exactly what I told you last time, Mr. Friedman," says the girl, walking through a door marked

Authorized Personnel Only.

"Tell him to fuck off," mutters the older woman She looks at me and smiles. "Sorry for the language."

"No worries," I say.

"What can I do for you?" she asks, setting her pastry aside and brushing her hands on her stretchy black pants.

"I'm actually wondering if Chief Gregory is here."

The woman shakes her head. "He's not in today. Is there something I can help you with?" The girl comes back into the bullpen.

"I was hoping to see the chief," I say. "I'm a reporter for the *New York Tribune* and . . ."

"Oh!" says the girl. "Did you write the story about Pessie?"

"Yeah. I did."

"It's *so sad,*" she says. "You know, I knew her a little bit . . ."

"You didn't even know her last name until you saw it in the paper," says the woman.

"So? I knew her. I mean, not *well*. But she was so nice. And her little baby."

"Chaim," I say.

"Yes!" The girl is very excited. "I saw her at the Stop & Shop every week. A lot of the Jews around here don't talk to us, but she complimented my nail polish one time in checkout and after that we'd say hi and chat and stuff. Poor thing! Do they really think she was *murdered*?"

"Dawn, sit down you're making me nervous," says

the woman. Dawn sits. "This is Dawn. I'm Christine."

"I'm Rebekah," I say. "I spoke to the chief over the phone yesterday but I wanted to follow up . . ."

"You should talk to Van!" Dawn jumps up. "He was the one who found her."

"He didn't find her, Dawn," says Christine.

"Well, he was there. I mean, he worked the scene. He told me all about it. I'll go get him."

Dawn rushes back through the AUTHORIZED PERSONNEL door.

Christine sighs. "You drive up from the city then?"

I nod. "I was meeting someone from Pessie's community earlier. I figured I'd stop by while I was in the area."

"It's been a challenge, all the Jews moving in," says Christine. "They're just so different, you know? And they don't seem to want to interact with us. I mean, Dawn says she talked to that poor girl in the grocery store, but Dawn talks to everybody. Talks at, more like. I guess they come up here to get away from the city and do their own thing, but there's not much respect for our community. I was born in the city, too. We came up here when I was a kid in the seventies. It's a nice place to live. People are friendly. But . . . it hasn't been easy. More and more are coming, and they have so many kids. It's a strain. It really is. And a lot of people are just sick of it. I think that's how Chief feels. You know, if they want to be left alone, fine, leave 'em alone. But then they come asking for our help . . ."

Dawn returns to the bullpen.

"He's on his way!" she practically sings. "Can I get you some coffee? I forgot to ask."

"I'm good," I say.

"Are you sure? I'm getting some for Van."

"Officer Keller," says Christine.

"He always says I should call him Van," says Dawn.

Christine shakes her head and picks up her pastry. A moment later, Officer Van Keller walks through a door on my side of the reception desk. It is immediately clear why Dawn was so enthusiastic about summoning him: he is hot. Like, homecoming king hot. Blue eyes and curly, tar-black hair, a thin nose, and laugh lines like parentheses beside his mouth. The muscles in his chest and arms press slightly against the inside of his blue short-sleeve uniform shirt. Immediately—unconsciously—my hand goes to my head. If I had my long hair, I'd run my fingers through it, but I end up just scratching the side of my neck.

"'Morning," he says.

"Hi. Thanks for coming out. My name is Rebekah Roberts. I'm a reporter for the *New York Tribune*." I have to concentrate to keep myself smiling. He is astonishingly attractive.

"When she asked about Pessie, I said she should talk to you," says Dawn. "Are you sure I can't get you some coffee?"

Officer Keller looks at me.

"Okay," I say. "Thanks"

"I'll put on a fresh pot." She bounces out of the reception area, humming.

"Why don't we head back into the offices," he says.

I follow Officer Keller through the door, down a narrow hall, and into a small room with a desk and three mismatched chairs. There are no photos or plaques or posters on the walls; no bookshelf, no personal touches at all. Just a desktop computer and some notepads and files.

"Dawn showed me your article," he says. "It's a little frustrating, actually. I mean, we're not the ones who insisted on burying her without an autopsy. I don't know why he called the newspaper instead of us if he had a problem."

"He said he called, but didn't hear back."

"Do you know who he talked to?"

"I don't," I say.

Dawn comes in and sets two mugs of coffee on the desk.

"I'll be right back with milk and sugar," she says, and seconds later she is back with milk and sugar.

"Can I get you anything else?" she asks.

"We're great, Dawn, thank you," says Officer Keller. I imagine he spends quite a lot of time being polite to Dawn.

"Holler if you need me," she says, beaming.

We each reach for our coffee and take a sip. I look up and he's looking at me.

"Didn't Chief tell you to call the State Police?" he asks.

"No," I say. "Should I?"

"We haven't had a homicide in Roseville in years, so Chief thought it was best if we hand the case over to the State Police. They have a lot more resources. That's where the crime lab is. Mostly we do drug arrests, assaults, robbery, DUIs. Water deaths are particularly tricky. Even with an autopsy it can be difficult to determine a cause—or a time—of death."

"That's what I've heard," I say. "So, I guess I should reach out to the State Police?"

Officer Keller nods. "I'm not sure who's assigned. I've actually been meaning to follow up, though. We didn't have much, unfortunately. The family was real adamant about getting her body to the funeral home. But I did get some photos." He pauses. "Chief's off today and he hates it when we call him for anything that isn't an emergency. How about I call the State Police and see what's going on?"

"Great," I say.

Van Keller picks up his phone and presses a single button.

"Hey Dawn, could you get me Kevin Durant at the State Police? Thanks." He looks at me and smiles. "She's a nice girl, Dawn."

"She definitely likes you," I say, although I know I shouldn't. I haven't felt even remotely attractive in months. Some of it is about my hair—or lack thereof. But the real truth is that it takes confidence to flirt. And when I received the news that Aviva was alive, the knowledge of her sudden proximity, her now-definite realness, sucked away almost all the confidence I'd built up about who I am and how I interact with the world. I couldn't find a way to imagine a future with her in it, and the notion of the emotional obstacle course I was going to have to conquer when she walked into my life seemed utterly exhausting, if not impossible. No matter who she is, I will have to find a way to live with her. Alone in my apartment, or bent over a computer at the city desk the past couple months, I did not feel up to the task. But now, sitting across from a stranger in whose eyes I am not an abandoned child but rather a professional woman from New York City, I feel stronger. When Van Keller looks at me he sees a reporter with the freedom and the curiosity to drive up to his little town and walk into his little police station and ask to see the chief. He sees a reporter with a source inside a notoriously tight-lipped community. Wouldn't it be nice if I could look at myself and see those things, too?

"Sergeant," says Officer Keller when Dawn connects him. "Thanks for taking the call. I wanted to follow up about the Pessie Goldin case." A pause. "Pessie Goldin. Mother from here in Roseville. Found in her bathtub." Another pause. Officer Keller squints like he's hearing something that confuses him. "Well, do you think you could double-check?" A pause. "Okay, thanks." He hangs up the phone. His smile is gone. "They're gonna get back to me."

"Cool," I say, trying to keep the vibe light.

Officer Keller pushes his coffee away. He seems flustered. "So, you said your source hadn't heard back from the chief?"

"Right," I say. "He said a neighbor had seen a truck they didn't recognize outside Pessie's apartment the day she was found. He said he gave the license plate to the chief."

"Really? When was this?"

"I'm not sure exactly. At least a couple weeks, I think. I've got the license plate number." I take my notebook out of my purse and flip it open. "Do you want it?"

"Yeah," he says, taking a pen from the drawer beside him. I read the number off and he writes it down. "New York plate?" I nod. He swivels his desk chair toward the computer and powers up the machine. "I think these things are older than you are."

"You should see the ones we have at the *Trib*."

"Oh yeah?"

"Oh yeah. It's bad. Honestly, it's kind of a miracle we get a paper out every day."

He laughs. "We didn't have the Internet on these until a couple years ago. Just this weird e-mail program and the state databases." Click click click. "Chief probably wasn't real friendly on the phone."

I shrug. "I'm used to it. NYPD almost never even calls back, so even an official 'no comment' is better than I usually get."

"You from the city?"

"No. I'm from Florida."

"Oh wow, that's a big change."

"The cold is killing me. Seriously."

I expect our banter to continue, but Officer Keller is suddenly still in front of his computer, mouth open. After a moment, he clears his throat and closes the page he was looking at.

"Do you, um, have a card?" he asks, standing up. "I should probably go ahead and let the chief . . . State Police should get back to me. I'll . . . I can give them your contact info."

"Okay," I say, scribbling my name and e-mail and cell number on a piece of my notebook paper. "Were you able to run that plate?"

"Um, no. I think it's a different database."

Everything about our interaction has changed. Whatever came up on the plate search spooked him, and now he wants me out of his office.

"I'll be in touch," he says.

CHAPTER ELEVEN

AVIVA

I landed at JFK Airport late at night. It had been twelve hours in the air and several sleepless nights preparing to leave Jerusalem. Etan wanted children; that was expected after we married. I was twenty-one and he was twenty-nine. He taught history at a yeshiva to boys who were just before bar mitzvah; they were still children in many ways, but Etan said that their minds were ready to take on serious ideas about the world. Etan had a lot of serious ideas about the world. Two months after we married we put on our gas masks and went to the roof to watch the missiles Saddam Hussein sent over. I did not love him, but like so many of the Israelis I met, he was passionate, and I trusted that he would be kind to me. I imagined I would have boyfriends, and I did. I agreed to marry because I could not bear living with my father's brother and his wife any longer, but I was afraid to live without my family's support. If I married Etan, his parents would give us an apartment in the Old City. Etan would teach and I would have babies. Until then, I would do for money what I had done in Florida: clean house.

I did not tell him about you, and I did not tell him that I was terrified of becoming pregnant again. I had never felt fear as strong as the fear I felt when I lay in bed and imagined becoming a mother again. I knew I would fail, and that my failing would spread misery. I had already left you and your father in the wake of my weakness; Etan would be disappointed, but he would be better off. I got the prescription from a Christian doctor, an American from New Jersey who was living in Israel while his wife wrote her dissertation. He was a nice man. After two years, I told Etan the doctor said I couldn't have babies, and he believed me. He could have asked me for a divorce then. His parents encouraged him to, but he thought that the righteous thing was to honor his commitment to his wife. He would help create a new generation for Israel as a teacher, not a father. But then he found the plastic disk of pills. They must have fallen out of my pocketbook. I had become careless, I suppose. Perhaps I wanted him to find them; perhaps I was finished with our life together. Or perhaps I just did not care either way. That evening he confronted me.

"Why are you taking these pills?" he asked as I walked into the front door of our little apartment. He came toward me, his eyes wide, waving the little pink case. "How long have you been taking these pills?"

I did not have an immediate answer. I hesitated.

"Aviva!"

"Not too long."

"I don't believe you."

What could I say? I do not lie well. I omit, but I rarely lie. He left the apartment and did not return until morning. He said that he wanted a divorce. He said that he was still young enough to have children and that he wanted a wife who wanted to give them to him. I know he felt betrayed. He also felt foolish. He had turned his embrace of my infertility into a kind of martyrdom, and now he saw that I had duped him. I asked him what he would tell people, and he said he didn't know.

"Tell them I was having an affair," I said.

"I might."

The terminal was empty when my plane landed. In the bathroom at the gate I changed into jeans and uncovered my hair, and at the luggage pickup I became a young American woman back from traveling abroad, not a sneaky frum failure. I took a taxi to the house in Coney Island, praying on the way that it was still a place for me. I imagined Saul in the kitchen. The front door was open and the people living there were asleep. I set my bags in the living room and walked to the beach. There had been changes in New York since I left. The Twin Towers had fallen only a month before. We watched them crumble from the television in the tiny triangle of a café on the corner of our street in Jerusalem. I remember that I'd thought about all the times I snuck into Manhattan as a child. I understood the grid, but the streets below Houston did not conform, and when I needed a marker to tell me where north and south and east and west were, I looked for the towers. What did people look for now?

I sat in the sand with my knees pulled to my chest. It was warm for October, and as I listened to the shuffle and fizz of the black waves sliding in, I thought about you. I had watched the American girls when I saw them in Jerusalem, on tours with their parents or a school group. I looked for you. I wondered if you'd been told about me. And if so, what you'd been told. I hoped that what I'd done hadn't hardened your father. He was such a loving man. His loving felt strange to me, but to you, I hoped, it would feel natural. I hoped you would always know what love felt like. I hoped you would feel it enough for both of us.

Saul no longer lived by the house in Coney Island. The two semipermanent residents were Yael, a woman from Crown Heights fighting an ugly custody battle over her three children, and a young man named Isaac who grew up in Williamsburg. Isaac was twenty and gay, and unlike Yael, who was always running off to meet a lawyer or see her children, Isaac had nothing to do, so we quickly became close. He took me downtown to see where the towers had been, and on Thanksgiving we served food to the men and women working on the piles. Before I left, New York had seemed to me such a rigid, angry place. Everyone fighting to get where they were going, everyone with their heads down, their worlds small inside the enormous city. But the New York I came back to in late

2001 was a place where people smiled at one another. Thankful, perhaps, that they—and their beloved city—had survived. I remember taking great comfort in the smiles of strangers. I remember thinking I had made the right decision by coming home.

Etan sent papers to sign and I signed them. I knew my family had moved to Roseville, and I wrote to my brother, asking after Sammy and my father and the girls. Eli did not write back, but little Sammy did.

CHAPTER TWELVE

REBEKAH

Larry isn't at his desk when I call to fill him in on what Van Keller said. I leave Nechemaya a message saying that I definitely want to talk to the neighbors about Pessie, and reiterating that I'd appreciate any leads on friends or family who could tell me about her. I look back through my e-mail and open the attachment the library sent on Pessie. Her address is just two miles from the police station, so I decide to do a drive-by before heading north to Ryan Hall's in search of Sam.

I pull into a Shell station along the main road to fill up and use the bathroom. At the pumps on either side of me are men in Hasidic dress, phones pressed to their ears, putting gas into minivans. In the convenience store, the shelves by the bathroom hold plastic-wrapped magazines, but instead of *Playboy* and *Hustler,* the titles are Yiddish, and the covers feature old men with white beards. Yiddish movies and music are stacked in a rotating rack, and I notice that no women appear in the images on the CDs and DVDs for sale. I pour myself a cup of coffee and as I wait in line I watch a man in sidecurls and a hairnet slide a platter of what looks like bread pudding into a heated serving tray. He sets a paper notecard atop the glass display case: *potato kugel*. Beside the kugel is a steaming tray of something that smells fantastic but looks like brown slop. It is marked "chulent." I've never had either dish and decide that, despite the possible inadvisability of eating gas station food, it's time to try. I motion to the man and point to the stew.

"What size?" he asks. He is very tall and thin, with olive skin and a black unibrow.

"Small. And I'll have a piece of that, too," I say, pointing to the kugel. Next to me, a woman says something in Yiddish to the man, who nods at her. The woman is dressed all in black except for the white-and-green floral-patterned scarf wrapped over her head. I look down at my jeans and Doc Martens and am conscious, for the first time, that I might as well be wearing a sign that says "not one of you." As the server ladles the chulent into a cardboard container and slides a lasagna-sized slice of kugel into a Styrofoam box, I wonder what this woman thinks of me. My first instinct is to imagine that she is jealous; that she would trade places with me and run off to the city for bacon and barhopping if it didn't mean losing everyone she loved. But that's me transposing my values onto her, and that's exactly the opposite of what a real journalist is supposed to do. I'm in this work because I'm curious about people, because I want to bring the truth of their circumstances into the light. If I can't even imagine outside myself, I can't do that. And I certainly can't do it if I feel sorry for everyone who doesn't live like I do.

I pull Saul's car to the parking lot beside the gas station and open the steaming cup of chulent. It is delicious: savory and sweet, hearty but not heavy. Jewish food, I think. Who knew? I put the container on the passenger seat and snap a photo with my phone, then send it to my dad.

Upstate on a story, eating Jewish food!

A minute later, he texts back:

Good for you, hon!

My dad still doesn't know that Aviva contacted me through Saul in January. I didn't tell him because I didn't really want to deal with his reaction—whatever it was. He deserves to know, I know that. I'd been thinking that I'd wait and tell him when, if, I actually meet her. But now that I'm upstate, where she is—or was when she called—I want to share what's happening with him.

He picks up on the second ring.

"Hi, hon!" he says. "You working?"

"Yeah," I say. "I'm up in a town called Roseville. A lot of Jews from the city moved up here, so there's a big Haredi community. This man named Levi reached out to me and Saul because his wife was found dead in their home. Everybody thinks it was suicide but he thinks it was murder."

"Goodness," he says. "That's terrible."

"Yeah," I say. "So, I didn't tell you this but Saul actually got a call from . . . Mom. Aviva. Apparently she's upstate. She wanted to meet me, I guess. I didn't call her back for a while, though. And now she's not answering her phone."

I spit the story out quickly and am glad I can't see my father's face when he learns, for the first time in two decades, that the woman who gave him a baby and then gave up is suddenly present in his life again. I know what I've just said has affected him because for the first time I can recall, my father is at a loss for words. Typically, his automatic response to sadness or distress is to immediately offer some verse or story or perspective; that's his role as the youth minister: to comfort and guide. He's good at it, especially when it's not his biological kids he's guiding and comforting. When my mom left, his church embraced him—and me—without reservation, and that, in some way, shaped his life after Aviva. *God's grace,* he called it. *I'd be lost without it.*

"Dad?" I say.

He clears his throat. "I'm here," he says. "I just wanted to shut the door. I'm in my office at the church."

"Are you okay?"

"Of course," he says. "Thank you for asking."

"Are you mad?"

"Why would I be mad?"

"I don't know. I don't want you to think I'm, like, betraying you by getting in touch with her."

"Don't be silly, Rebekah. I hoped one day she would reach out to you."

"Do you think you'd want to see her?"

Another long pause. "I don't know," he says finally, slowly. "She gave me you, and I am thankful to her for that. But I love you so much more than I ever loved her. I never wanted to say anything negative about her to you. That was very important to me. I can't say what I might have done in her shoes, but she brought great pain into my life, Rebekah. I'm happy with what I have now, but I'm a different man than I was before she left us. It was so sudden. And what she did took something from me. My innocence, I guess you could say. I hadn't understood that people really did things like that to each other." He pauses. "In some ways, I know, the experience made me a better counselor to those in pain, and brought me closer to the Lord."

Whenever my dad says things like "brought me closer to the Lord," I cringe. It's such a corny, awkward thing to say. I always imagined he was trying to convince me of something, trying to push me to believe what he believes by exaggerating a relationship with the God he is so devoted to. But just because such a thing would never come out of my mouth doesn't mean he isn't telling me the truth. And if I actually want to understand him—which is something he deserves after all these years—I have to assume that when he says things like that he is being sincere.

"I don't look forward to having that pain in my life again," he continues. "But I'm a big boy, honey. I can handle it."

And I know he can.

"Thanks, Dad," I say. "I'll keep you updated."

"Be safe, Rebekah. Promise me."

"I promise. I love you, Dad."

"I love you, too, honey."

When I hang up the call I am trembling. Did Aviva just help bridge a gap between me and my dad?

I pull out of the gas station and follow Roseville's two-lane main street east past several more strip malls, each with about half the signs in Hebrew and half in English. The road has no sidewalk, and little shoulder, but scores of men and women in black walk alongside it nonetheless, hands holding hats and head coverings against the wind, arms weighed down with shopping bags and briefcases. After about a quarter mile the buildings become residential. I turn off the main road and wind through a neighborhood of two- and three-story apartment buildings, most shabby and utilitarian with beige vinyl siding and long orange rust stains bleeding from metal handrails down bare concrete front steps. Plastic children's toys and strollers are scattered on tiny lawns and recently poured sidewalks; minivans abound, the better to carry all the kids in, I guess. The neighborhood reminds me of the low-rent sprawl that popped up outside Orlando before the real estate crash. Every week some new development broke ground. Their names were all stupidly sunny, referencing either the warm weather or their proximity to Disney World. Most of them filled up fast and are now half empty, with absent or incarcerated landlords, falling into disrepair from neglect. Here in Roseville, on the other hand, the buildings appear worn down by use.

After a few blocks, I pass an enormous yellow brick and stone building that looks like a cross between a castle and a banquet hall. My guess is that it's a synagogue. Three rows of silver Hebrew letters make a rainbow shape above the entrance. Men, all hatted and in black coats, move along the walkways of the building like ants, scurrying here, stopping to talk or smoke there, then off again. Most have what look like leather binders under their arms.

Pessie's apartment is on the first floor at the far end of a row of apartments two blocks from the synagogue. The street dead-ends into a wooded area and through the still-bare trees I can see another, similar street of beige buildings. Aside from the toys—the same plastic cars and slides and blocks and bicycles that litter lawns across the country (across the world?)—there is little personalization. No seasonal flags or window boxes of flowers; no decals in the windows, no bumper stickers on the cars. I park at the end of the street. A woman pushes a stroller in the direction of the synagogue, and another, just one door down from Pessie's apartment, is unloading groceries from her minivan. Two little girls are with her, squealing and chattering at each other, happy to be outside. The mother yells at one, who stops her sprint up the walkway and turns to catch as her mother tosses a set of keys into her hands. Her little sister claps, delighted, and the girl resumes her race to the door, which she unlocks and props open with a plastic bin of toys. I get out of Saul's car with my notebook tucked in my jacket pocket and walk toward the woman as she is sliding the side door of the minivan shut.

"Hi," I say.

"Hello," says the woman, not smiling but not unfriendly. The older daughter runs to her mother's legs and hangs on, looking up at me.

"Bring your sister, Shaindy," says Mom.

"Who's that?" asks Shaindy.

"Bring your sister!"

Shaindy twirls off, a clumsy ballerina in black tights and a puffy black coat. She hollers for her sister, who appears in the doorway. Shaindy wraps her arms around the little girl, and picks her up. The little girl does not like this. She squirms backward, nearly toppling them both, but her big sister rights them and waddles toward us.

"Let her *go*! If you break your glasses again Tatty will be furious."

Shaindy lets go.

"I'm sorry to bother you," I say.

"We have a birthday party today," she says. "They are showing off."

"We are *not*!" shouts Shaindy, stamping her feet.

Both girls are wearing headbands, each adorned with little black bows. The mother's wig is a beautiful shade of auburn, cut with side-swept bangs. Fastened around her head is a piece of shimmery black and blue fabric that looks like a cross between a headband and a handkerchief. She has small features and well-drawn eye makeup.

"I'm wondering if you knew Pessie Goldin," I ask.

"Pessie died," says Shaindy.

"Hush!" says the woman. "Go play with your sister."

Shaindy makes a dramatic and ugly whining noise, but seems to know she has tried her mother's patience as far as she should, so she takes her sister's hand and lumbers toward the bin of toys.

"They're very cute," I say.

"Thank you," she says, smiling at the compliment. "Some days I think so, too. You are a friend of Pessie's?"

"No. I'm actually a reporter from the *New York Tribune*."

"You wrote the article? Everybody is talking about it!"

"Oh?" I say. "Did you know her well?"

"Yes, of course! We live next door. Levi thinks someone killed her?"

"He's not sure. But he wants the police to look into it."

"Her sister Rachel said it was a horrible accident. She slipped in the shower! My husband said they should sue the landlord. These apartments are very bad. But that is not true?"

"I don't know for sure," I say. "Did you happen to be here that day?"

"Yes," she says. "The girls both had the flu."

"Do you remember anything odd? Like, a car or a truck you hadn't seen before?"

"I did see a truck, yes. I came out from the bathroom and when I walked past the front window I saw them circle at the end here and then drive off."

"Them?"

"Two men. Goyim."

"Did you recognize them?"

She shakes her head. "They were from the heating company, I thought. Everyone is having trouble with the heat. The basements are flooding all the time when it rains. Pessie complained that the landlord kept sending people who told her nothing was wrong, even though she knew something was wrong. I thought maybe she called someone outside the community to fix it."

"Was there a decal or a sign on the truck?"

"I don't remember seeing one, but there could have been. I was running back and forth from the kitchen to their bedroom all day. You have children?" I shake my head. At least she didn't ask if I was Jewish. "They were very sick."

"Do you remember anything else about he truck? The color? One of your neighbors got the license plate number. I guess she thought it was suspicious."

"Yes? Who? Mrs. Silver? She thinks everything is suspicious."

"Where does Mrs. Silver live?"

The woman points to the apartment above Pessie's. "Pessie and I, we are a little more modern. Mrs. Silver wouldn't let a goy rake her lawn. She thinks everyone outside the community is a thief or a rapist. Her children are grown now and they don't see her."

"Maybe I'll knock on her door and see if she's home."

"I don't see her car."

"Is there anything you can tell me about Pessie? What was she like? You said she was a little more modern?"

"Pessie was very smart. Most of the women in Roseville just follow what their husbands say, but Pessie did things her own way. And you know what I liked about her? She did not gossip. The women here, they talk talk talk talk. Always talking. But not Pessie. Some people said she thought she was better than everybody, but I don't think so. She did not need to be Miss Popular. If she had something to say, she'd say it. But she didn't just go on and on like some people. I think she struggled."

"Struggled?" I ask, scribbling as fast as I can: *most wom rose follow husb say, but P things own way. didn't gossip. mos wom talktalk; not need miss pop; if had some to say say it.*

"She had been engaged before Levi," says the woman, lowering her voice. "I don't know the story, but I think the young man broke it off. There were lots of crazy stories. Like I said, talk talk talk. It must have been very hard for her. She asked me once, when she was pregnant, how long it took for me to love my husband. I told her that I knew I loved him when our Shaindy was born and he was so gentle with her. He kissed her little toes! She said she hoped that the same thing happened to her. She said she and Levi slept in different rooms, but she knew that when the baby came they would have to share because they only had two bedrooms."

"That's sad," I say.

The woman shrugs. "Love is not everything. There are different kinds of love."

"Do you know if she was still in touch with the ex-fiancé?"

"I don't know," she says. "I didn't think it was right to ask."

"I've been told his name was Sam Kagan. And that he left the community."

"Could be," she says. "My husband and I are not from Roseville. I grew up in Pennsylvania. Asher came here for his work in . . . Oh! You should go to Pessie's work. Something happened there, a week or two before she died, I think. She didn't want to talk about it but I heard there was a big scene."

"Where did she work?"

"She did the books at the women's clothing store in the shopping center. Go there."

"I will," I say. "I'm Rebekah, by the way. Can I ask your name?"

"I am Raisa. But I do not want to be in the newspaper."

"Okay," I say. "Could I just call you a neighbor?"

She considers this. "Don't write about the bedrooms."

"No," I say. "Of course not. I just want to be able to give people a sense of who she was. You said she didn't gossip. And that she did things her own way."

"Yes," she says. "That is fine. Have you spoken to Levi?"

"I have," I say.

"Poor man," she says. "Pessie said he was a very good husband. Very patient and understanding. What a shock it must have been to him! If you see him, please tell him we are thinking of him and Chaim."

Raisa gathers the little girls and takes them inside. Once she closes the door, I climb the steps to the apartment above Pessie's. I knock several times, but there is no answer. The blinds are closed in Pessie and Levi's apartment, so I can't even try to peek in. Before I leave, I snap a photo of the building with my phone. I don't think I have enough for a follow-up yet, but just in case, I'll have art.

The shopping center Pessie worked in looks like a typical big-box supermarket, until you get up close. Posted at all three entrances are big signs: PLEASE RESPECT OUR MODEST DRESS CODE: No Shorts, No Midriffs, No Bare Feet. The old me would have gawked at this sign. I probably would have made a big show of taking a photo and posting it to Facebook with some snarky remark, maybe even gone back to my car and dug around for some sandals to walk in wearing, just to see what would happen, just to show all these strangers that their rules are sexist and stupid and that I'm better than them. But I don't feel like doing that today. Let them have their dress code, I think.

The first floor of the center is a grocery store, and according to a sign just inside there is a women's clothing store, a boys and girls clothing store, a wine and liquor store, a toy store, and a Judaica shop upstairs. A woman with a crooked wig and a walleye stands at the main entrance holding a plastic bag. The man walking in front of me drops a dollar in and she barely registers a response. Her gaze remains in middle distance. The grocery area appears bustling, but upstairs is quiet. I follow a long, wide corridor to the back where I see a sign that says LADIES LINGERIE. A bell rings when I walk in. The store is crowded with racks of long dresses: crushed velvet and rayon and sateen, mostly black and dark blue or green or purple, some with a lace overlay or a bow or smocking at the neck. High collars and long sleeves. Two women are deep in conversation as they stand between racks of seemingly identical black mid-length skirts. Both women wear scarves around their heads, their hair presumably tucked beneath. I find another woman in the lingerie section, which consists entirely of apparel in three colors: black, white, and flesh-toned. Long old-fashioned cotton nightgowns, girdles and shape-wear, nursing bras, and full-coverage panties.

"Excuse me," I say to the woman, who is tagging boxes

of panty hose. "My name is Rebekah. I'm a reporter for the *New York Tribune*. I was just speaking with one of Pessie Goldin's neighbors and she told me that Pessie used to work here."

The woman, who appears to be in her fifties, puts down her tagging tool.

"I saw your article," she says. Her wig is cut in a shorter style than Raisa's. It is more matronly, with blond feathering around her face. She shakes her head and purses her lips. "I did not wish to gossip, but if her husband is asking questions . . . Pessie was being stalked."

"Stalked?"

"He came to the store a week before she died. She did not wish to see him. She had Chaim with her—sometimes she would bring him to work, he was such a good little baby. Men are not allowed in the store, but he would not go away. He was yelling and yelling. He pushed right past me! Pessie gave Chaim to me and went out to talk to him. I told her not to! I called shomrim but he ran off before they got here. And she would not say who he was."

"Do you remember anything else about him? What he looked like?"

"He was Chassidish but dressed like a goy. Clean-shaven. He was very upset. I think maybe he was on drugs. He kept saying he was sorry and that she didn't understand."

"Didn't understand what?"

"How should I know?"

"Could his name have been Sam?"

"She wouldn't tell me. Pessie was very private. Not friendly like the other girls here."

"What did you think when you heard she had died?"

"It was terrible!"

"But did you, like, think something might have happened to her? That maybe it wasn't an accident?"

She shrugs. "What do I know?"

"Have you told anyone else about what happened?"

"Yes," she says. "Maybe. Why shouldn't I?"

"I'm just wondering if you've . . . would you be willing to talk to police?"

"Police? Puh!" She makes a spitting sound. "My son got hit by a car while he was walking to shul and the Roseville policeman said it was *his* fault. His leg was broken! They said he shouldn't have been walking along the road. But where else will he walk? *Where else will he walk!* Police are bad here. They do not like Jews."

The woman refuses to give me her name, but says that I can call her one of Pessie's coworkers. Aside from Levi, I still don't have a single named source on the record.

CHAPTER THIRTEEN

AVIVA

Sammy's letters were always short.

> *Dear Aviva,*
> *Tante Penina says you are my sister. She says you live in Israel and that is why we do not see you. I hope we will meet someday.*
> *Sincerely, Samuel Kagan (your brother)*

His handwriting slanted backward and the piece of paper was fraying at the side where he must have torn it out of a notebook. I wrote him back immediately, telling him that I now lived in Brooklyn and that I would like to meet him, too. I made no more attempts to contact Eli or my father or my sisters. I had become used to loneliness in Israel, and I knew how to bear it. They did not wish to understand me, and I did not wish to force them to. I had made some friends in Coney Island. Isaac and I became very close. He reminded me how young I had been when I had you. He reminded me how lost I was, and how, frankly, stupid. I thought because I had seen movies like

Fast Times at Ridgemont High and *Splash* that I understood life outside the shtetl. I found work cleaning houses again. It suited me perfectly. I could work when I wanted. And every day I learned more about the goyim but I did not have to face the embarrassment of interacting with them for more than the few minutes it took for them to let me in their homes. I cleaned apartments in any neighborhood I could get to on the subway: Brighton Beach and Park Slope and Greenwich Village. Once I had a job at an apartment on the same block as the Strand bookstore where I met your father. After I finished work, I went in and walked the aisles of books slowly, hoping as I turned each corner that your father would be there. That you would be there. You were not, of course. What would I have said if you were?

Sammy's next letter came two weeks later.

> *Dear Aviva,*
>
> *Feter Eli told me I should not write to you anymore. Will you ever come visit us in Roseville?*
>
> *Sincerely, Your brother Sammy*

I wrote Sammy back saying that I would like to visit him, but that I did not think Eli would like that. I asked him to tell me about himself. *What do you like to do? Who are your friends? What do you want to do when you grow up?* In his return letter, he answered my questions in a list.

Dear Aviva,

I like to go fishing with my cousins. I like to eat ice cream. I like to catch frogs. I like to ride my bicycle.

My best friend is Pessie Rosen. She isn't like most girls. She catches more frogs than me. She has a very pretty singing voice. My cousin Dovid is also my friend. Last summer we built a fort in the woods. But it fell down in the snow.

When I grow up I want to move to Israel and study Torah.

Sincerely, Your brother Sammy

Sammy was an eleven-year-old boy living in frum family. It made no sense that his best friend was a girl. There were only two explanations: either my family had become less observant since I left them, or he was not being properly looked after. I doubted very much that my family was less observant; like most of the people Isaac and I grew up with they had probably gotten even stricter. I discussed it with Isaac, and he agreed that something seemed strange. We asked around and found someone who had grown up in Roseville. The man's name was Schlomo and he was in the process of divorcing his wife. He had to go to court in Rockland County almost every week because he was trying to get visitation with his children. Schlomo reported back that Sammy was living with Eli and Penina and their four children, and that one of the children was severely disabled. He was almost nine years old but could not speak or feed himself or use the toilet and had to be moved in a wheelchair. My father was also living with them, but had become a recluse. He no longer even went to shul. While I was in Israel, Diny had written me a letter once a year telling me of my family's marriages and births and movements. She and her husband had also settled in Roseville, as had one of my younger brothers and his wife. My two little sisters, it seemed, had been passed between Diny's and Eli's households. Diny had mentioned nothing in the letters about a disabled child, or about my father.

"And there's something else," said Schlomo. "Sammy has accused a man of sexual abuse."

"What do you mean, accused?" I asked.

"My brother attends shul with Eli," he said. "He told me that Eli was very upset about it."

I waited for more. "And?"

Schlomo shrugged. "And?"

"What's being done? Who is this person?"

"Eli told my brother that it was someone at Sammy's yeshiva. He went to the rebbe and the rebbe told him that the man denied it, and that one little boy's story was not enough to take the matter further."

Isaac and I looked at each other. We both knew that sexual abuse was not discussed in the community. Men were accused quietly. Occasionally, someone left a job at a yeshiva. The secular authorities—the police—were never involved, at least not for long. A *moser* was the lowest of the low.

"When did this happen?"

"My brother was not specific," said Schlomo.

"Is Sammy still attending the yeshiva?"

"I do not know."

We were all silent for what seemed like a very long time. I took a bottle of wine upstairs with me and as I lay in bed I decided that I had to try to help Sammy. You were safe with your father and his family; I would not have made your life better by entering it after so many years. But Sammy needed me. And I was not going to run away from him.

Isaac drove with me to Eli's house. I had not been to Roseville since Rivka died there twenty years earlier. I couldn't fathom why my family would live in the place that had killed my sister. Isaac said the rebbe had encouraged people to leave Brooklyn in the years following the riots in Crown Heights, and my brother was not one to disobey the rebbe.

I don't know how I expected Eli to react to my surprise visit. I suppose I thought my presence, after so many years, might soften him—or at least shake him into recognizing how terrible what had happened to Sammy was, and how important it was to show him that he would be protected in the future. But that is not how he reacted.

"This is not a good time for a visit, Aviva," said Eli when he answered the door.

"I am not here for chitchat," I said, pushing past him. Penina was sitting on the sofa bed, her hair beneath an ugly velvet snood, feeding the disabled son something from a jar. He sat in a wheelchair, his head propped up by a kind of collar connected to the back of the chair. Half of what should have gone in his stomach was smeared on his bib.

"I want to know what you are doing to keep Sammy safe. Have you reported this man to the police?"

Eli sighed. In the ten years since I had seen my brother he had aged tremendously. Both he and Penina had gained weight. Their skin was yellow and their eyes were gray and their home stank of grease and spoiled milk and urine.

"Aviva, I do not know what you have heard. . . ."

"I have heard Sammy was molested! Is that true?"

"That is what he says."

"What he *says*? Are you saying you don't believe him?" I had gotten myself worked up on the drive; I anticipated his condescension and I practiced the way I would respond. I would make him see how he had failed. I would make him see that Sammy needed me.

"I am not saying that," said Eli.

"How could you let this happen! How could you not do anything!"

The boy in the wheelchair grunted. His sidecurls were flat, one halfway in his mouth, caked with food.

"Aviva, please," said Eli, walking toward the boy. "Not so loud. David . . ."

"Where is he?" I said, ignoring my brother's plea. "I want to speak with him."

"Sammy is at yeshiva . . ."

"You sent him *back there*?" I screamed.

Before Eli could answer David swung his arm forward, knocking the spoon and jar from Penina's hands, sending them flying into the wall. He began screaming, high-pitched shrieks in short bursts. Penina stood up and went to the kitchen without a word. She returned with a towel and a new spoon. She wiped the spilled food from the wall and the carpet, and then sat back down on the sofa. Her face was slack. David kept screaming. The noise was terrifying. A boy his size behaving like an infant, like an animal.

"I know you do not care about our community anymore, Aviva," said Eli, raising his voice above his son's cries. "But I spoke with the rebbe and he does not permit taking an accusation to police if you have not witnessed the crime with your own eyes."

"The rebbe? Who gives a *shit* what the rebbe says! Sammy is your brother. Can't you think for yourself, Eli? Can't you *feel*! Sammy *needs* you!"

Eli was unmoved. "He will attend a different yeshiva next year. A big fuss will make shidduch difficult for Sammy and the girls. And we just can't be sure."

And that was the end of it, as far as Eli was concerned. How can you argue with someone so brainwashed that he is more concerned about a fuss than the rape of his brother? You cannot. But I was no longer twenty years old and frightened. Eli could not shame me into running off and leaving him to do what was "best" for my family. On the drive home I told Isaac I wanted to move upstate.

"I can't live in Roseville," I said. "But I have to be closer. I have to be there for Sammy."

Isaac told me he had heard about a house like the one in Coney Island—a house for wayward Jews—in New Paltz.

"I'll go with you if you go," said Isaac. "I'm done with Brooklyn."

A month later, Isaac and I moved into the *farkakte* house in New Paltz. The yellow paint was chipping and the porch sagged and the bedrooms had been partitioned off like a bunkhouse, with patchwork carpet and sloping floors. The house belonged to a man from Marine Park who'd bought it in foreclosure and turned it into a temporary residence for Jews coming from Brooklyn or Israel. He'd separated the three bedrooms upstairs into a maze of six little rooms each with space for a single bed or a bunk bed and a pile of clothes in a basket in the corner. When Isaac and I moved in there were two families living there, each with three children. We had to walk through one another's bedrooms to get to the upstairs bathroom. Outside, there was space for a little garden, and you could walk to the main street. I bought a Nissan from a graduating senior at SUNY New Paltz and put paper fliers advertising housekeeping on bulletin boards around the campus. Soon, I had as many clients as I could handle.

I wrote to Sammy with my new address and he wrote back. When I called, he picked up the phone. He asked if he could come visit me and I didn't bother telling him to ask Eli. The next Sunday morning I picked him up a quarter mile from his house, behind a ladies' clothing store, and we went to Stewart's for ice cream cones. We sat on the bench outside and watched the people come and go, filling up their cars with gas, buying groceries and lottery tickets. I didn't ask him about yeshiva, and he didn't mention it. Sundays became our day. That summer we had picnics in Harriman State Park and when it got cold we went to the Galleria mall in Poughkeepsie and saw movies at the theater. Sometimes Isaac came with us, and sometimes Sammy helped us with projects at the yellow house. Within a year, the families had left and it was just me and Isaac, plus the occasional Borough Park refugee needing a place to stay for a few days or weeks. We tore up the ugly carpet and got on our hands and knees to sand the floors beneath. We dug a garden, and by the third year we were growing tomatoes and herbs and green beans and squash. Sammy loved it. Manual labor was not encouraged in Roseville; extra time is spent studying. Isaac had begun working odd jobs for a contractor in New Paltz, and he taught me and Sammy how to use an electric drill and a level. For my birthday one year, Sammy surprised me with a window box for flowers. He said the work made him feel strong. He asked me and Isaac if we thought someday he could make a living using his hands.

"There are people moving to Roseville all the time," he told us. "Maybe I could help build houses like Isaac?"

"You can do whatever you want," I told him. "You have so much life ahead of you."

One week, a girl was with Sammy when I got to our meeting spot.

"Can Pessie come, too?" he asked me.

"Why not?" I said. And off we went, with Pessie in the backseat. Immediately I could see why Sammy liked Pessie so much. She had as much energy as he did, and a wild, fantastic imagination. She reminded me a little bit of Gitty when she was a girl, although she wasn't as mischievous. Pessie could make up a story that took an hour to tell. She could stand in an empty yard and find as much to do as if she were in the middle of Times Square. She was a tiny thing, with frizzy brown hair and an underbite. She wore the frum uniform—blue button-up blouse, long black skirt, ballet flats—which made her look ten even as she turned into a teenager. She was very different from me at her age—I had been more restless, always looking for a button to push, a dark place to explore—but when I looked at Pessie I remembered how little I knew about the world as a child. And when she came to me and asked about the blood in her underwear I knew they still weren't teaching girls about their bodies. We went to the drugstore for pads and the bookstore to look at *Our Bodies, Ourselves*. Pessie couldn't take a book like that home, but I bought it for her, and she read it when she came to visit.

Sammy was more alive with Pessie beside him. They talked over each other, excited and overflowing with stories and details about this neighbor who smelled bad and that cousin whose wife had stopped shaving her head. One afternoon, as we sat around my kitchen table drinking Cokes and eating Doritos Cool Ranch chips—Sammy's favorite—Pessie said that her older sister had just gotten engaged to a boy from Borough Park.

"She is scared," Pessie said.

"How old is she?" I asked.

"Eighteen."

"Does she love him?"

Pessie shrugged. "No. But my mommy says that eighteen is too young for love. She says you get married first and then Hashem brings you love."

"I fell in love when I was eighteen," I said. "With a goy."

For a moment, Pessie and Sammy, who were probably sixteen at the time, were speechless. They looked at me, and then each other, and then Isaac, trying to decide if I was teasing them.

"No, you didn't," said Sammy, his lips furry with yellow powder.

"I did," I said. "His name was Brian."

"Was he Chassidish?" asked Pessie.

I shook my head. "He was studying to be a Christian minister."

They looked so shocked, I laughed.

"Does Eli know?" asked Sammy.

"He only knows I left with a man for a little while. He doesn't know what happened while I was gone."

"What happened?" said Pessie, leaning in, ready for gossip.

"Can you keep a secret?"

"Yes!" screamed Pessie. Sammy and Isaac exchanged a look. Perhaps I should have read something into it, but I didn't. I was ready to tell them. I was thinking that knowing something about my life that no one else in the family knew might make Sammy feel closer to me. I told them about the bookstore in Manhattan and the pool at the YMCA and the trips to Coney Island and the bus to Florida. I told them about living in the college dorm and about your grandfather's job at Disney World. Pessie asked lots of questions, but Sammy was quiet. I keep looking at him, trying to figure out what he was thinking, but his face gave nothing away.

"What was your wedding like?" asked Pessie.

"We did not get married," I said.

"Sammy said you were married, though."

"That was later. In Israel. Brian and I were engaged, but things changed." I looked at Sammy. I needed to see his face as I said this. "I had a baby."

Pessie gasped. "A baby!" Sammy looked up, finally. Curious.

"A little girl," I said. "I named her Rebekah, after our sister Rivka."

"Did she die?" asked Sammy.

"No," I said.

"Then why did you come home?"

"I came home because Mommy died and you were born," I said. It was not a good excuse, but it was better than the truth—and it was partly true. I skipped the part where I snuck out in the middle of the night, and I skipped Gitty entirely.

"I was very young. I did not know how to be a mother."

Sammy and Pessie were both silent for a few seconds. I couldn't tell what the slightly scrunched expression on Sammy's face meant. Pessie spoke first.

"Do you miss her?"

"Yes," I said. "Every single day."

"Where is she?" asked Sammy.

"She is in Florida, with her father." As I said it, though, I realized I wasn't certain. All those years talking to you, Rebekah, I did not allow myself to imagine that something might have happened to you. Or to Brian. I suddenly felt unsteady. What if I was talking to a ghost?

I must have looked as woozy as I felt because Pessie put her hand on mine.

"Don't worry, Aviva," she said. "We promise not to tell. Right, Sammy?"

Sammy nodded. After we dropped them off in Roseville that evening, Isaac and I went out to dinner at a tavern near campus.

"I wish you hadn't asked them to keep a secret," said Isaac.

"What do you mean?"

"This man," he said, and the way he looked at me told me that he was talking about the person who had molested Sammy. "The way he talks about him . . . one minute he is almost . . . tender. And then he becomes angry and embarrassed. He said that when he thinks about the man he sometimes gets . . ." Isaac did not finish, but I understood.

"He said that?" I whispered.

Isaac nodded. "Not in exactly those words, but yes."

"Did he say what happened?"

"He said it started with washing. Washing their hands together in the yeshiva kitchen. He said the man taught him to bake challah. I believe he may have been the school cook, not a teacher, although Sammy won't tell me his name. He said soon after they would wash their whole bodies. The man washed Sammy, and then had Sammy wash him. And then . . . then he told Sammy to touch him. Kiss him . . ." Isaac took a deep breath. He wasn't giving me all the details, but I didn't push. It was enough.

"And he told Sammy to keep it a secret," I said, feeling feverish with dread, abandoning my meal.

"Yes."

I closed my eyes. I should have known better.

"I have read about men like this," Isaac continued. "They find the boys with difficult family lives. They do things that are too shameful to say out loud. Sammy knows what the man did was wrong, but I think he is almost as afraid of people knowing as anything else. And now that he is becoming a man, he is mixed up. He asked me if I thought he was gay if it feels nice when he thinks about kissing a man instead of a woman."

"What did you say?"

"I said I didn't know. I said that if he is gay, there is nothing wrong with that. I told him that just because a man made him . . . do sexual things, it doesn't mean he is gay. But if he is gay, it may be one of the reasons this man chose him. Men like that—they can tell who is different."

The next time I saw Sammy he didn't mention my secret or his, and when he turned eighteen, he told us that he and Pessie were engaged.

"Are you happy?" I asked him.

Like me, Sammy was not a good liar. "Pessie will make a good wife," he said, but his voice did not sound like his own.

Two months later, Sammy broke off the engagement and Eli sent him to a camp that was supposed to fix gay boys. Three weeks in, he shaved off his sidecurls and came to live with me and Isaac in the yellow house.

A month after that, he met Ryan Hall.

CHAPTER FOURTEEN

REBEKAH

According to my GPS, it'll take about an hour to get from Roseville to 444 County Route 81, the address for Ryan Hall. The Google map says the location is between a small airfield and something called Winters' Feed. I get on the Thruway and head north toward the Catskill mountains. Signs indicate ski areas and campgrounds, farm stands, firewood, and county fairs. I pass apple orchards and creeks running under the highway, and start seeing license plates from Quebec.

I take the exit for Catskill and follow Route 145 to Route 81, but my reception is spotty and I overshoot the address and end up back on 145, somehow. The roads are badly marked, and there are huge spaces between the houses. I've been spoiled reporting in the city the last year. It's hard to get really lost in New York—there's always somebody around to ask directions, and 178 Broadway is right next to 180, which is right next to 182. At first I was always forgetting to ask whether it was East or West Fourth Street, or if it's Third Street not Third Avenue, but in most cases—except when you're on Staten Island, where I haven't been since my car died—you can hop on the subway and get back to someplace you know easily. In Florida, and up here, county routes become different county routes without signage. Landmarks—a gas station, a house with a purple barn—are how you tell where you are, but if you've never been to where you're going, landmarks are meaningless.

I double back and ride the brakes (much to the chagrin of the Chevy behind me) for about a mile until I spot a crooked mailbox set inside an old milk jug with three stickers—444—affixed to the side. I can't see a house from the road. The trees are bare, but thick, and the dirt driveway is dotted with rusted NO TRESPASSING! signs posted on both sides. A low fence strung with barbed wire enforces the dictate. After a few hundred yards, a clearing appears, and in it are a two-story house that looks at least a hundred years old and three mobile homes—one half-destroyed by fire. A dark-coated pit bull-rottweiler-lab mix comes racing toward my car, barking a manic fit two feet from the driver's side door. My first guess is that no one is on the property. The only vehicle is a gray minivan, its back window taped over with plastic and weeds growing up past the floorboards. The blue paint on the house's siding is chipped and faded to nearly white, and there is a scar across the façade where an overhang was once affixed. A gutter that should probably be somewhere along the roof is leaning against a tree. There are shutters on two of the four front windows, and an assortment of chairs—including a wheelchair—on the front porch. The dog feels like it is barking inside my head, the noise pushing on the dull ring from that stupid gunshot. I am about to back up when a girl about my age flings open the front door of one of the intact trailers and screams, "Junior!"

The dog looks at her, but keeps barking.

"Junior get the fuck over here!" She slaps her thigh and waves at me. "Junior NOW!"

Junior obeys.

"Sorry!" she shouts, waving at me. And then she addresses the dog: "Sit down, Junior. DOWN!" Junior does not sit down. She points her arms toward the old house. "JUNIOR! Go back home. GO! JUNIOR GO!"

Junior goes. He trots in front of my car and goes to stand on the porch.

"It's okay," she calls to me. "He's harmless."

I doubt that, but I get out of the car anyway. The trailer this girl is calling to me from—its skirt rusted and come undone, a piece of plywood serving as entry ramp—looks as uncomfortable as any dwelling I've ever seen. The girl at the door is wearing an extra-large New York Jets sweatshirt and stretch pants. Baby-blue terry cloth slippers on her feet, mismatched wool socks, hair in a ponytail, nickel-sized black plugs in her earlobes.

"Hi," I say, standing at the base of the plywood ramp.

"Sorry about that," she says.

"It's okay," I say. "I'm Rebekah. I'm actually looking for Ryan Hall."

"Ryan? I haven't seen him in . . . a while."

"Oh," I say. "So he doesn't live here."

"Fuck no," she says. "Not anymore."

"Oh" I say.

"Hey, do you like jewelry?"

"Jewelry?"

"Come in," she says. "I want you to try something on for me. If you have a sec."

The rules are that I'm supposed to tell her I'm a reporter now. But I'm not just a reporter. Yes; I'm looking for Ryan to find Sam because he's connected to Pessie. But also—okay, I admit it—because I'm looking for Aviva. If anyone asks, I rationalize quickly, I can say I was just gathering information, off the record. For personal reasons.

"Okay," I say.

Inside the trailer looks much better than outside. It is tight, but clean, and smells of baby powder. The enormous television is the dominant feature in the main room. Spreading like tentacles from its base is an impressive video game setup, with lots of plastic gadgets and knobs and weaponry. *Charmed* is on, but the girl has got the TV on mute and is instead listening to talk radio through an open laptop. A familiar and repugnant man's voice growls about Obama. Beside the TV is a playpen, and inside the playpen is a little girl wearing a diaper and a t-shirt with a monkey on it. She grips the railing with her pudgy little hands and stares at the big screen. Beside the playpen, on what might once have been the kitchen table, is a little workshop. Silver and bronze and gold earrings hang in pairs on a neatly framed piece of window screen near the sink. Pliers and a small hammer lie beside a metal toolbox, drawers open revealing little loops and beads and chains. A mannequin's torso is strung with necklaces of varying length, including a sleek pendant made of what looks like hammered brass. If it weren't a swastika I would compliment it.

"I'm Mellie," she says. "Do you want something to drink? The coffee's decaf." She touches her belly; she is pregnant. "I'm supposed to be off caffeine."

"Decaf is cool," I say. "Thanks."

"That's Eva," says Mellie.

Hearing her name, Eva turns toward her mother. She is a beautiful little girl with a round face and big, hazel eyes. I'd guess she's around one, but I don't really know much about babies.

"Hi Eva," I say.

Eva is sucking on a pacifier. She looks at me, then back at her mom, then returns her gaze to the television.

"I need a model for some new earrings," she says, pointing to the table. "The lightning bolts. I don't have to use your face or anything, if you don't want. Just, like, a close-up of your ear."

I look at the earrings she is talking about—a pair of silver SS lightning bolts, each about an inch long. Beside those are other similarly dainty designs: Celtic crosses, suns, swastikas, and several versions of the number fourteen. I'm not going to say yes to having my picture taken in this stuff—I wonder if my ears would catch fire?—but I don't need to say no right away, either.

"A lot more girls are doing the shaved head thing. If I wasn't so fat I'd cut mine. Maybe after the baby comes. Hank would love that. Did you shave it yourself?"

I rub my hand over my head. "No," I say. "It was kind of an accident."

"Have you ever done any modeling?" she asks, pouring me coffee into a mug with a deer and the words ADIRONDACK STATE PARK on it. She takes some milk out of the fridge and I add a little, wave off sugar. "I know a guy who makes t-shirts and panties and stuff and he's always looking for hot skinhead chicks. Do you have tattoos?"

"No," I say.

She shrugs. "Well, anyway. He's up in Troy. I could give you his number."

I suppose I should take this as a compliment. Wait till I tell Iris: I've been spotted by a Nazi model scout!

"You sell online?" I ask.

"Yeah," she says. "Online and at shows. I did pretty good on Etsy for a while but I got kicked off last year—which is total bullshit. If you say your swastika's *Buddhist* you can sell whatever you want. And people can sell *vintage* SS pieces." She shrugs. "I do other stuff, too, like hoops and stars and crosses. But the white power stuff sells the best. There aren't that many other people making it. I've got a pretty good following now. Valentine's

Day and Christmas are my big holidays. And I've done a couple wedding parties. It's kinda slow right now so I'm trying some new stuff. I like the lightning bolts 'cause they're subtle, you know? Like, if you want to represent at work but your boss is a liberal or a nigger or something."

I've never known how to respond to people who use racial slurs easily. I don't encounter them much, fortunately—although there is one photographer for the *Trib* who talks like he's living in 1950s Alabama—but when I do it's always a little shocking. Mellie looks perfectly normal. Throw a pair of boots on her and she'd blend right in on Bedford Avenue.

"Have you been doing it a while?" I ask.

"A couple years. I started right around when I got pregnant with her. Hank goes to the gun shows with his dad and there's always all these wives and girlfriends wandering around kinda bored. Nan—that's his grandma—used to bitch about how there's never any good accessories for women. Nothing, like, feminine. That's sorta what I'm known for. We go to bike rallies, too, and the patriot marches. Here," she says, opening a plastic file box that's tucked beneath the kitchen table. She hands me a shiny black business card with a Web site address printed in hot pink: WWW.WHITEGIRLPOWER.COM.

"Cool," I say again. "So when are you due?"

"July eighteen. It's a boy. Thank God. Hank's obsessed with the bloodline. Well, really it's his dad, Connie, who's obsessed. But Hank, too. Him and his dad are really close.

Especially now that Ryan's a faggot. . . ." She pauses. "Wait, how do you know him again?"

"I'm actually looking for a friend of his. Sam Kagan?"

Mellie's expression changes. She raises an eyebrow. "You're friends with Sam?"

"Well, no. I've never met him. I'm looking for him because . . ." I don't want to tell the whole story, so I use shorthand: "I'm adopted. And I think Sam might know my birth mom."

"You're adopted?"

"Yeah," I say, hoping I don't have to extend this lie too much longer.

"Me, too."

"Oh yeah?"

"My birth mom was a junkie. She got locked up when I was a baby and my dad wasn't in the picture. I was in foster care for a couple months then my mom's cousin ended up adopting me." She looks up expectantly. It's my turn.

"My mom gave me up. She had me really young."

"So you've never met."

I shake my head.

"Oh wow," says Mellie. She lowers her voice. "Sam's a Jew, did you know that?"

"Oh?" I say.

"Yeah. One of those crazy *black hat* kikes. Like, with the coats and the . . ." She makes a spiral beside her head.

"Huh," I say, trying to sound like I don't quite know what she's talking about.

"Do you think you might be *Jewish*?"

"I don't know," I say. It's not a lie. Okay, it's a lie. I am denying my Judaism in the home of a Nazi.

"I hope not, for your sake," she says. "They're really dangerous. I mean, they're breeding an army down there in Rockland County. You know they all have like ten kids. At least! And they're all on welfare. I mean, they're seriously worse than niggers and spics on that. But nobody knows about it. That's what so crazy. They're taking over the school boards and the city councils and they're all fucked up sexually. They have arranged marriages, like the Muslims. And men and women can't even touch. And they *let* people molest their kids. Seriously."

"Huh," I say again.

"Fucking Sam," she says, shaking her head. Eva spits out her pacifier and starts whining. "You hungry?" she asks the child, already reaching for the refrigerator door. "If you see him, tell Sam to stay the fuck away from here. Connie'll shoot him if he sees him. I might, too." She pours whole milk from a plastic gallon jug into a bottle, twists the cap on, shakes it, and hands it to Eva. "He's caused *a lot* of drama. First of all, he's a total liar. Him and Ryan both. I can't even get into it it's so bad. People are always trying to infiltrate the Brotherhood, so Connie thinks he's a narc. I don't know if he's like, FBI, or some Jew mafia, but the point is that now, even though we're *supposed* to be saving for a place of our own that isn't right on top of his whole family, Hank's basically spending all our money on guns."

"Guns?"

"Connie says it's an investment. All this shit with Ryan and Sam has got him paranoid. I mean, race war is coming. If you look at *history*. And Connie says the first battle is gonna be with the Jews. He's like, the Jews are *organized*, you know? Niggers can't stop shooting each other. He's got a connection down in the Carolinas and him and Hank have been bringing the guns up so when Obama really cracks down we can sell 'em to everybody who didn't see it coming. We've already sold some, since fucking Cuomo's fascist new law. People are starting to see what's happening, finally." She sighs and sits down at her jewelry table. "So, I get it. I do. But honestly, I kind of wish Hank would just get a *job*."

I've interviewed a lot of wacky people in the past six months at the *Trib*. In October I was on a day-long stakeout in Tribeca for a banker who'd been arrested for rape when some guy latched on to me and swore up and down he'd been "investigating" the bankers moving into the area and found a secret apartment they kept to take girls and torture them. He tried to convince me he had paperwork proving that Goldman Sachs was paying for everything and that if I came up to his apartment he'd give me an exclusive. Needless to say I did not go up to this man's apartment. I expect conspiracy theories from people—but race war?

Mellie continues. "Hank practically blew himself up a couple weeks ago trying to make some stupid pipe bomb.

I love him but sometimes he's a fucking idiot. That other trailer is, like, basically unlivable now." She shakes her head. "I mean, I'd like my kids to grow up with a father, you know?"

Junior starts barking outside, announcing a car. It is, I decide, time to go.

"I should probably take off," I say, setting my coffee down.

Outside, a man shouts, "Shut up, Junior!" The dog shuts up. A car door slams. Another creaks open.

"Oh wait, what about the earrings?"

I have the front door open. "My holes are actually a little infected right now," I say, stepping outside. "I wouldn't want to, like, contaminate them."

In the dirt circle linking Mellie's trailer, the old house, and the site of her boyfriend's apparent attempt at becoming the Unabomber, a man who looks about fifty is lifting a wheelchair out of the bed of a pickup truck.

"Hank ain't home yet?" the man asks Mellie.

"Nope."

The man is wearing a long-sleeved Orange County Choppers t-shirt and jeans tucked into what look like surplus military boots. He is very lean, with a close-trimmed gray beard, and most of his skin not covered by clothing is inked. From here, I see a spiderweb with a swastika at the center on one side of his neck and a large shamrock on the other. Each knuckle is adorned with some kind of symbol or letter or God-knows-what, and the back of both his hands have skulls on them. In Roseville, the women seemed to assume I was Jewish, but apparently I blend in here, too. I look at Saul's car and suddenly realize there is a very real possibility that something—a Yiddish language flyer or a parking pass for a shul—might be visible. I should get out of here.

The man rolls the wheelchair to the passenger-side door, then lifts an old lady who is missing both legs into it.

"Who's your friend?" asks the old lady, her voice rattling like a lawnmower.

"Rebekah," says Mellie.

"Love your hair, Rebekah."

CHAPTER FIFTEEN

AVIVA

For several weeks after he left Roseville, Sammy barely went outside the yellow house. He did little but sleep and talk to Pessie on the phone. I told him I thought it was unhealthy to be so attached. I said it was unfair to her. But he said I was wrong and that they understood each other. She came to the house every week with food and they cooked dinner together. I told her I thought it was very nice of her to be his friend after what he had done.

"Sammy didn't like to hurt me," she said, looking down at her feet, which were still too long for her little body. She'd never grown into them, and at eighteen years old she barely looked fourteen. "Hashem has plans for him. He is going to help the other boys. But he cannot stay in the community. And I understand. Perhaps he is a little like you?"

I asked Sammy what Pessie meant by helping the other boys, and he said she wanted him to start a group for Chassidish boys who'd been molested.

"Are you going to do that?" I asked.

"Probably not," he said.

"What are you going to do?"

Sammy shrugged.

"You know," I said, "I had a very hard time after Mommy died and I went to Israel. I went to talk to a doctor and he gave me medication. It made me feel better."

"I don't need crazy pills, okay? I just need to be left alone."

I decided not to argue, and a few weeks later I saw a HELP WANTED sign in the window of a Mobil gas station that was walking distance from the house. I convinced Sammy to go apply, and he got the job—which wasn't much of a job: just a six-hour shift unloading trucks of beer each Monday and Thursday. On the second Thursday, Sammy met Ryan Hall.

Ryan was riding in the truck with his father, who worked for a beverage distributor out of Albany. He invited Sammy to a bar to hear a band that night. At first I didn't realize he'd fallen in love. Sammy hadn't said he was gay, and I assumed he broke off the engagement to Pessie because of the abuse, or maybe because he didn't want to live a frum life and she did. But after that first night, all he talked about was Ryan. I didn't mind Ryan. He was polite and I was glad Sammy had a friend who wasn't Pessie. But then I saw the tattoos. Ryan was coming out of the shower with just a towel around his waist one evening as I was coming up the stairs to drop my things after work. He turned the corner to go into Sammy's bedroom and there on his right shoulder blade was a swastika.

I went to the kitchen and waited for them to come down. I waited for hours. The sun went down. I drank a whole bottle of wine as I waited. Our mother survived the Nazis. She was born in the Warsaw ghetto and in 1942, when she was six months old, her parents got notice they were to go to Treblinka to a work camp. They died there, of course, like everyone else, but before they went they left her with my father's former employer, a Catholic butcher named Josef Soskowitz. The penalty for protecting a Jew was death, but Josef and his wife told the Nazis my mother was theirs. There was so little food in the ghetto that my mother barely weighed ten pounds, so the officers believed the Soskowitzs when they said she was a newborn. When the war was over and my grandparents—like three million other Polish Jews—did not come back, the Soskowitzs followed the instructions they'd left and wrote to an uncle in what would soon be Israel. A few months later, Josef escorted four-year-old Bracha to Switzerland, where her mother's cousin met them and brought my mother to Jerusalem to live with his family.

My mother told this story to us every year on *Yom HaShoah*. When I was ten, someone spraypainted a red swastika on the outside of our shul and my mother took us to see it.

"This is why we live the way we do," she said. "This is what they want to do to us."

I had nightmares about the swastika. Over and over, I dreamt that the man who painted it was chasing me, spraying poison. My mother told me that she had nightmares, too, and that the nightmares were Hashem reminding us that the world is a dangerous place for a Jew.

But Sammy never knew my mother. He never heard her tell her stories. When he and Ryan finally came downstairs they were high. Sammy kissed the top of my head and Ryan opened the refrigerator door and brought out three cans of beer. Suddenly, he frightened me. I thought, if I confront him now he will kill us both. I got up and told them good night and then I went upstairs and threw up the wine. It came out in a tidal wave. Sammy and Ryan went out and Sammy didn't get home until the next afternoon. I was still in bed. I felt paralyzed by what that swastika on Ryan's back meant. Sammy had to have seen it. Did he think it didn't matter? When I heard him coming up the stairs I opened my door and he smiled at me. He looked happy.

"I wish you had come," he said. "The music was really good."

"Does Ryan know you are Jewish?" I asked him.

He looked puzzled for a moment, then he leaned against the door frame and looked down. "Yeah," he muttered.

"And what did he say about that?"

"He doesn't care."

"Are you certain about that?"

"I don't consider myself Jewish anymore," he said.

"It doesn't matter what you consider yourself, it is what you are."

"It's not what I *am,*" he said. "I don't believe any of it. Neither do you."

"That doesn't mean I go with people like him!"

"You don't even know him."

"I know he has a Nazi tattoo."

Sammy rolled his eyes. "It's an old tattoo. His dad made him get it, okay? What do you care? You hate them, too. *You're* the one who said it was a cult. I mean, Shoah was, like, a hundred years ago but all they do is talk about how it excuses everything. It's bullshit."

"Sammy," I said, slowly, "Shoah is not bullshit."

"You know what I mean."

"Where did you get an idea like that?"

"Like what? I'm saying they're corrupt. They don't care about me or you. They only care about everybody following the rules. Like robots! *That* is bullshit."

"It is one thing for it to be bullshit and another thing for you to bring a Nazi into my house."

"He's not a Nazi!"

"When Isaac finds out he won't want him to come here."

"Why would you tell him? *It doesn't matter!*"

"It matters to me. And it will matter to Isaac. What about his friends? All these people you are hanging around with. Are they all . . . like him?"

"You don't know what you're talking about, Aviva. You're making a big deal out of nothing. Maybe you should take your medicine and call me in the morning."

He laughed, suddenly confident, alive in his meanness. I had never seen him like that before and I was surprised at how much it hurt. I thought I knew him because I knew his secrets and he knew mine. I thought we were the same because we both left. But we are not the same.

After that, Sammy didn't bring Ryan around anymore. And he started staying away for days at a time. He didn't return my phone calls, and when he did come home he barely spoke, just locked himself in his room. I spent most of those next few weeks in bed. Every time I heard the front door open, I sat up and waited for him to knock on my door so I could tell him how much I loved him and that I just wanted him to be safe and happy. But he never knocked. And I started to feel sick again. Sammy was the last piece of family I had, Rebekah. He was the boy I was supposed to save. I slept and slept and it was never enough to make me feel awake. I stopped going to my cleaning jobs. I didn't bathe. Isaac came upstairs with peanut butter sandwiches and glasses of water. Sometimes I ate them. When Sammy had been gone a whole month, I pleaded with Isaac to find him and bring him to me. Please, I said. I need him.

"Give him space," said Isaac. "He's in love."

But he couldn't stop me. The next Thursday I got out of bed and drove to the Mobil station and waited for Ryan and his father. His father was covered in tattoos. He had a skull and the SS lightning bolts on his enormous arms. He had a spiderweb on his neck with a swastika in the middle. Ryan was wearing shorts, and I saw he had a skull on his leg. The skull had an open mouth and wild eyes. It was laughing at me. They were both wearing sunglasses and to me they looked like soldiers. Soldiers without an army, with only their anger. I almost ran them over, right there in the parking lot behind the gas station. I wish I had. Instead I followed them. They drove out of New Paltz and up the Thruway past Kingston. After almost an hour, they turned west onto a state route I'd never been on. I was down to an eighth of a tank of gas when I followed the truck down a dirt driveway under a thick patch of trees. Three trailer homes and one old house shared the entrance. One trailer was new, but the other two were sagging, aluminum skirts cracked and split and missing in places, one just sitting on cinder blocks. On the porch of the old house sat an old, legless woman smoking cigarettes. She was sitting in a wheelchair wearing a long t-shirt, the stumps dangling over the edge of her seat.

Ryan and his father got out of their truck and both immediately walked toward me.

"What the fuck do you want?" The father was wearing blue jeans and a black sleeveless t-shirt with a faded yellow Batman insignia across it. Both their heads were shaved. I rolled up the window, locked the doors and pressed on the horn.

The father started screaming and banging on my window. I closed my eyes. I was here for Sammy. I had to get

Sammy. The father banged and banged and then I heard Ryan say my name. I kept honking.

"Aviva! It's okay," he said, putting his palm on the passenger-side window. "I know her!"

"Tell her to shut up!"

"Aviva, please stop," said Ryan, his face close to the glass. "Please."

I stopped. The horn was very loud and it hurt my head. The father kicked my car door.

Ryan tried the door but it was still locked. "He's not here," he said to me through the glass. He looked almost as frantic as I felt.

"Who the fuck is this bitch?" shouted the old lady on the porch. Her voice sounded like a robot's. Another man, closer to Ryan's age, came out of one of the trailers. He was shirtless, with an enormous eagle tattooed across his chest, and holding a shotgun. He shielded his eyes from the sun.

"It's okay, Hank," said Ryan. "I know her."

"She needs to get off our property," said Hank.

"Aviva, please, let me in."

I shook my head.

"Ryan, you fucking this chick?" asked the father.

Ryan didn't answer.

"Tell him to put the gun away," I said.

"Hank go inside, it's fine!"

"I'm not going anywhere," said Hank.

"Don't be an asshole, Hank."

"Fuck you, Ryan. Handle your fucking pussy."

"You're freaking her out, Hank. Gimme a break here."

Hank lowered the firearm. I cracked the passenger window open. Ryan grabbed ahold and shoved his mouth as far into the car as possible.

"Sammy's not here," he said. "This is my family's place. Please, they don't know."

At first I thought he meant that they don't know Sammy is Jewish, that he was trying to protect my brother. But then I realized he was talking about himself: his family didn't know that he had sex with men. I let him in the car.

"I want to see Sammy," I said.

"Fine," he said. "Just go. Now."

I backed out of the driveway and he directed me into town, past the A&P and the McDonald's to the Dollar Store. We turned right and he told me to stop at a two-story apartment building.

"Thank you for not saying anything," said Ryan.

"Where is Sammy?"

"He's probably inside. I'll take you."

"What do you want with him? What does your father want?"

"My father?" Ryan was a little older than Sammy. Twenty-two or so. And he was very handsome. He had dimples in both cheeks. I remember noticing them in our kitchen once, before I saw his tattoo, when he and Sammy and Isaac and I were laughing about kugel. Ryan told us there was a similar word that meant an exercise for your vagina. It was a fun night. I remember being happy for Sammy that such a good-looking boy liked him. I thought it would be good for his self-esteem.

"Look," said Ryan, his leg bouncing so wildly it kept knocking against the bottom of my glove compartment. "My family isn't like you. It's *not* okay to be . . . gay." He stumbled over the word "gay," like it hurt to say. It was almost funny: it is not okay to be gay in Sammy's family, either. But to Ryan, I was Sammy's only family. Me and Isaac. "Please don't say anything."

"We're Jewish," I said. I said it proudly for the first time I could remember. Like it meant something strong and positive.

"I know," he said. "I'm not racist. I know the . . . thing on my back is awful. I'm real sorry about that. I knew you saw it but I didn't know what to say. I got it when I was sixteen. It was kind of a thing in my family. Everybody has one. But I'm not like that. That's why I moved out."

He was very convincing.

"Outside of work I never see my dad and my brother. Really. They've only met Sammy once. We said he was German."

"German?"

"Because you guys have an accent."

"We're not German!"

"I know, but my family doesn't know accents. And he's blond."

It was so outrageous I couldn't even respond. Could

Sammy have possibly allowed this? I turned off the ignition and we got out of the car. The building was faced with dingy white aluminum siding, and when Ryan opened the door to the first-floor apartment I could smell the marijuana from the landing. Sammy was on the sofa with a video-game controller in his hands. He was playing some sort of war game and the volume was turned up very loud. Gunshots and screams and the sounds of bodies struck by bullets filled the room. There was a thumping kind of music beneath it. Two girls were sitting at a kitchen table, putting pot into plastic baggies. At first, none of them noticed we'd entered, then the girls looked up. The one dressed like a boy acknowledged me with a slight backward nod. The other girl, who had bright pink hair and a tattoo covering her entire upper right arm (flowers, it appeared, not swastikas) looked at me and then looked at Ryan for an explanation.

"Sam," he said. Sammy looked up and smiled when he saw me, which made everything better.

" 'Viva," he said. "You found me."

"Can we talk?" I asked.

Sammy stood up. He was wearing a white tank top and new jeans that were too big for him. He hugged me and his arms and chest felt harder than I remembered.

"We'll go outside," he said. As we walked to my car, he lit a cigarette and offered me one. I rarely smoke, but I did not want to say no. I did not want him to think I was rejecting him.

"Please don't cut us off, Sammy," I said. "I love you."

"I know," he said. "But you can't tell me what to do. I've had enough of that for a whole life. I get to pick what I do now, Aviva. Me. Not you."

"I know," I said. "But this Ryan . . . his people, they are bad people."

"They're okay," said Sam, kicking the dirt. "They actually think like I do about a lot of stuff. Like, how the government is trying to take away our rights. I mean, that's what the rebbes do—and the government is totally involved. The politicians look the other way so they can get elected. I'm supposed to have the right to an education, but all I know is Torah! And they want to tell us who to marry and what we can read and eat and do and wear. They take away our right to be *free*! This is a *free country*! And they get us to go along because they say it's good for the community. But that's *communism*! What about the individual?"

"That is not all they think, Sammy. That is not what that swastika means. That means they want Jews to die. That means they are full of hate. Are you so full of hate?"

"Fuck yeah, I'm full of hate," said Sammy. His face was pink. He was getting worked up. "I'm never going to be normal, Aviva, because of what they did to me. You get that, right? And *nobody cared*. Nobody cares now. I don't matter to them. You don't matter to them. Eli knew what was happening to me. I told him about the bleeding. *I told him!* And he didn't care! Do you know what Ryan's dad would have done if he came home bleeding like that? He would have killed the guy. Shot him dead and fuck the consequences. But all Eli cared about was making sure no one could say anything bad about us. How fucked up is that! It's totally okay to do bad, sick things but you just can't talk about it? Rebbe Taub basically told Eli it was worse to report on a pedophile rapist Jew than *be* a pedophile rapist Jew! How is that okay? How are they *all* not in jail!"

What could I say? He was right. And I, too, had done nothing.

"You do not have to let that man ruin the rest of your life, Sammy. You are a smart boy. There are people who can help you. Professionals . . ."

"I'm not going to therapy. I don't want to *talk* about it. I want to forget about it. I want to *move on*."

It was a reasonable request. But by then I knew enough to know that trauma doesn't let you move on. Whether you inflict it on yourself—like I did by leaving you—or have it forced upon you like Sammy did, shame and fear implants inside you like cancer. Sammy, I knew, would never go a day without being assaulted by that man, just as I had never gone a day without seeing your father's face when he discovered that I was gone.

"Is this really how you want to live? With these people?"

"They're my friends! Until I met Ryan, all I thought about was killing myself."

"Sammy!"

"What? What did you think I was doing in that room all day? I had it all planned. I would go into the mountains where we used to hike and jump off a cliff. But now everything's changed. Can't you see I'm happier, Aviva?"

"But this can't be what you want to spend your life doing?"

"Aviva, I have so much life ahead of me!" He laughed. "Since I left I've learned more about history, and the way things work in the real world, than twelve years in yeshiva. It's such bullshit the way they make us afraid of everyone who isn't like us. You can't just come to America and pretend you're better than everybody else. It's supposed to be a *melting pot*."

"I don't think your friends with the swastikas believe in the melting pot, Sammy."

"You know what I mean!"

"They're going to find out you're Jewish."

"I'm not Jewish anymore."

His naïveté shocked me. "Being Jewish isn't like a hat, Sammy. You can't just take it off."

He made a little gesture with his hand like he was tossing something away. "It's gone."

"How can you pretend to be a Nazi?"

"I'm not pretending to be a Nazi!"

"What's going to happen when they see you've fooled them?"

"Would you shut up about it, Aviva?" The meanness

fell over his face like a metal gate closing over a store. I was back where I started. How could he not see that this was ridiculous? How could he not see that it would turn out badly no matter what? But I was not going to win this fight—at least not today—and I would not allow myself to lose him.

"Okay," I said.

"Don't worry, okay? Ryan's not close with his family. He just sees his dad for work because he has to."

"I think he is the wrong man for you, Sammy," I said, speaking slowly, thinking that perhaps if I enunciated perfectly, he would agree. "Please come home. It is not safe with all that pot around. The police will put you in jail."

"It's not that much," he said. "You want some?"

I said, no, I did not want any pot. Sammy promised to come visit soon, and as I drove home, I began to see how I had opened this path to him. When I told him about you, I taught him that keeping secrets was normal. If I could live with a secret daughter, he could live as a secret Jew. And if big sister Aviva sometimes drank too much or smoked some pot, why shouldn't he? When he first ran off the derech I imagined that getting a little tipsy or high together was a way to connect with him as a new adult—but I set a terrible precedent. Sammy was just weeks out of a life where every choice had only one right answer: whatever the Torah says, or the rebbe, or his elders. Suddenly, he could do anything. And why not try? But I should not have made it look like it was all without consequences. He needed to know about the hardships of this life. He needed to know that he would get hurt, and that he would hurt others. He needed to know that, sometimes, people die.

CHAPTER SIXTEEN

REBEKAH

Half a mile away from the Halls I call Kaitlyn's cell.

"I'm sorry to bug you again," I say. "I was just out at Ryan's family's place in Greenville . . ."

"You went out there?" she says, interrupting me.

"Yeah. I was just trying to track down Ryan and Sam."

"Well, they definitely aren't gonna be out there."

"Right," I say. "I guess I didn't know . . ."

"Ryan usually gets back to me quick but I still haven't heard from him. I'm home now. Do you wanna come over?"

I plug her address into my phone and then call Larry to see if he's gotten a name on the license plate number from Nechemaya.

"Nothing for you," he tells me. "We're not really supposed to run plates. I asked my guy for a favor but I don't want to bug him too much. What did Roseville PD say?"

"The chief wasn't there but I talked to the cop who was first on the scene when Pessie died."

"Great! Can you write it up?"

"He wouldn't go on the record. He told me the chief had turned the case over to the State Police, but the chief didn't mention that to me when I talked to him. I gave him the plate number and when he looked it up . . . it was weird. He was all friendly and then he clammed up."

"So nothing for tomorrow?"

"I got a little bit from a neighbor and one of Pessie's coworkers. Apparently she had a fight with someone at work about a week before she died. It might have been this ex-fiancé."

"What was the fight about?"

"She didn't know. She said the guy was really upset."

"But she doesn't know his name?"

"No."

"It's a little thin. I'd rather advance the police angle. Have you called the State Police yourself?"

"No."

"Do that. Call me back."

I pull over at a Stewart's gas station and Google "State Police Rockland County" on my phone. A woman answers.

"Troop F," she says.

"Hi," I say. "My name is Rebekah Roberts and I'm a reporter for the *New York Tribune*. I'm working on an article about a possible homicide in Roseville. A woman named Pessie Goldin. Do you know who I might speak to about that?"

"Hold please."

I hold. About a minute later she comes back on the line. "I'm gonna have to take a message."

I leave my information and call Larry back.

"I feel like I'm making progress," I tell him. "I definitely want to stay up here tonight. That's still okay, right?"

"Do you really think there's a story there?"

"I do," I say. Should I tell him about Mellie? I can't use anything I saw there—or at least, I shouldn't—since I didn't ID myself as a reporter. There's a story there, obviously, about white supremacists buying and selling guns in preparation for some race war, but it's not Pessie's story. I decide to wait. I can pitch it later. "Something is definitely fishy with the cops. I just need to, like, give it a little time."

He considers. "Okay. But if you don't get anything for tomorrow's deadline I can't justify expenses, or keeping you out of rotation."

"I know," I say, thinking, is this when people like Jayson Blair started making shit up? "I'll get something."

I follow my GPS through Cairo's "main street," which consists of a feed store, a combination lawyer/real estate office, a hair salon, a sandwich shop, and a post office. There are many more storefronts, but they are all vacant. Outside the post office is a folding table manned by a man and a woman who look sixty-ish. Draped over the table is a carefully hand-lettered sign that reads IMPEACH THE DISHONEST LIAR OBAMA. I wonder if they bought a gun from Connie or Hank Hall recently.

I turn left just past a Dollar General and come to a stop at a two-story apartment building with moldy white vinyl siding and a handful of cars parked on the grass where the landlord was apparently too cheap to create a parking lot. I call Kaitlyn and tell her I am outside. A moment later a girl with a phone to her ear opens a ground-floor door and waves. I tuck my notebook and pen in the pocket of my jacket, lock Saul's car, and greet her.

Kaitlyn is barely five feet tall; she probably weighs less than a hundred pounds. One side of her head is shaved and the other is dyed a faded pink over blond. Her apartment is shabby—a low ceiling and cheap Berber carpet—but like Mellie's place, well taken care of. A vanilla scented candle is burning on the kitchen counter, and a futon and two fold-out camping chairs face the TV, which is tuned to E! Joan Rivers is making fun of someone.

"You want something to drink?" asks Kaitlyn.

"I'm okay," I say.

"You've kinda got me nervous," she says, sitting on the futon, leaning forward. Her left arm is covered with a sleeve of flower tattoos. "When did Pessie die again?"

"March fourth."

She thinks a minute. "That's right around when Sam stopped coming to work."

"You guys work together?"

She nods. "At a big nursery outside Catskill. It's kind of seasonal. We're out on a crew doing gardens and stuff May to, like, October. Then we do shifts at the store in the winter, but the hours are erratic. Sam's been sorta . . . different since he got back from prison. Gina—that's our boss—she took him back, but he kept showing up late.

And sometimes he'd be high. I thought she fired him but she said he just stopped coming in."

"Why was Sam in prison?"

"We all got arrested—him and Ryan and me and this other girl—about four years ago. It was really stupid. The neighbors called in a noise complaint and the cops found all the pot we were bagging for Ryan's dad. Plus a couple guns, which I didn't know they had. I got lucky 'cause it was my first arrest. I just got probation and the landlord even let me stay here, thank God. But Ryan and Sam had priors and they both got jail time. Ryan got out after like six months and he totally straightened out. He stopped working for his dad and got back in school. Now he's doing vet tech work in Hudson. Sam was in for a lot longer, though. He just came back around Thanksgiving."

"Why was Sam in longer?"

"Something happened in there. I don't know the details, but they sent him up to state prison. Which is a whole other ballgame."

"Do you know where he was living after he got out?"

"I think he has a sister in New Paltz."

"Aviva?"

Kaitlyn shrugs. "Maybe? I didn't know her. I think he was back and forth between her place and Ryan's."

"How long have you known Ryan?"

"Since we were kids. My mom and his mom were close. Ryan had it really rough. It's a miracle he turned out as normal and nice as he is. His dad was in prison for a lot of his childhood. And his mom killed herself while he was gone."

"Wow."

"It was really fucked up. She shot herself and Ryan found her. He was, like, eleven, I think. Him and Hank pretty much ran wild out there. Their grandma and grandpa took care of them until Connie—that's their dad, Connie for Conrad—came back. The grandpa was from the South, I think. He was in the KKK. I heard he moved here because he'd, like, killed some black guy down there. He died of a heart attack or something before Connie got out. And the grandma . . . she drank a lot. Got both legs amputated from diabetes or something."

"I think I met her."

"I can't believe you went out there," she says. "Connie used to come to Little League games and yell at people and start fights with the other parents. My mom totally blamed him—and the grandma—for Beth's suicide. She said they treated her like a servant. I think she had a couple miscarriages after Ryan and Hank and they were, like, pissed she didn't make more Aryan babies."

"Aryan babies?"

"I told you, they're crazy. Hank dropped out in tenth grade but Ryan graduated and they always gave him shit, saying he thought he was better than them. He got a job at the hardware store but it was just part-time, not enough for rent or anything else. He ended up going to work with his dad to make enough to move out. Ironic, right? That's how him and Sam met. Sam worked at a place on Connie's route."

"Connie's route?"

"Connie's got a gig delivering beer for a distributor in Albany. I mean, that's, like, the cover. He's always got whatever else you want, too. Pot and pills, heroin."

And guns, I think.

"After Ryan got out of jail, he cut ties with his dad. He was like, I'm *not* going back in."

"So when did Ryan come out to his family?"

"Are you kidding? They don't know he's gay. They'd probably kill him."

"The girl I met out there, Mellie?" Kaitlyn nods. "I think she knew. She was like, tell them not to come around here. She seemed really pissed."

"Fuck," whispers Kaitlyn. "I can't believe Ryan didn't tell me. I wonder if he even knows. Him and Sam were pretty careful. They only went to clubs and stuff down in the city or up in Albany and they never hung out at the bars Hank and Connie and their friends go to. Sam was kinda messed up about being gay, too. Actually, the one time me and Pessie really talked, that's what we talked about. She came over right after Sam got out of prison. We had kind of a welcome home party. She brought some really good food and she was telling me about where they grew up. I didn't know anything about Jews and Sam never talked about it. Anyway, she said she used to think gay people were evil. But she and Sam were really close—I actually thought they were brother and sister at first—and she said she realized that Sam, like, couldn't help how he was. That he must have been born that way and that if God made him that way he must have had a reason. She was really nice. I can't believe she's dead. I can't believe Ryan didn't tell me."

"When was the last time you talked to him?"

"Ryan?" She sighs. "That's the thing. We had a fight a few weeks ago. I love Sam, I do, but I told Ryan I didn't think their relationship was healthy anymore. I was, like, Sam needs help. Ryan knew, but . . . I mean, they're in love. And Sam wasn't always the way he is now. He changed a lot in prison. We used to kind of make fun of all the shit the Halls believe—race war and Obama the monkey and whatever stupid cliché crap they spout. Ryan doesn't believe that stuff at all. I don't think he ever did. But after Sam got out, he was talking like Ryan's dad."

"You didn't think that was weird? A Jewish kid talking like a neo-Nazi?"

"Of course I thought it was weird! It's fucking insane. But, I mean, that's how it is. Was." She pauses. "You know, Ryan and Sam used to talk about running off together. Going down South, someplace warm where nobody knew them."

"You think they might have left town?"

She shrugs. "If they didn't, maybe they should."

CHAPTER SEVENTEEN

AVIVA

Sammy moved into the pot apartment. He stopped working at the gas station and, for the next few months, every time the phone rang I thought it would be the police or the hospital. But when Sammy finally did get arrested, he didn't call me: he called Conrad Hall.

"It was no big deal," Sammy told us a couple weeks later. Every month or two he showed up, usually without notice, for Shabbos dinner. Isaac and I have been OTD for a long time, but we both keep Shabbos, in our own way. We like to make dinner, and, if we can help it, we don't drive. I make my own schedule, and I do not take jobs on Saturday. Isaac's work with the contractor was sporadic and he got a part-time job at one of the shops on the main street near campus, selling t-shirts and incense and CDs. He couldn't always take Saturdays off, but when he could, we spent the day together. We both like science fiction books, and sometimes we read aloud to each other while we cook. Sometimes I just sleep, or drink wine or take a bath. I try to take time for myself, to remember to be calm in my mind. Sammy doesn't keep Shabbos; he once told me that he makes it a point to expend as much energy as possible on the day of rest. When he came for dinner, he was always on his way somewhere else.

"It wasn't my fault, anyway," said Sammy, when Isaac pressed him. "Ryan got a DUI and I was in the truck."

Isaac was skeptical.

"I had a little pot on me, okay?" said Sammy, mouth full.

"And they just let you out?"

Sammy kept eating. He poured himself some more wine.

"Please answer my question, Sammy," said Isaac. Isaac feels tenderly toward Sammy, but he does not know how to connect with him anymore. Isaac was the one who realized immediately that Sammy and Ryan were having sex. Isaac said he tried to talk to him about it, just to let him know that he had a friend, but Sammy wasn't interested in talking.

"Fuck you, Isaac," said Sammy.

"Sammy!" I said.

"It was nothing," said Sammy, hissing into his chicken. "Ryan's dad bailed us both out, okay? He felt bad because it was Ryan that got us in trouble. It was nothing. I wouldn't have even *told* you but I put this address down."

"Our address?" The Nazis knew our address?

Isaac put his fork down. "Sammy, I do not think it is safe for you to be friends with those people."

"*Those* people? You mean goyim?"

"You know exactly what I mean," said Isaac, his voice rising. Isaac is a quiet man. We had been living together for almost ten years and, until that evening, I had never seen him angry. "I am not stupid. I know who Conrad Hall is. I know what you must be involved in if he is using his money to get you out of jail."

"Oh yeah? What do you think I'm involved in, Isaac?"

"Drugs, obviously."

Sammy rolled his eyes.

"Now you owe Connie Hall a favor."

"No I don't," he said, automatically. But you could see it dawn on him that Isaac was right.

I looked at Sammy, trying to get him to look at me.

"Come live here," I said. "For a little while. Just until . . ." I did not know how to end the sentence. It didn't matter. "Come stay. There are plenty of rooms."

"I hate it here," said Sammy, finally lifting his eyes, which had softened. "Do you know how stupid I feel with all these college kids around? I can barely read a book in English!"

Isaac and I looked at each other. Isaac knew exactly how poor a yeshiva education in Roseville was. He knew that just like in Williamsburg, the rebbes censored whole portions of textbooks; he knew that words like "university" and "dinosaurs" were blacked out with markers, just as Pessie's "anatomy" lessons had been conducted without mention of entire regions of the human body.

"You're smart, Sammy," I said. "You will fit in when they get to know you."

Sammy made an ugly face. "I don't want to live with a bunch of hippies."

Isaac and I exchanged a look. Hippies?

"What do you mean?" asked Isaac.

Sammy sighed dramatically. "It's just not me, okay?"

"What's not you?"

"All my friends are in Greene County."

"Ryan's friends," I said.

Sammy glared at me. His moods changed so quickly. "They're *my* friends! I have my own life!"

"What do you think Conrad Hall is going to do when he finds out his son is having sex with a Jewish boy?"

"I'm not a boy!" screamed Sammy. He brought a fist down hard on the table. The wine glasses jumped; his glass fell into his food.

"You think there won't be consequences?" asked Isaac, his voice steady. "If you think they are going to keep believing you are a German exchange student you are being very stupid."

"Who the fuck do you think you are, Isaac? You're not my father. You're a fucking old faggot."

"Sammy . . . ," I said, standing up. "I love you."

"Whatever, Aviva. I came over for Shabbos, like you're always *begging* me to do. This is why I don't want to live here. I'm eighteen years old! I can do what I want. And I don't want to live with you."

Four months later, Sammy got arrested again. The charges were more serious, and this time Conrad Hall didn't come to the rescue.

At the jail, the woman behind the bulletproof glass

told me his bail was set at $50,000.

"That seems very high," I said.

"It's because of the gun," said the woman.

"What gun?"

"There's a weapons charge," she said, and directed me down the street to a bail bond office where a man took my money order. After we moved to New Paltz, Isaac and I both put a little bit of money aside each month. The man who owned the yellow house took only a few hundred dollars in rent from us—just enough to pay his taxes. He had no mortgage and was grateful to have caretakers continue his work, housing people who were leaving the community. We joked that we ran a secret bed-and-breakfast. Once Isaac brought little chocolates home and we put them on the pillows in all the bedrooms, just to be silly. Some months there were half a dozen people in and out of the house; some months there was no one but us. We opened savings accounts at the same bank on the same day, and ten years later, I had almost ten thousand dollars in mine. Before I went to the bank for the bail money, Isaac told me he hoped Sammy knew how lucky he was that he had a sister who loved him so much. I don't know, Rebekah. That day—and most days—I felt certain I had failed my brother.

I waited two hours for Sammy to come out. He was silent almost all the way home, staring out the window.

"You have a gun?" I asked finally, almost whispering.

"It's not really mine," he said. "I was just borrowing it."

"What do you need with a gun?"

Sammy sighed. "For protection, Aviva, don't be stupid."

It hurt to be called stupid. But this was not about me.

"Protection from what?"

Sammy didn't answer immediately. We drove through town. When I moved here, I looked at the main street and all the happy college students and felt fortunate. I knew I could blend in. Sometimes it was sad knowing that all this learning was going on around me and I would never really be a part of it. Sammy could. But he did not want to.

"You know I'm a really good shot," he said, finally. "Ryan learned to shoot when he was a kid and he's been teaching me. We go to the range and sometimes out in the woods to practice. I could maybe have been a sniper in the army or something."

I wasn't sure what to say. I have never held a gun in my life. I have never wanted to.

"I wish I'd had a gun when I was ten," he said. "I would have killed him, Aviva. Boom. And everything would be different."

"You think you would have been happier if you had murdered the cook?"

"He deserves to die," said Sammy. "You know that."

What could I say? He was right.

The next morning when we spread the paperwork on the kitchen table in the sunlight, we could see that Sammy was in a lot of trouble. He was charged with possession of marijuana and three kinds of prescription pills with intent to distribute, and criminal possession of a weapon. We called the phone number for the public defender and two days later I drove Sammy to his office. He told us that it was not good news.

"Six months ago I could maybe have gotten you probation and community service," he said. "But the prosecutor has a hard-on for gun crimes. He's trying to get on Cuomo's good side for an endorsement since he's up for election in November. And you've already got this other misdemeanor. I suggest you take a plea. I can probably get the sentences to run concurrently. Three months—give or take—then community service, maybe a fine."

"Three months in jail?" I said. I didn't like it. I have been to a lot of ugly places in my life, but jail was about the ugliest.

"I can do three months," said Sammy.

"There is something else," said the lawyer. "I see you were arrested with Ryan Hall. In his apartment. Do you live there?"

"Sort of," he said. "But I'm not on the lease or anything."

"Okay, that might help you. I'm guessing the prosecutor hasn't looked too hard at the file yet, but I think I'm likely to hear from him about this. Here's the thing: If the drugs and the gun you had on you *weren't* yours. If they belonged to the Halls, say . . ."

"You want me to snitch on the Halls?"

"I'm not saying one way or the other," said the lawyer. "I'm saying it may be an option."

"You're the lawyer," I said. "What do you think he should do?"

"It's up to you."

"I'm not going to get Ryan in more trouble," said Sammy. "I can do three months."

And that was that. Sammy stayed by us in New Paltz until his court date. He rarely left the house, and spent most of his time asleep or on the phone with Ryan. God knows what they were talking about.

Pessie came to visit several times, but Sammy did not want to spend much time with her. Like me, Pessie had been worried about Sammy's new life, but unlike me she seemed confident he would come to his senses. I had always liked Pessie, and as she got older, I liked her even more. I had never met anyone like her. She loved Sammy no matter what he did. She even liked me, despite the fact that I represented everything she was supposed to be afraid of: alone, unpious. Sammy was always trying to get her to leave the community, but she did not want to. She said she loved Hashem. She said that Jews needed to be strong to survive and that our strength came from unity. She said she was doing her part. But I do not think it was easy. She defended the community when Sammy made blanket statements about how evil and corrupt everyone was, and I imagine that, occasionally, she defended those of us gone off the derech when her friends in Roseville called us crazy. She told me that as more people went OTD there was opportunity to merge the interests of the two communities. She said one of her friends started a group for people whose family members had left and she hoped she could help with that.

But once we learned Sammy was going to jail, I began to see that she wasn't as certain about her future as she pretended. One afternoon, she came over with a chulent and Sammy wouldn't come out of his room to see her, so she and I ate together in the kitchen. She told me that there was a man from Israel who wished to marry her.

"Do you like him?" I asked.

"He is very nice. Not too old." Pessie paused. "Did you know your husband in Israel for long before you married?"

I shook my head and told her the story about Etan: that he was related to the man and woman that lived down the hall from my aunt and uncle in Jerusalem. He came to Shabbos dinner at their apartment one Friday and I happened to be there. He asked after me and we met again, more formally. My aunt and uncle did not mention that I had been off the derech for more than a year as a teenager, and his family did not ask.

"Did you tell him later?" asked Pessie.

I shook my head. "Why should I?"

"So he would know you?"

I remember being puzzled by what she said. It had not ever really seemed possible that Etan would know me.

"Do you think that if you had told him about Florida and Rebekah that things might have been different?"

"I don't know," I said, and I didn't. "I think the way things turned out was probably for the best."

"Did you love him?"

I almost lied, but Pessie deserved the truth. "No," I said. "But I liked him. Most of the time. I think maybe love is . . ." Love is, what? I never saw anything that looked like love between my parents. They did not kiss or hug or hold hands. They did not say, "I love you." But I think they had a good marriage. As good as any I've seen.

"I always thought I would be Sammy's wife," she said. "I know I am not supposed to want so much. But when I imagined being married, and having children, I imagined being with Sammy. And it seemed like fun." She shook her head and bent forward to sip her tea. "It feels very different now."

Isaac and I both went to the courthouse in Catskill for Sammy's sentencing. For some reason, I kept thinking my father might appear. Part of me wished that he knew what was happening with Sammy, although I know Sammy would not have wanted him to. He hates my father—who was more like a distant uncle to him than a real father—and I could tell, as he stood there in Isaac's too-big suit coat, shoulders bent before the judge, that Sammy was scared. He, too, had failed at life outside the shtetl and he would never want my father to see him fallen this low. I knew the feeling and it broke my heart.

I wrote him a letter every few days. He wrote me back only once. Nobody called me when he was in the infirmary. And nobody called when he stabbed the black man.

CHAPTER EIGHTEEN

REBEKAH

I leave Kaitlyn around 5:00 P.M. and drive south toward the New Paltz address from the library, my heart beating in my teeth. *A sister in New Paltz*. It has to be Aviva, right?

Saul doesn't answer his phone when I call, so I leave a message: "I think I might have found her! I talked to somebody who said Sam had a sister in New Paltz. And there was a New Paltz address on the backgrounder the library gave me. I'm going there now! Call me!"

The evening sky is the color of Orange Crush as I turn onto West Pine Street. Number 781 is a two-story yellow house with a driveway leading to a small shed in the back. I pull in and turn off the engine. Breathe in. Breathe out. The house is dark. A wind chime trills in one of the trees in the yard. Someone has draped a kind of black netting over bushes along the front of the house, protecting them from winter, I assume. It does not appear that anyone is home, but I knock anyway. I knock again. The curtains are drawn in the two first-floor windows. The street is quiet, a few lights on in the nearby houses, but almost no one out walking, which means no one to get suspicious if

I sneak around the side yard. Which I do. There are still patches of snow on the lawn and ice in the corners of the small deck attached to the back of the house. I climb up three steps to a door with a window, cup my hands around my face, and look into the kitchen. I can't make out much beyond the lines of the counters and a glowing clock on the microwave. There are papers and magnets on the refrigerator but I can't tell what they say. Does she live here? I try the door, but it's locked. What would I have done if it wasn't? Walk in and crawl in her bed? Wait for Mommy to come home?

I go back to Saul's car and turn on the engine. She is bound to be home soon. After about ten minutes, Nechemaya calls.

"Pessie's neighbors do not wish to be in the newspaper. They are concerned that whoever did this might target them."

"Okay," I say. "But I don't know if my editor is going to let me stay on the story if no one from the community is willing to go on the record."

"I understand," he says. "I am doing what I can."

I pull out my notebook and open my laptop to transcribe what Kaitlyn told me. I've already missed the deadline for tomorrow's paper, so I decide not to e-mail Larry with my new information about Pessie coming to Sam's welcome home party. Instead, I click into an open Wi-Fi network (gotta love a college town) and Google "Conrad Hall." The first few results are contact listings that refer me to the property in Greenville, but at the bottom of the page a 2011 article from the *Albany Times-Union* pops up.

MAN WITH TIES TO HATE GROUP QUESTIONED IN TROY DOUBLE HOMICIDE

By Marisol Lopez

An ex-con with ties to a right-wing hate group was questioned in relation to the murders of Quantrell Hamilton and Michael Wilkins, police sources say.

Conrad "Connie" Hall, 56, was questioned and released Thursday.

Hamilton and Wilkins were shot execution-style in their Troy apartment on February 19. Police suspect that the murders were drug-related.

Hall has a long criminal history, including a nine-year prison term for manslaughter. He was arrested in January 2009 with members of the so-called Greene Freemen at a demonstration on the day of President Obama's inauguration. Hall and about 20 protesters, some carrying firearms, attempted to enter the Capitol building. Charges against him were later dropped.

The Greene Freemen are listed on the Southern Poverty Law Center's Hatewatch as a white nationalist group.

Neighbors told the *Times-Union* that Hamilton and Wilkins had recently moved into the Troy apartment and were believed to be using it as a holding place for guns and drugs.

A woman who answered the phone at Hall's residence refused to comment on the case.

I copy and paste the article's URL into an e-mail and send it to Larry, along with a note:

The guy Pessie used to be engaged to is/was in a relationship with Conrad Hall's son Ryan. Do you know what happened with this homicide? Anyone ever caught? Thoughts?

The Southern Poverty Law Center's Web site lists more than forty New York-based organizations that they consider to be "hate groups," including the Radical White Persons Party and the Suffolk County Aryans. The Nation of Islam makes the list, too. The Greene Freemen—who the SPLC identify as both white nationalist and Aryan Nations—don't appear to have their own Web site, so I click on a link for the Rochester-based Caucasian Caucus and am redirected to a no-frills Web site called The Protected. The banner at the top of the site reads, in flashing red letters: WE ARE THE WHITE MINORITY! PROTECTED BY GOD! SWORN TO FIGHT FOR OUR RACE! Below the banner are dozens of discussion threads, beginning with "Introduction to the Protected," then "Rules of the Board," then "News Links," "International," "Money," "Self-Defense," "Strategy," "Events"; there are even threads for "Poetry," "White Singles," and "Ladies." I click into "Strategy" and see that there are more than two hundred pages of discussions with thousands of views. I scroll down and click on a thread called "The Problem with Jews." The post is written by a user named John March. He starts by telling readers that although they might think Jews are just harmless white people in funny hats, they are actually responsible for the destruction of the white race and "civilized" society more than any other group—"even niggers." He goes on. Jews are parasites who suck the life out of whatever country they are in, and then move on when there is nothing left. They are also sexual perverts who encourage pornography, masturbation, bestiality, and all manner of ugly stuff to keep the white race weak and distracted from their evil ways. He goes on and on, linking to various speeches and videos, several by David Duke, and then turns to "History," tracing the origins of modern Jews' use of sexual perversion as a weapon to Freud. Finally, he takes on "The Holocaust Myth." I click out, disgusted. Obviously, it's not a surprise to me that neo-Nazis and white supremacists exist; I mean, I'm from Florida. I've seen plenty of trucks flying Confederate flags, and I've spent at least a couple weekend afternoons half-watching cable news documentaries about Aryan prison gangs. I saw *American History X* like everybody else. What I didn't understand, though, and what this Web site proves, is how much thought, how much *imagination*, these people put into building their ugly theories and alternative histories. It's not posturing. It's not just provocation. It's fucking serious. John March is an articulate writer. He doesn't sound unhinged or particularly angry. In fact, the post reads like an above-average academic paper—he even embedded images of newspaper articles from during World War II. Someone predisposed to hating Jews would find much to bolster their beliefs in this post. And someone who had been the victim of sexual abuse by a Jew—someone like Sam—might find an easy excuse to think that what happened to him was part of some larger, ongoing conspiracy. As if the poor kid's mind hadn't been fucked with enough.

I've been sitting in Saul's car for almost two hours when my phone rings. It's a number I don't recognize.

"This is Rebekah," I say.

"Rebekah? This is Officer Van Keller."

"Hi," I say. "How are you?"

"I'm calling you from my cell. Are you still in town?"

"I'm in New Paltz," I say.

"Can we meet?"

"Now?"

"If possible. I'll come to you."

We agree to meet at a diner just off the New Paltz exit from the Thruway. I order a bowl of potato soup and send Levi a text asking him to call me. If I can get him to comment on Pessie's apparently secret friendship with her ex, that might be enough for a story. After about an hour, Van Keller appears in the doorway dressed in jeans and a Carhartt jacket. I wave to catch his attention and he slides into my booth.

"Must be important," I say, trying to keep my smile salutary, not flirtatious. It's difficult. Poor guy; must be annoying to have every woman he meets turn into a giggling, stuttering teenager in his presence.

"Yeah," he says, taking off his coat. "We're off the record, okay?"

"Okay."

He nods. The waitress appears and he orders a Diet Coke.

"I'm probably going to lose my job for talking to you," he says. "But I'm not sure what else to do. You've already written about the case, so it makes sense that you'd keep digging. I read your other stuff. About that murder in Brooklyn? I guess this is your beat. So. And you have that plate number. I'm sure somebody at the *Trib* can figure out who it belongs to. Maybe you already have. Have you?"

I don't answer immediately, which he takes to mean yes. He's nervous, talking fast, tearing at the paper napkin in front of him.

"Right, yeah. So the truck Pessie's neighbors saw is registered to a man named Conrad Hall. You're not from around here so you probably haven't heard of him, but Connie Hall is a bad dude. He's Aryan Brotherhood. You know them?"

I nod.

"I don't think he advertises it, but that's blood in blood out. The Brotherhood controls most of the drugs and the guns coming into the state—outside of New York City.

Heroin has become a *big* problem here in the past couple years. Everybody hooked on prescription pills is losing their prescription since they started cracking down on doctors, and heroin is almost as good, and cheaper. Most of the robberies we see are heroin-related. Junkies stealing just enough to get a fix. Breaking into cars and houses. It's not as bad in Roseville, partly because the Jews aren't into that shit and they're more and more of the population. But the rest of Rockland and Orange County. Plus Dutchess and Greene and Ulster and up in Albany. And if they're not robbing—and they're white—they can sometimes make a little cash moving product for people like Connie. Which means they want to carry a gun. And if you've got a record, you can't get a gun in New York State. Well, you can't get it *legally*. But the Brotherhood has people all over, so they bring guns up from the Carolinas, Virginia, even Pennsylvania. And guns just up the ante for everybody. Now we gotta think about getting shot every time we pull over some stoned asshole, you know? I mean, it happens. Last year a probation officer got killed checking on a meth head in Woodbury. He knocks, and the guy's out of his mind, and armed. Shoots the officer through the door. Cop's wife had just had a baby. And, like, even the tweaker, he didn't know what he was doing. Without that gun he'd have gotten violated, sure, but now he's life without parole for capital murder."

Van Keller is talking alternately to me and to the napkin he has now torn to confetti. He pauses, looks at the shredded paper, then makes a kind of disgusted exhale out of his nose, and pushes the pile aside.

"I don't know if you know this already," I say, "but I've talked to two people who told me that Connie Hall's son, Ryan, is gay, and that he's in a relationship with a Jew from Roseville named Sam Kagan. Sam Kagan used to be engaged to Pessie."

Van Keller blinks. "Are you kidding me?"

"No," I say, and tell him about my visits with Mellie and Kaitlyn. He takes in what I am saying with eyes wide, mouth agape.

"So," he says, after I finish, "Connie could have gone to Roseville looking for Sam."

"Right," I say. "Except Sam hasn't lived there in years."

Van falls silent. He wipes his hand across his face, thinking.

"I read an article about Connie Hall being questioned in a double homicide in Troy," I say. "Did they ever get anybody for that?"

Van smirks and shakes his head. The waitress sets down a glass of Diet Coke and a paper-wrapped straw. "They indicted a kid connected to Connie."

"Connected?"

"Friend of one of his sons, I think. I'm not sure which one. A small-time dealer, full-time dirtbag named Tim Doyle. But he didn't make it to trial."

"Didn't make it?"

"He died in jail a couple days after they booked him."

"How?"

"Hung himself was the official word," says Keller. "But the Brotherhood has a lot of people. And it's not like they did an autopsy."

"You think Connie Hall had him killed?"

"I think that being close to Connie Hall can be deadly. And I know that I do not want him and his racist friends in my town. I know the Jews are weird, I get why some people think they aren't good neighbors. But they deserve to live in peace. That's my job. That's my chief's job."

"Does he see it that way?"

Van almost smiles. "Good question, Rebekah. Good fucking question. You didn't hear this from me, but you can look it up easy enough: Connie Hall is Chief Gregory's stepbrother."

"How is that possible?"

"What do you mean?"

"How'd he get to be chief if he's related to a . . . criminal?"

"Being related to a criminal's not a crime," he says. "Ever hear of Whitey Bulger?"

"I'm not sure."

"Big-time mobster from Boston. They say he killed, like, thirty people over the years. His brother was a state politician. Got reelected I don't know how many times. People believed he was on the right side of the law."

"Was he?"

"Who knows," says Van. "Nobody ever caught him doing anything illegal."

"But he had to know what his brother was doing."

"You'd think so," he says. "Chief's dad married Connie's mom back in the seventies. From what I've heard, Chief's dad was a real bastard. Drank too much, beat his mom when he was little, which led to the divorce. Chief had a lot of experience with cops coming to the house and having to pry his dad off his mom. I think he thought of the guys as heroes. So he joined up. Connie went the other way, and since they have different last names and live in different counties not that many people know. But the State Police have never heard of Pessie Goldin, and the thumb drive with my pictures from the scene is gone from our evidence room."

"Do you think he . . . did something with it?"

"I don't pretend to know what he did. But I know he didn't pass the information along like he said he would. And if he told Connie that someone saw his truck in Roseville, that could be very dangerous for whoever that person is—or whoever Connie thinks that person might be. I'm guessing you probably don't want to tell me who your source is, but you should make sure they know what's going on. Connie's not a reckless man. He's not going to make noise until he needs to. But now that Pessie's name is the paper, if he's connected to her death, he'll be watching."

CHAPTER NINETEEN

AVIVA

"He's not here," said the woman at the jail when I called to be put on the visitors' list.

"What do you mean he's not there?"

"I mean he's not here anymore. He's been transferred."

"Transferred where?"

"You have to call the DOC for that. All I can see is that he left here two weeks ago."

It took three days of phone calls to find out that Sammy was at a state prison almost 150 miles away. Isaac got on the computer and looked up the visiting procedures and we made a plan to drive there the next week. I dreamt of Sammy in a cage of animals. Shirtless, bleeding, swinging at them, exhausted and outmatched, knowing it was only a matter of time until he was torn to pieces. At the prison, a man escorted the visitors in the waiting room through a metal detector and a set of heavy sliding doors. We sat down in a booth and Sammy came out. There was glass between us; we spoke through telephones.

"Are you okay?" I asked.

"I had to do it, Aviva," said Sammy. He had a poorly

stitched-up cut above his eye and a chipped front tooth. He seemed smaller, somehow, and he couldn't sit still. He looked around constantly, like he was waiting for someone to jump on him. The man attacked him once, he told us, whispering into the telephone. When he tried again, Sammy was ready with a weapon made from springs in his bed.

"But why did they send *you* away? You were defending yourself!"

"They don't care," said Sammy.

"How long will you have to stay here?" I asked.

"They added four years to my sentence," he said.

"Four years!" I must have screamed because the guard came immediately.

"Calm down, ma'am," he said, standing above me.

I began to cry. Isaac took the phone and told Sammy we would come back as often as we could. He told him not to forget that we loved him. That Pessie loved him. That we did not blame him, and that we would be here when he came home.

Sammy got paroled three years later, just before Thanksgiving. It had been more than two years since I'd seen him. The last time I visited he told me not to come back. He said it was better if he didn't think about anything outside prison while he was inside. He said it made him weak. I didn't argue. I did not like seeing him in there. I did not like the way his voice sounded, and the way he couldn't seem to look me in the eyes anymore.

He was getting bigger—from lifting weights, he said—but all those muscles did not make him seem stronger. It took days, sometimes more than a week, to clear my mind of the way he looked in that jumpsuit, his skin gray, his eyes rimmed with red. I had to take more pills and drink more wine to sleep than was good for me. I could not stop imagining all the things that could happen to him—that were happening to him—in there. The crushing loneliness; the fear. The shame of where he was. The secret of who he was.

It was cold on the day we picked him up at the prison, and Sammy slept the whole ride home, huddled in the backseat with an old blanket over him. Isaac drove and I rode in the front, peeking back at him, wondering who we were bringing home, wondering what would happen next.

Sammy's parole officer explained the conditions of his release: He would be tested for drugs every week. He needed to find a job. And he could not affiliate with criminals.

"What does that mean?" I asked the parole officer.

"What I said. He can go back to prison if I find out he is hanging out with anyone else with a criminal record."

I looked at Sammy, but he was looking at the ground.

"Did you hear that, Sammy?" I asked.

"I'm not deaf, Aviva," he said.

"You better check your attitude, son," said the parole officer. "I have no problem violating you."

For the first week, we left him alone. He slept all day and lay in front of the television all night. Finally, one night at dinner, we broached the subject of work. Isaac said that he could get Sammy a couple shifts a week at the store where he worked part-time.

"The hippie place," said Sammy.

"What is this hippie thing?" asked Isaac. "It is a job."

Sammy rolled his eyes. "I'm not going to sell incense and beads to college students, okay?"

Isaac took a deep breath. "You think it is beneath you?"

"I think it's fucking lame," he said.

"Why do you think it is okay to insult Isaac?" I asked.

"I'm not insulting Isaac," said Sammy. "He can do what he wants. I'm not into hippies, okay?"

Isaac shook his head. "You have to work."

"I'll find a job."

"Doing what?" I asked.

"I don't know," he said. "I'll pump gas. Whatever."

"Well," said Isaac, getting up with his plate, "you better get started."

Sammy stayed at the table, pushing his food around.

"I know this is hard, Sammy," I said. "Don't let this change who you are. Don't let this get in your way."

"You don't know shit about who I am, Aviva," he said. "You know that, right? You know you bailed on our family. You know you left me alone with Tatty and Eli and the sicko molester freaks. Why didn't you take me with you?"

I didn't know what to say. I didn't take him for the same reason I didn't take you. I didn't think I was good enough. I had nothing when I came back to Borough Park. Who was I to take a baby from his home? I couldn't even get a job. I was broken to pieces and needed time to create a life for myself. Just like him now.

"Whatever," he said, when I didn't answer fast enough. "This is who I am. Sorry if you don't like it. If you want to be a mother so bad now, go find Rebekah. Maybe she still cares."

PART 3

CHAPTER TWENTY

REBEKAH

It's nearly 11:00 P.M. by the time I check into a ground floor room at the Comfort Lodge between New Paltz and Poughkeepsie. There is a piece of duct tape over a crack in the window and water stains in the toilet, but at seventy-two dollars a night, I'm way under budget. I turn the room's heat up high and e-mail Larry to relay what I've learned from Van Keller, then send Nechemaya a text saying we need to talk. I haven't heard from Saul or Iris. After about twenty minutes of CNN, I turn off the bedside lamp and, with the hotel's floral blackout curtains drawn, fall into the big silence of the little room.

The sick feeling begins in my dream. Mellie is in front of the synagogue on Ocean Parkway shouting *Junior! Junior!* But instead of emitting a human noise, she barks. She barks and barks and then she pulls a handgun and points it at me. Van Keller is at my side, his arm around my waist. Mellie pulls the trigger and it makes a barking sound. The bullet hits my stomach and I think, I will never meet my mother. And then I am awake. I keep my eyes closed—sometimes, I've found, I can return to my dreams. I always imagine that I can change the outcome, but usually I'm just back in the pain, as ineffectual as before. Mellie shoots me again. I am on the ground but this time Saul is beside me instead of Van Keller. *Take her gun!* I shout. He waves his arms, like he is directing traffic. Someone has painted a swastika on the stone steps. The paint drips white. *Where is she?* I yell. Saul says nothing, but suddenly I can see her. Her back is to me, her long red hair. She is walking away. And I can't get up.

At 7:30 A.M., Larry calls.

"Connie Hall has a gay son?" he says. "Unbelievable!"

"You know him?"

"Sure," he says. "I was the Albany stringer back in the eighties. I covered his manslaughter trial. He ran a guy down with his truck. They couldn't prove intent so he only got, like, eight years. He pops up every now and then, waving his Nazi flag on Hitler's birthday, shit like that. People always said he ran drugs and guns for the Aryans but nobody could ever make anything stick."

"I actually went out to where he lived yesterday and talked to his son's girlfriend. She said they're stockpiling weapons for a race war."

"She said *what*?! Is this on the record?"

"No," I say, throwing off the hotel covers and sitting up, trying to fling out the fear left in my stomach by the dream. I'm going to have to use the bathroom soon. Fucking anxiety. I always laugh when movies and TV shows portray mental illness as, like, glamorous. *Oh, that poor, sensitive girl*. I'll tell you what's not glamorous: diarrhea. "I was . . . I wasn't sure it was, like, safe to say I was a reporter. I kind of just went poking around, trying to find the son or his boyfriend, Pessie's ex."

"Have you talked to him?"

"The son?"

"Or the ex."

"Not yet. I've left messages but I haven't heard back."

"So, what do you have on the record?"

"I have that Pessie was still hanging out with her ex and that he spent time in prison. I guess I need to confirm that with the DOC. The girl I talked to used to live with the gay son and the ex and told me they used to deliver drugs for Connie. She said they all got arrested about four years ago. Plus, we have the license plate number of the truck a neighbor saw at Pessie's. The cop told me it's registered to Connie Hall, but that's off the record. But if we could confirm on our end . . ." I trail off, hoping he'll interrupt with an idea.

"His truck being seen at the apartment doesn't mean he killed her, but clearly it means they have to talk to him—it's not exactly his neighborhood."

"Not at all. And if the Roseville chief is related to him, that's a pretty major conflict of interest."

"I can get the library working on confirming a family relation between a possible murder suspect and the chief supposed to be investigating the case. I think that's the best lead. The whole gay son, ex-fiancé thing feels iffy.

I don't want to write about a relationship if we haven't talked to either of the people supposedly in it. You make sure the State Police never got a call from the Roseville chief. You also want to get them to say that, yes, murders in towns with small forces are typically kicked up to them. Your first story already made the point that police didn't seem interested. We need to advance that with specifics. Can you get the neighbors on the record saying they gave the plate number to the cops?"

"They didn't actually give it to them—they gave it to my burial society guy and he gave it to the cops."

"Is he on the record with that?"

"No."

"You need to get this stuff on the record. I'll try to confirm that the plate is Hall's. Meantime, get the chief's response as if we know for sure. Does he deny getting the plate? What's his comment on it being Hall? Does he think he's got a conflict of interest? And ask about Hall's son. Does the chief know about this relationship with Pessie's ex? I'll loop in the city desk."

"Tell them I have a photo of Pessie's apartment."

"Great. That'll help. E-mail it to me."

"What about the guns at the Halls?"

"Pessie wasn't shot, was she?"

"No," I say. "Well, I don't think so."

"No autopsy, right?"

"Right. But my cop and the husband both saw her and neither mentioned a gunshot wound or anything like that."

"Okay, let's keep the stockpiling in our back pocket. One thing at a time. Actually, now that we have all this new information, why don't you go back at the husband. Get his reaction to her hanging out with these people."

"Okay," I say.

"Let's regroup around noon."

I head to the toilet and then turn on the shower. I breathe in the steam and close my eyes beneath the water, but the sharp fright of being shot at in my dream won't dull. I've made myself a target again. I've pushed into another ugly little world that doesn't want me.

When I get out of the shower, I take a pill to try to ease the terror that the water didn't wash away. On my phone is a text message from Iris.

I love you, too. everything ok up there?? Call me

I call immediately. I hadn't been letting myself think too much about what it might mean if Iris really closed herself off from me, let alone if she moved to Asia. She is all I have in New York. Iris and the *Trib*. And only one of them gives a shit about me.

"Hi," she says. "Where are you?"

"I'm at dumpy motel near Poughkeepsie."

"Awesome. The *Trib* really lays out the red carpet for you guys, huh?" I hear a bus backfire. Iris is probably walking toward the subway from our apartment. She's kind of living the dream. A working girl in New York

City. A good-looking, gainfully employed boyfriend. She wouldn't have dared dream it a year ago. Or maybe she did dream it. I look in the mirror beside the TV. I'm sitting on a motel bed wearing a towel. The motel room is being paid for by a newspaper. I am here reporting a story about the overlooked death of a young mother. I have a source in the police department. On paper, this is my dream. Maybe someday living my dream won't make me feel sick.

"I'm lucky I got them to agree to cover an overnight at all," I say.

"I'm sorry I didn't call yesterday. I just needed to, like, feel bad for a minute."

"I'm really sorry I ditched you guys. I'm . . ."

"It's okay," she says. "I'm glad you're working. What did Saul say?"

My conversation with Saul in front of The Doom Room feels far away. "Aviva's mom died when she was in Florida with us," I say.

"Wow. She's motherless, too."

"Yeah," I say.

"And her phone is still off?"

"Yeah. I think I found her house, though. I went by last night but it was all dark."

"Holy shit. Are you sure it's hers?"

"Not a hundred percent," I say. "But I talked to a girl who said Sam sometimes lived with his sister in New Paltz, and this was the New Paltz address the library found when they ran his name."

"Have you found Sam?"

"No," I say. "The girl I talked to used to be his roommate but she said she hasn't heard from him in a while."

"Do you think they're together?"

"Him and Aviva?" That hadn't occurred to me. "Maybe."

"Will you be home tonight?"

"I don't know," I say. "Larry said I had a hundred and fifty for a hotel, but I only spent half that so I'm hoping maybe I can squeeze another day out of him."

"I'm about to go underground," she says. "Keep me updated, okay?"

"I will," I say. "I'm really glad you still love me."

She laughs. "You should be."

We hang up and I feel marginally calmer. Calm enough, I decide, to try Aviva again. I go RECENT CALLS on my phone and press "Mom." The call goes straight to a voice mail message saying this mailbox is full. So much for the calm. Something feels wrong. What if this Sam guy is dangerous? What if he's done something to her?

I pull on new socks and underwear and then the same bra and jeans and purple sweater I was wearing yesterday. My hair is already dry—a perk, I suppose, of having almost none of it. At just after nine, Nechemaya calls. I tell him who the plate belongs to.

"You need to be careful," I say. "It sounds like Sam was dating this man's son. Secretly. Conrad Hall is . . ."

"I know who Conrad Hall is," he says.

"You do?"

"We are not naïve, Rebekah. We know our enemies."

"I'm going to call the chief now and confront him about getting the plate and doing nothing. Can I use your name?"

"Yes," he says. "He knows my name. I made no secret when I called."

"What about for the newspaper?"

He is silent a moment. "All right."

"Thank you," I say. "And listen, I don't want to tell you what to do, but there's a cop in Roseville I think you should call. He's a good guy . . ."

"I am through with the Roseville police. We have a connection with the district attorney. We will be meeting him tomorrow."

I scribble "call DA" in my notebook and then dial Van Keller's cell.

"Officer Keller? It's Rebekah. Can you talk?"

"I just left the station," he says, breathing hard.

"Did you talk to your chief?"

"Hold on." I hear a car door slam. "He denied getting the plate from your man. I told him I'd run it to Connie Hall and he ripped me a new one. Bunch of shit about chain of command."

"Does he know we've been talking?"

"No. I didn't tell him, anyway. And I swore Dawn and Christine to secrecy."

"I tried to get my guy from the community—the one that gave him the plate—to call you but he says he's going to the district attorney."

"I don't blame him."

We agree to stay in touch and before I have time to think too hard about the conversation I'm about to have, I dial Roseville PD. Dawn answers and I ask for the chief.

"Him and Van just got in a big fight," she says, her voice low. "I swear I didn't tell him you were here though. Cross my heart."

"I believe you," I say.

Dawn puts me on hold and about twenty seconds later Chief Gregory picks up.

"Chief."

"Hi, Chief Gregory, this is Rebekah Roberts from the *New York Tribune*. We spoke the other day . . ."

"I know who you are."

"Oh. Great. Okay, well, I've been told by a member of Pessie Goldin's community that one of her neighbors saw an unfamiliar pickup truck at her home the day she was found dead. He said he passed the license plate to you but never heard back."

Nothing.

"Can you confirm you received a license plate number?"

"No."

"Are you saying you didn't receive it?"

"I'm not saying anything."

"Well," I say, "I've been given the plate number and my desk tells me it belongs to a man named Conrad Hall. Can you confirm that?"

"Nope."

"Is it true that Conrad Hall is your stepbrother?"

There is a pause, and then the call ends. Chief Gregory has hung up on me.

I go into the bathroom to brush my teeth and as I am spitting into the sink I feel a kind of whoosh and suck in my ear. The ringing is gone. "Huh," I say out loud, looking at myself in the mirror. The water sounds loud, like it's pouring into my brain instead of the sink. For a moment I am dizzy. I close my eyes and shake my head, knocking my jaw around, opening my mouth extra wide, and hearing the pop of cartilage in my ear. The relief is powerful. Two months of tinnitus, gone, just like that.

I take out my notebook and dial Levi, who picks up after several rings.

"Yes?"

"Levi," I say, "hi. This is Rebekah. From the *Tribune*."

"Hello."

"How are you?"

"Things have been difficult with Pessie's family since your article came out. They are very angry."

"I'm sorry," I say.

"It is not your fault. I am the one that came to you."

"Right," I say. "Do you have a minute to talk? I've learned a few things that I thought you might want to know, especially before I put them in the newspaper."

"Go ahead."

"Okay, well, first of all it seems like Pessie was still

pretty close with her ex, Sam Kagan." I wait for a response, but Levi is silent. "I don't know how often they saw each other, but I talked to a girl who used to live with Sam up in Greene County and she said she'd seen Pessie several times, including right after Sam came home from prison."

"He was in prison?"

"Yes," I say. "For drugs, I think. It sounds like he was pretty troubled. I spoke with a man who grew up in Roseville, and he told me that Sam had been a victim of . . . abuse."

"Abuse?"

"Sexual abuse."

"I see."

"Did Pessie ever mention anything about that?"

"No," he says. "But several months ago there was a story in the news about a Chassidish man in Brooklyn who was sentenced to life in prison for sexual abuse. Pessie followed the case very closely. Most of the people in the community thought the sentence was too harsh. Some people said the boy who testified was lying. We had some of her family over for Shabbos dinner just after the trial ended and there was a big argument. Pessie's mother said that the boy was a drug addict and mentally ill and that she was donating money to the fund to defend the man in an appeal. Pessie screamed at her. I had never seen her so upset. She threw her parents out of the apartment and said that if they gave the man their money she never wanted to see them again. She said she would keep Chaim from them. I told her she was overreacting. I told her she should apologize to her mother." He exhales. "No one mentioned a word about this Sam. Nothing!"

"I'm sorry," I say again, because nothing else seems appropriate.

"Was she having an affair with him?"

"I don't think so," I say. "Apparently he's gay."

A pause. Levi lowers his voice. "Pessie once asked me if I knew anyone who was gay. I told her yes. My oldest brother. She asked if I ever saw him, and I said no, although that wasn't because I didn't want to—he joined the IDF when he was eighteen and after his service he moved to Indonesia. But we wrote letters, and I still get an e-mail from him now and then. She asked if I thought it was his fault that he was gay. I said I didn't know. I wasn't sure how she felt about it and I didn't want her to think I was too . . . tolerant. Pessie's family is more conservative than mine and you have to be careful. I thought maybe she was testing me. I don't know why I did not just ask her."

"Did she ever mention anything about work? I spoke with one of the women at the clothing store who said a man came in and they had a big argument. I think it's possible it was Sam."

"When was this?"

"The woman said it was about a week before she died."

Levi sighs. "My work has been very demanding over the past several months. The company I work for is opening a location in Chicago and I have been traveling back and forth to supervise. The whole situation was very stressful and when I was home we mostly talked about Chaim, and made arrangements for when I was away again. I did not think the traveling would last for long. I thought it was a period we had to get through. And Pessie never complained. She seemed to be doing much better. She took care of everything at home. When something was broken she knew who to call to get it fixed. She never talked about her work and I did not ask. When I came home she seemed pleased to see me, but . . ." He hesitates a moment, then exhales heavily. "I thought she was happy with our life, but there was so much we did not know about each other. I wanted to know more about her. I *wanted* her to tell me what she thought. I assumed that would come with time. I never imagined our time was nearly up."

I tell Levi that I will keep him informed as I continue reporting and he thanks me for taking an interest in his wife's death. I type up what Levi said and start drafting a new article with the headline, "Dead Roseville Mother's Secret Life." I figure it's worth at least sending to Larry since I don't have anything from the State Police yet. I am a paragraph in when Saul calls.

"Can you pick me up the train station in Poughkeepsie this afternoon?" he asks.

"Sure," I say. "Did you get my message?"

"Yes," he says. "I am sorry I did not call you last night. I wanted to wait until I had confirmation. You are right.

Aviva has been living in New Paltz for almost ten years. I spoke with her roommate Isaac yesterday. Something is wrong, Rebekah. Her roommate says he hasn't seen her in almost a week. He is very worried. And I think he is the only person she has to worry about her."

CHAPTER TWENTY-ONE

REBEKAH

Saul's train from Grand Central is scheduled to arrive at 3:15 P.M. I arrive at the old brick station a little early and sit waiting on one of the long wooden benches, seat backs at ninety degrees, forcing a kind of posture that feels as historic as the space. Almost no building in Orlando is more than fifty years old, and here below the soaring arched ceiling, red brick walls, molded columns, and iron gas lamps, I feel suspended in time. People have been waiting for trains in this room, according to the plaque on the wall, since 1888. I imagine waiting for Aviva here. Waiting a hundred years. Lights going off and on, sun up and down, people in and out, and me, sitting upright, elbowing away despair.

"Could you stop that?" says the man next to me. I look at him and he looks at my right leg, which is popping up and down like it's plugged in. "You're shaking the whole bench."

I stand up. "Sorry."

Saul's train arrives on time.

"I had a friend run a criminal background check on Sam," says Saul as we get into the car. "He was arrested for drugs about four years ago and got three months in jail."

"One of the girls I talked to said he got transferred to state prison."

Saul nods. "According to my source in the DOC, he stabbed another inmate. Repeatedly. The man survived, but his intestines were significantly damaged. He has to wear an ostomy bag for the rest of his life. Sam's sentence might have been more like ten years, but apparently several witnesses testified that the man sexually assaulted Sam and he was defending himself from further attack. Wardens won't always take something like that into account."

"It doesn't exactly seem right to call him lucky," I say, quietly.

"No," says Saul. "It doesn't."

We cross over the Hudson River, wide and white-capped in the wind.

"It's pretty," I say, aloud but to myself.

"Yes," says Saul.

We ride in silence for a while, and within just a few minutes arrive in New Paltz. A sign announces the SUNY campus. College kids in hooded sweatshirts, backs bent beneath overstuffed backpacks, cigarettes and enormous mugs in their hands, trudge down a main street with hippie clothing and incense shops, a couple bed-and-breakfasts, a taco joint, a Starbucks, and a record store. It's no use trying to pretend I'm not in agony. *What if she is there? Around the corner.*

"I wonder if Aviva went to college," I say.

"It's possible," says Saul.

As an adolescent, I sometimes imagined that Aviva had taken off to fulfill some wild, lusty dream of life. I assumed she'd never tell anyone about me because she'd all but forgotten. But I thought that before I had any idea about her life at all. Now, I know she didn't run off to Mexico or Bali; she went back home to Brooklyn, then to Israel, then back to Brooklyn again, and then to a sleepy town upstate. Not exactly *Eat Pray Love*.

We turn right off the main drag and immediately see the flashing lights. And the black smoke.

"What's going on?" I ask, although clearly Saul has no more information than I do.

"I don't know," says Saul.

I get out of the car and start running. I run past half a dozen gawking college students, three police cars, and two fire trucks before I see the yellow house. The front window is shattered and the wood above it turned to black, smoldering charcoal. Smoke rises weakly from inside the ruined center of the home. The black netting I'd seen over the bushes has melted, creating a row of monstrous little shrubs that look like creatures from hell. Red and blue emergency lights shine off the little pond in the yard, left, I assume, by the fire hoses. A stream of water pours off what's left of the front gutter. I grab the first official-looking person I see, a pimply twenty-something in a jacket that says University Police.

"Is everybody okay?" I ask.

"They took one guy in an ambulance," he says.

"Was anyone else inside?"

"I don't know," he says.

"Rebekah!" Saul comes running from behind with my coat.

"What happened?" I ask the university cop, my teeth chattering with adrenaline.

"Some kind of explosion," he says. "I was over on Main Street and I heard a crash. Like glass breaking. I came running up the hill and the fire was pouring out of that window. It took them an hour to put it out."

"Do you know the people who live here?" asks Saul.

Good question. I am completely off my game. I am not thinking like a reporter; I am not really thinking at all.

"No," says the cop. "I don't think they're affiliated with the school."

Behind him, some of the students who had been lingering across the street begin walking toward us.

"I'm a reporter," I blurt out, grabbing my coat from Saul and pulling my notebook and pen from its pocket.

"Oh yeah?" he says. "Your friend is already here."

"My friend?"

"From the school paper. *The Oracle*?"

"I'm from the *New York Tribune,*" I say. "From the city."

"Wow," he says. "You got here fast."

"We sort of know them," says one of the girls behind

the cop. Her hands are plunged deep into the front pocket of her SUNY hoodie. Her bottom lip is pierced. "Aviva cleans our house. She's really nice, right, Bree?"

The girl next to her—Bree, presumably—nods. "The cops said Isaac was the only one home."

"Isaac?" Saul pulls out his phone. "Excuse me," he says, and steps away.

"They said he was going to be okay," says the first girl.

"What happened?" I ask.

"We heard a crash, like everybody else," says Bree. "And then the fire."

"Did you see a car or anything?"

Bree and lip-pierce shake their heads. "I was in the back of the house," says Bree. "Somebody broke their kitchen window and spraypainted a swastika on the front door a week or two ago."

"Aviva and Isaac are Jewish," says a young man wearing a Mets cap.

"So's half the school," says lip-pierce.

"They're different kind of Jews," says Mets-cap. "They're the black hat kind."

"How do you know?" I ask.

Mets shrugs. "I'm from Marine Park. We have lots of them in my old neighborhood."

"But they didn't, like, dress funny," says Bree.

"Not anymore," he says. "Isaac was gay, too. I mean, so's everybody, but he's older. Maybe that has something to do with it?"

"Since when are you best friends with them, Matty?" asks lip-pierce, not pleased.

"We talked," he says. "She's nice. But somebody was definitely messing with them."

"Did they say anything about who might have done the vandalism?" I ask.

"No. Isaac asked me to watch out. Let him know if I saw anything suspicious, but I didn't."

"So he was worried?"

"Definitely," he says. "He got a motion-sensor light right afterward."

"Did they call the cops?"

"I'm not sure," says Matty.

"They've been rolling by a little more often," says Bree.

"Do you mind if I get your names?" I ask. Look at Rebekah, acting like a professional.

Without hesitation, Bree, Matty and lip-pierce (Liza) provide first and last names, ages, and phone numbers for possible follow-up.

"Will this be in the *Trib*?" asks Matty. "My mom'll love that."

"Maybe," I say.

"I wonder where Aviva is," says Bree. "She's been gone a while."

"Yeah?" I say.

"I haven't seen her car for at least a week, now that I think about it. Since right after the swastika thing."

Saul returns and ushers me away from the students

and the university cop.

“The hospital is very close,” he says. “I think we should go see Isaac.”

“Those kids said Aviva’s car hasn’t been here for a week.”

“Rebekah!” Saul and I turn and see Van Keller jogging toward us.

“What are you doing here?” I ask.

“I have a buddy at the State Police barracks nearby. I came up to talk to him about Pessie and heard this on the radio.”

“What happened?”

“It looks like somebody threw some kind of incendiary device—like a Molotov cocktail—in through the front window. There was some nasty shit in it. Acid, I think.”

“Acid?”

“Ate right through the firefighters’ boots.”

“Jesus.”

“Middle of the fucking day,” says Van. “*Crazy* brazen.”

“Did anybody see anything?”

“Staties are doing a canvass,” says Van.

“The woman who lives here is related to Pessie Goldin’s ex-fiancé,” says Saul.

“What? How do you know that?”

“Because she’s my mom,” I say.

Both Saul and Van look surprised.

“Your *mom*?”

“I never met her. She abandoned us. Then she reached

out a couple months ago but she's, like, disappeared. And so has her brother. Sam. The one I told you about—the one that's dating Connie Hall's son. I just talked to these neighbors and they said someone painted a swastika on the door a couple weeks ago and they haven't seen her since. And Pessie, and now this . . ."

"Rebekah," says Saul, putting his hand on my shoulder. I am talking too fast.

"I didn't realize this case was . . . personal for you," says Keller. He is unnerved.

"I should have told you," I say. "I just . . . I didn't know for sure. At first."

"I looked up Sam Kagan last night," says Van. "He has a criminal record. A *violent* criminal record. And you're telling me he is your uncle?"

"I think so. But I've never met him."

Van raises his eyebrows. He doesn't believe me.

"She is telling the truth," says Saul.

"I'm sorry," says Van, "who are you?"

"Saul Katz," he says. "Retired NYPD. Rebekah and I have worked together in the city. I do private investigations now." Van looks mildly suspicious.

"Have you interviewed the man who was in the house yet?" Saul asks.

"No," says Van. "This isn't my investigation."

"The man's name is Isaac. He and Aviva—Rebekah's mother—have been roommates for more than a decade. Apparently, Sam was living with them, on and off."

"Sam Kagan was living in this house?"

Saul nods. "I spoke with Isaac last night. He was very concerned. He said he hadn't heard from Aviva or Sam in a week. We are going to the hospital to see Isaac now."

Van brings Saul over to his friends in the State Police cars while I take a photo of the burned house with my phone and e-mail it to the city desk. Minutes later, my phone rings.

"It's Rebekah."

"Rebekah, hold for Mike."

I hold.

"Rebekah! Great shot. Give Cathy what you have from the scene. State Police radio said something about a possible domestic terror connection. Did you hear anything about that?"

"Not exactly," I say.

"Well, give her what you've got. Can you stay up there tonight? Dig around tomorrow?"

"Sure," I say.

"You can expense a hotel room."

Mike transfers me to Cathy and I give her the quotes I have from Bree and Liza and Matty, and tell her that one person was taken away in an ambulance.

"I'm headed to the hospital now," I say. "I'll call the night desk if I get anything."

Saul and I arrive at the hospital a little before 7:00 P.M., with Van just behind us. The guard at the information booth directs us to the third floor, and as we get off the elevator, two state policemen in plain clothes, badges at their waists, step on.

"How is he?" asks Van.

"He'll make it," says the taller Statie.

Keller's badge gets us past the nurse and we find Isaac in the bed by the window. He is attached to several machines, tubes going into his nose, his arm, beneath his gown. His entire left arm and part of his chest are wrapped in white gauze, blooming with the red and yellow seeping from the wounds beneath. His eyes are closed when we walk in.

"Isaac," says Saul.

Isaac opens his eyes, and sees me first.

"Aviva," he says, groggy. "What happened to your hair?"

Saul looks at me.

"I'm Rebekah," I say.

Isaac closes his eyes again and, perhaps I am imagining it, smiles slightly. He lifts his good arm. He wants me to take his hand. I do.

"You are so beautiful," he whispers, eyes open now. "You look just like your mother."

"You know about me," I say. A mix of pride and relief catch in my throat. Yes, I am that girl. Yes, I have made my way to you. To her.

"I found your articles in the newspaper," says Isaac. He winces, and presses a button that I imagine delivers pain medication.

"She wanted to tell you about Sammy. I told her it wasn't the right time to call, but she wasn't going to change her mind." He pauses, licks his cracked lips. There is a plastic cup of water with a straw in it beside the bed. I pick it up and he nods and opens his mouth slightly, drinks as I hold the cup for him. When he is done, he nods.

"Your mother . . . sometimes she gets hold of things in her mind and she can't let go."

Sounds familiar. "She called and then she disappeared," I say.

"She turned her phone off. Sammy knows about technology and he had her worried they were tracking her."

"They?"

"The Halls," he says, slowly, now looking at Van.

"This is Officer Van Keller from the Roseville Police," I say. "He's trying to find out what happened to Pessie."

Isaac looks skeptical. Saul says something to him in Yiddish. Isaac says something back.

"We trust him," I say, chiming in.

Isaac nods, and continues. "They seem to be . . . working up to something. Last time it was a swastika on the door."

"Are you sure that was the Halls?" I ask.

"I did not see them, if that is what you mean. Just before the New Year, someone vandalized a yeshiva in Roseville. Same thing. Broken windows, swastikas. Everyone was talking about it on Facebook and the blogs. I heard that the caretaker got the license plate number of a pickup truck, but that the police said there was no such number."

"No such number?" asks Van.

"The caretaker had written it down wrong, I guess," says Isaac.

Van shakes his head and takes out his notebook. "I never heard that anyone got a license plate number connected to that."

Isaac continues. "Everyone was talking about how the fact that there was no arrest meant that the community was right to be annexing more land and taking a greater role in the city government and on the school board. That this was just more proof the goyim could not be trusted."

Isaac's speech is slightly slurred. He looks at the cup again, and again, I bring it to his lips. As he sips, he closes his eyes. When he is done, he lies back. After a few seconds, he speaks again, slowly, his eyes still closed.

"Since he got out of prison Sammy wasn't coming around much. But he showed up the day after we heard Pessie had died. And he was scared. He wouldn't say anything for days. He said he was sitting shiva but really he was hiding. He told us he did the vandalism. He said that Ryan's father and brother had done it with him, but that it was his idea. He kept saying that. 'It was my idea.' "

"You said Ryan's father and brother. Not Ryan?" asks Van.

Isaac shakes his head. "Ryan is a good kid. He hated his family as much as Sammy hated his. But it wasn't as easy for him to cut ties."

"Why not?" I ask

"Sammy had a path out. He had Aviva and me. More and more people are going OTD. And Sammy knew they would let him go. But I got the sense Ryan was afraid that no matter how far away he ran, he'd always be looking over his shoulder for his father."

Van raises his eyebrows and nods almost imperceptibly. I remember what he said about the kid "connected" to the Halls who died in prison.

"What about Pessie?" I ask.

"Sammy wouldn't tell us anything specific, but it was clear he knew whatever happened was not just an accident. He begged us to believe that he had nothing to do with it. Aviva did. It was easy for her to believe that one of the Halls killed Pessie and then threatened to kill Sammy—to kill all of us—if he told. That's what she thought the swastika was. A warning. What I didn't understand was why they would want to kill Pessie in the first place. Sammy wouldn't explain, except to say that it was his fault. If it hadn't been for him, Pessie and them would have never crossed paths."

"So Sammy said the Halls killed Pessie?" asks Van.

"He didn't ever say. But it is what Aviva and I assumed."

"Why didn't you go to the police if you thought Pessie had been murdered?"

Isaac pauses for a breath. Talking is taking a lot out of him.

"Aviva thinks it is her fault Sammy turned out the way

he is. She thinks she should have protected him better and she is terrified of him going back to prison. She was afraid that if she went to the police they'd suspect Sammy. I respected her wishes. And I did not have any real knowledge about what happened."

"Do you think he could have done it?" I ask.

"If Sammy killed Pessie," he says slowly, "it had to have been some kind of accident. He loved Pessie as much as he loved Ryan. As much as he loved anybody. And Pessie was the only one of us who had never let him down—at least that's how he saw it. She was steady as a rock. I don't think Sammy ever thought he would have to live in a world without Pessie Rosen."

None of us say anything for a few seconds.

"When was the last time you saw Aviva? Or Sam?" I ask.

"I haven't seen either of them since the night after we found the swastika. Aviva packed a bag and made Sammy come with her. When I talked to her last she said they were staying at one of the houses she cleans, but she didn't say which one. The number she called from is in my cell. I think it was a landline. I told her she was being paranoid, but she said they weren't finished killing people. And she was right. I was upstairs when that thing came in. If anyone had been in the living room they'd be dead."

Saul and I check into a Super 8 just outside New Paltz a little before 10:00 P.M. The barely legal desk clerk tells us that the only room they have available has a king-sized bed.

"I don't mind sharing," I say.

Saul looks at the clerk, who is back to watching *Family Guy* on a tiny tube television behind the counter, and then at me.

"I will sleep on the floor," he says quickly.

"Whatever you want," I say.

We get our key and walk outside, climbing concrete stairs to the second floor room.

While Saul is in the bathroom, I fold the shiny floral bedspread into a sleeping mat on the floor, and set a pillow at the head. When we parted ways at the hospital, Van asked me not to inform the newspaper tonight that Isaac named the Halls as probable suspects in the firebombing.

"Give me twelve hours," he said. "I don't want to give them a heads-up we're onto them just yet."

I told him I could do that, but that I planned to call Nechemaya.

"They should be on the lookout, don't you think?"

"Yes," he said. "They should."

In college, we had a guest speaker from *The Miami Herald* come talk to our long-form class. She made a big point of telling us that it was unethical to insert ourselves, as journalists, into a story in any way. She told us about a series she wrote about a family in Naples whose McMansion had been foreclosed on. Once, she said, the mother had an interview for a job in the next county, but the father had to take the one working car with him or he'd get fired. I had a car, she told us, but I didn't offer to drive her, because then my presence would have altered their story. I remember thinking that was some pretty lame logic. Iris and I talked about it afterward and we both agreed we would have taken the woman. Because we are human beings before we are journalists. Warning Nechemaya that a neo-Nazi may be on the hunt for a former member of his community is definitely inserting myself in the story, but if I've learned anything over the last couple months I've learned that it's a crock of shit to pretend that once you've decided to write about something you aren't a part of it—in some way.

Nechemaya does not answer his phone, so I leave a message with as much detail as I can. Hopefully, he'll listen to his voice mail.

Saul comes out of the bathroom, takes off his shoes, and lays down. He's wearing a white undershirt beneath his long-sleeved blue button-up, but is apparently going to sleep fully clothed. He doesn't even remove his belt. I brush my teeth and change into my t-shirt and sleep pants. It occurs to me that because we met in the dead of winter, Saul has never seen me in anything but long pants and sleeves—and a hospital gown.

"I'm sorry this makes you uncomfortable," I say. "Are you thinking I'm, like, shaming God by sleeping in the same room as you?"

"Not at all," he says. "I am marveling at how easy it is for you to interact with people. All kinds of people. It took me many years to look at people who were different from me as people at all, really. And more years still to see them as unthreatening. In some ways, working for the police department helped with that. In some ways it probably hurt. Seeing people at their lowest times, on their worst behavior."

"That's sort of how I see people as a reporter," I say. "At the worst times."

"Yes," he says. "But you are so young. And it seems to come naturally to you."

"Bugging people?"

"No," he says. "Flexibility. Empathy. You encounter people who are different from you and you are able to connect to them instantly. You see similarities, not differences. You look for a way through what divides you."

I've never been great at accepting compliments; I don't like the way it tilts the balance of power, even if for just a moment. But if I could let myself believe what Saul has just said about me, I could be pretty happy.

"Thanks," I say.

"No need to thank me," he says.

"Just say, 'you're welcome,' Saul."

Saul chuckles and lays his head on his pillow on the floor. "You're welcome."

I am about to turn out the lamp beside the bed when my phone rings with a blocked number. The city desk, I assume.

"This is Rebekah," I say.

"Rebekah? This is Ryan Hall."

CHAPTER TWENTY-TWO

REBEKAH

Ryan insists I meet him alone, I insist we meet in a public place, and Saul insists I call Van to tell him where I am going before I leave the motel. So, at just before midnight, I pull up to the same diner where Van and I met last night, knowing he and Saul will be parked with sights on the building. Just in case.

I see Mellie as soon as I walk in. She is standing beside the booth against the far wall, bouncing Eva on her belly, looking like she hasn't slept since I was in her living room yesterday. When she sees me, she scowls.

"Ryan," she says, "that's her."

Ryan, who is sitting in the booth, bent over with his hand on his forehead, looks up. He squints at me, then pops up, nervous.

"Thanks for coming out," he says, gripping my hand. Ryan looks weary, but wired. He is tall and thin, with brown hair grown a little shaggy over his ears and half a week of stubble on his face. His blue scrubs have the words Hudson Animal Hospital embroidered on the chest.

"You didn't say were a reporter before," says Mellie.

"Shut up, Mellie," says Ryan. "Tell her."

"You tell her first."

"Maybe we should sit down," I say. There are people in a booth at the other end of the restaurant who appear to be in a study group. The lone waitress is behind the counter, filling ketchup bottles. Nothing screams ambush, but I'm going to sit facing the door anyway.

I pull out my notebook as Mellie slides in across from me toward a child's car seat. Eva, dressed in footie pajamas with bunnies on them, is whining, twisting backward and trying to hurl herself out of Mellie's arms. Mellie presses her into the car seat and struggles to strap the child's limbs down beneath the various belts and buckles required to make her stay. She produces a teddy bear from the diaper bag on the table and drops it in Eva's lap, but the stuffed animal does nothing to quiet her crying. She pulls a baby bottle, a water bottle, and some sort of tin from the bag. Ryan watches, standing, chewing on his fingers. I can hear his teeth *tick tick tick* as he pulls away cuticle flesh.

"Sit down, Ryan," she says. "You're making Eva nervous."

"Tell her," says Ryan, still standing.

"I have to make this fucking bottle!"

"Shhhh," hisses Ryan, looking around.

"Sit down or I'm leaving," she says.

"You're the one that called me!"

"Shhh," she hisses back. These two really don't like each other.

"Ryan," I say, "why don't you sit down? I'm glad you called."

Ryan points to the duffel bag on the seat next to me. "Open that."

I bring the bag to my lap. It feels empty. "What's this?" I open it. Inside the bag is hair.

"It's Pessie's," says Ryan.

"Pessie's?"

"She wore a wig."

Of course she did. Pessie's wig is in this bag.

"Where did you get this?" I ask. My head feels light. Keep it together, Rebekah.

"I'm sure there's DNA on it; they'll be able to get him with that."

"Get him?"

"My dad," he says. "My dad killed Pessie."

"Ryan!" says Mellie, her teeth clenched. "Sit the fuck down."

Ryan sits. Falls, more like. The burden now out of his chest and into mine. My head begins to sweat and I pull off my knit cap. I have the feeling that I am standing above the table watching myself, giving myself orders. Maintain eye contact. Zip close the duffel bag. Set it aside; it is evidence. Breathe. Breathe again.

"How do you know?" I ask, my voice tighter and higher than when I last spoke.

"I was there. Okay? But I'm not going down with him. No fucking way. He's already ruined my life. He's like the plague. He just *spreads*."

"Can you tell me what happened?"

Ryan looks at the ceiling. He's calmer since he sat down. More focused. "I don't even know where to start."

"How about with you being a faggot?" says Mellie, shaking the powdered milk mix for Eva.

"Hey," I say quietly. But she doesn't even look at me.

"There you go," says Ryan. "My dad and Hank didn't know I'm . . . gay." It's hard for him to say the word. "I've known since junior high, but Sam was the first, like, relationship I've ever had."

Mellie makes a kind of snort. Ryan ignores her. "When we met I was still working for my dad and the Brotherhood. I mean, what did I care? I was like, twenty-one, and it was good money, easy work. I was living with my friend Kaitlyn, and Sam started crashing with us there. My dad and Hank saw him, maybe, three times that whole first year. We made up this story that he was a German exchange student Kaitlyn met at work. My dad got a kick out of that. When he saw him he'd be like, Heil Hitler. I thought it was fucked up, but Sam thought it was funny. He really hated where he came from.

"And after he got out of prison, he hated it even more. He blamed everything on the way he grew up. On how, like, they didn't protect him. I mean, I get it. But you gotta move on eventually. Anyway, I thought he was back working with Kaitlyn, but it turns out he was also delivering for my dad again. Behind my back."

"Why do you think he did that?"

"When he was inside he stabbed somebody who'd been hassling him and it turned out that the guy was somebody the Brotherhood wanted out of the picture. The guy was dealing inside and, I don't know, it was some sort of turf thing. Anyway, word got back to my dad and he sort of got Sam protection for the rest of the time he was in there. Obviously, he didn't know Sam was gay, either. And then when he got out, Sam felt like he owed him. Plus," Ryan sighs, "he liked my dad. I can't spend ten minutes in a room with him. Nigger this and spic and faggot. That's all normal to them." Ryan lowers his voice. "But especially after prison, Sam was a lot angrier. And honestly, he's kind of racist. It's the one thing I really didn't like about him. He's not as bad as my family, but sometimes he'll talk about how black people are dirty and descended from, like, some Biblical character who was cursed. I don't know. I tried to ignore it. Anyway, so him and my dad just . . . got along. Sam used to say that everyone where he grew up was weak. That they didn't teach kids how to defend themselves. He dug how my dad was the opposite of that. He'd be like, nobody messes with your dad. After prison, Sam was kind of obsessed with being all macho. Lifting weights and shooting and—"

"Sucking dick," says Mellie, interrupting him.

Ryan ignores her. He's racing to get the story out.

"At some point he started carrying a gun my dad gave him. He didn't tell me. He probably knew I'd freak out. A gun is a major parole violation. Like, do not pass Go, go directly back to prison. It was a couple weeks before Pessie . . . died. I found an apartment in Hudson that's nearer to my work and Sam was helping me move in. He was staying with his sister, on and off, but he didn't really like it there."

"Aviva?"

Ryan looks surprised. "Yeah," he says. "How'd you know that?"

The words rise up fast, proud: "I'm her daughter."

"Her . . . ?" Ryan puts his hand over his mouth. "Oh my God. You're from Florida?"

"She told you about me?"

"She told Sam. Wait. Do you know where they are?"

"Aviva and Sam? Are they together?"

"I don't know! Sam won't return my calls since . . ." Ryan inhales deeply. "I don't blame him. If he hadn't met me Pessie would be alive."

"What happened?" I ask.

"Okay. So, Pessie came over to my new place with Chaim; that's her son. He's like, one, I think. He crawls but he can't walk. So we're just hanging out in the living room and Chaim is sitting on the floor and Sam's backpack is by the couch and Chaim, like, pulls it open and Sam's gun slips out and Chaim picks it up. I didn't even notice, and then Pessie screamed. She grabbed Chaim and went ballistic on Sam. Saying how reckless and thoughtless he was. How she didn't understand him anymore and she couldn't believe he'd put her child in danger. She was *shaking*. She looked like a totally different person. Pessie used to visit a lot before we got locked up—before she got married and had the baby—and she was always really, like, even-tempered. She didn't come around as much after Sam got out and it was clear she was being a little cautious with him, but I never saw her get mad about anything. She told Sam she didn't want to see him again. She said she had to take care of her own family now and he needed to, like, get his shit together.

"Sam was *crushed*. He loved her. Him and Pessie were like . . . they just understood each other. Or at least, Sam thought Pessie understood him. He barely left the apartment for a week and then he went down to Roseville to try and apologize, but she wasn't having it."

"He went to her work," I say quietly.

Ryan nods. "So, about a week later, me and Sam were at my apartment when my dad and Hank come barging in. I guess the door was unlocked. I was on the couch and Sam was, like, coming out from the bedroom, I think. My dad went over and just coldcocked him. He was, like, are you two faggots? Sam was on the floor. And I was just like, fuck it. Yeah, we're fucking faggots."

"How did he find out?" I ask.

"Apparently my dad has a monthly drop in Albany and the pickup guy used to bounce at a club we went to before

Sam went away. Sam filled in doing the drop and the guy recognized him. The next week the bouncer gave the regular guy some shit. He was all, since when does the Brotherhood run with fags? I guess the regular guy told my dad."

"Your dad had a right to be pissed, Ryan," says Mellie. "He was *employing* your fucking fag boy and you're both totally *laughing* behind his back."

"We weren't laughing behind his back, Mellie. You're insane. It doesn't make it okay to fucking *kill* an *innocent girl*!"

Mellie puts her hands up in a weak surrender.

"Pessie must have driven in a couple minutes after my dad and Hank. She probably wanted to make up with Sam. When she walked in with Chaim, Sam was on all fours on the floor, bleeding from his mouth, and my dad was kicking him in the stomach. Hank had my arms behind my back and was holding a fucking *knife* to my throat. My brother. *Your* fucking baby daddy. I was just trying to get *through* it, you know? But Pessie started screaming. Loud. My dad was like 'Who's this bitch?' And Sam and I were like, 'Leave her alone.' My dad told her to shut up and she didn't. She backed toward the door and he went to grab her hair. But, you know, she wore a wig. And it came off. He was like, what the fuck? Then he started laughing. I swear to God. He got a handful of her real hair and dragged her over to Sam and he was like, 'This is your fault, faggot. You did this.' And then he . . . it happened *so fast* . . . he put one of his hands in her mouth and one on the back of her head and snapped her neck."

His fists are clenched, and when he falls silent I realize that mine are, too. I exhale and it feels like fire coming from inside. She just wanted to make up with her friend. That was it. Sam wanted one kind of life and Pessie wanted another, but she refused to give up the boy she had always loved. Why should she have to? And it killed her. All her empathy, all their memories together, meaningless against the gale force of a bigot in a rage. I look over at Mellie and, for the first time since I arrived at the diner, she appears uneasy. She is bent forward, one hand on the edge of Eva's car seat, rocking the little girl as she sucks on her bottle, the other hand holding her head up, hiding her face.

"She was a tiny thing," whispers Ryan, his face now red. "She fell like . . . boom. I mean, there was no question. She was just . . . gone. Sam started screaming and the baby was screaming and my dad and Hank bailed. They were like, this is your problem." Ryan looks down at his hands. "It was Sam's idea to take her home. We wrapped her in a blanket and laid her down in the backseat of her car and put the baby in the front seat. He was still all strapped in. I drove my truck and Sam drove her car. Her husband wasn't home and we used her keys to open the door. We brought her in and at first Sam said to put her on the bed. Like maybe she'd died in her sleep. But I'd just seen this show on TV—I think it was *48 Hours* or something—about this woman whose body was found in a bathtub and they were trying to prove her husband killed her but they couldn't because apparently it's really hard to prove how somebody died when there's water involved. So I said we should put her in the tub and turn on the water.

"I drove Sam back to New Paltz and then took the truck—which is my dad's, technically—to the McDonald's in Cairo and called a buddy from work to pick me up. I texted my dad that I didn't want the truck anymore and that he should come get it."

Ryan stops talking. I haven't written down anything he said. For a moment, all three of us sit in silence.

"Why didn't you go to the police?" I ask, finally.

"Because I've got a record. They'd think I did it. And I am not going down for them. But now . . ." He looks at Mellie. "You have to tell her."

For a moment Mellie acts like she hasn't heard him. She keeps her eyes on Eva. "Connie and Hank are planning something."

"Something?" I say.

"Hank's been all secretive lately. I thought he was fucking around but . . ." She pauses. "Connie has cancer. Bad cancer. He told us last month and he said the doctors told him he has, like, a couple of months to live. He wouldn't even know if he hadn't gone to take Nan to the doctor. Usually I do it but Eva was having a meltdown and he offered. I guess he rolled her into the exam room and the doctor took one look at him and was like, what the fuck? His skin was all yellow. I mean, I'd noticed he looked kind of sickly, but what do I know? Anyway. They did some tests and apparently it's all up in him. Too late for chemo or whatever else. He's saying he'll be dead by the Fourth of July."

"Which means he has nothing to lose," says Ryan.

"Right. But Hank does. And so do me and Eva and the new baby. Connie can go out in a blaze of glory but I don't want Hank involved."

"A blaze of glory?" I say.

"Look," she says, leveling her eyes at me, "you didn't tell me you were a reporter, okay? Which has to be, like, against the law, right? This is Off. The. Record."

"Jesus, Mellie! If Hank and dad kill a bunch of people you're *going* to be in the paper! You're going to be on CNN getting led into *Guantanamo*, okay! Stop being so fucking stupid."

"Kill a bunch of people?" I say. But Mellie and Ryan don't hear me.

"That's why I called *you*! Not the fucking cops or the *media*. I'm still here, okay? I need your help. Hank is never going to choose me over your dad. He's too attached. But he'll listen to you. Your dad is out for *blood* on you being a fag and he's got Hank convinced they have to make this *stand* for the race."

"That's so fucking stupid!" shouts Ryan.

The people in the booth on the other end of the diner look back at us. So does the waitress. Somehow, she seems to know not to come over.

"Well, it's fucking happening," says Mellie. "So you need to deal with it."

"What, exactly, is *it*?" I ask.

"Hank won't tell me."

"Do you have any ideas?"

She shrugs.

"Because somebody threw a Molotov cocktail into Aviva's house in New Paltz this afternoon."

Ryan's face goes white. "Was anyone . . . ?" He can't bring himself to say it.

"The guy who lived there is burned really bad."

"Isaac?"

I nod. "He'll make it though. No one else was home."

Ryan coughs, sucking back the sobs I can practically see filling his chest. "Oh thank God," he says.

"I don't think that's it," says Mellie. "A Molotov cocktail isn't, like . . . that's not a big enough deal. Who's gonna remember that?"

"It's true," says Ryan. "If Dad could pull off Oklahoma City in Roseville he would."

I open my mouth but nothing comes out. *They seem to be working up to something*. The canvas duffel bag with Pessie's wig inside is beside me. I look over and imagine the secret of her death unzipping the bag and wafting out, creating a vision in fog. A warning. I pull my phone from my coat pocket and with shaking, sweat-slick fingers, text Van: *get in here*

"Who are you texting?" asks Mellie.

"Nobody," I say. "When is all this supposed to happen?"

"Hank said it was supposed to be April twentieth."

"Unbelievable," says Ryan. "It's such a cliché. Dad's gonna kill Jews on Hitler's birthday."

"Kill Jews . . . ?"

"Let me *finish,*" says Mellie. "It was *supposed* to be April twentieth, but Connie moved it up."

"To when?" I ask. My eyes are now on the front door. Please let them be close.

"Soon. I guess."

"Which is why I called you," says Ryan, leaning toward me. "You've got connections. We read your articles about that lady in Brooklyn."

"I didn't read your fucking articles," mutters Mellie.

"Me and Sam did," says Ryan. "You tell the cops what Mellie said. They'll believe you."

And that's when I see Van's flashing lights. He pulls in fast, his Roseville police car taking up four parking spots in front of the diner.

Mellie tries to glare at me, but the fight has gone out of her. "Bitch called the cops."

Ryan looks stricken for a moment, then he nods. "Good," he says. "Good. This stops now."

"So much for off the record," she says.

"Oh my God, Mellie, shut up. What was she gonna do? *Not* tell the cops that two completely *insane* people are plotting a *terrorist* attack!"

"They're not *terrorists*! They're patriots! They're *Christians* who hate all the niggers and kikes *leaching* off white people."

"Christians who hate . . ." Ryan shakes his head. "They've got you deep, Mellie. You realize that that's insane, right? You realize all that shit you think is so cute, making your little swastika earrings, that the rest of the world knows you're *crazy*? If Dad's gonna die in a month he is a ticking time bomb. You're fucking stupider than I thought if you don't get that."

"Call me what you want. I don't talk to cops."

But she doesn't have to. When Van and Saul get to our table, Ryan tells them enough to warrant Van calling his friend at the State Police. When he does, he learns that, based on Isaac's suspicion about who threw the Molotov cocktail, officers have been camped out at the Hall compound since midnight.

"Apparently the only person there right now is an old lady," says Van after he gets off the phone. "But Ryan, if you're willing to repeat what you told me, they can probably get a judge to sign off on a warrant to search the place."

Mellie, who has been slumped low in the booth, expelling her nervous energy by knocking her tongue stud against her teeth, suddenly looks nervous.

"If you know something I highly suggest telling me now," says Van. "Unless you want to have that baby in prison."

"I don't really know anything," she says softly.

"You don't *really* know anything?"

And then, before Mellie can stonewall him some more, my phone rings. Caller ID says: MOM.

"Hello?" I say, standing up, widening my eyes at Saul, who has been sitting quietly at one of the barstools along the diner's counter.

"Rebekah! This is your mother. This is Aviva. My phone was . . . Rebekah, you have to help. Sammy has taken my car. Something is happening."

Her voice is low. Not quiet—she is panicked and practically shouting—but a good octave below most women's. She has an accent that, if I didn't know was a product of speaking Yiddish, I might call Russian. Her words come from the front of her mouth.

"Hi," I say. "Are you okay?"

"Sammy has taken my car! He was tracking Conrad Hall."

"Tracking him?"

"Rebekah, I am so sorry to talk to you like this!"

"Like . . . ? It's okay. Hold on, I'm here with Saul. Do you want us to come get you?"

"Yes. I will explain everything."

She gives me the address and I tell her we will be there as soon as possible. When I hang up, I feel strangely calm. I am conscious of the fact that everything before I picked up the phone was "before Aviva," and the rest of my life will be after. I am ready.

CHAPTER TWENTY-THREE

REBEKAH

The morning sky is pink when Saul and I turn on to the street where Aviva is hiding out. Van is behind us in his cruiser. At the diner, I asked him if we could have a little time alone with her before he rolled in. He said he'd give us five minutes.

The driveway leading to the enormous house winds through maybe a quarter mile of woods. Saul and I haven't said much to each other since getting in the car. I think we are both a little stunned by what Ryan and Mellie told us, and as Aviva looms just ahead, I imagine we're both having conversations with her in our heads, conversations too intimate to share.

We park and get out. The weak sun is almost warm, and here among the trees and the quiet, it feels like it could be a beautiful day. Aviva opens the front door and she is exactly as I should have imagined her. My height, but thinner, a little too thin. Her hair less vibrantly red than mine, streaked now with bits of gray. She is wrapped in a puffy black winter coat, jeans, off-brand sneakers.

"Rebekah," she says, stepping outside. I walk toward

her, and she walks toward me. When we meet, she grabs my hands. "You are so beautiful."

"So are you," I say. Because she is. There are tiny crow's-feet at her eyes and she is smiling. At me.

"I am so proud of you, Rebekah," she says, squeezing my hands. "Look at you. A big reporter. And you still have your father's little ears. Of course!" She is giggling. We both are. I've played the moment I meet her in my head all my life but I never imagined us laughing. I never imagined thinking she might be someone I would actually like.

"I will explain everything to you, Rebekah."

"Okay," I say. I almost say, *it's okay,* because it kind of feels like it is. Or rather, like it will be.

"Can I hug you?" she asks.

I nod and open my arms and we fold together. I have a feeling like I am holding a baby, something delicate and precious. She holds tighter than I do. Less wary, I suppose.

When we part she looks at Saul and blushes. They don't hug, but they both seem to want to.

"Thank you for coming," she says, speaking now to him.

"Are you all right?" he asks. "What is happening?"

"Sammy left just before I called you."

"What did he say?"

"Nothing! I woke up and he was gone."

"Where did he go?"

"I don't know!"

"Do you have any idea?" I ask.

"He was tracking a man. A Nazi. Sammy put an app on his phone."

We all turn to the sound of tires on gravel. Van in his Roseville Police car is coming up the driveway.

"Who is that?" says Aviva, stepping back.

"We know him," I say. "He found Pessie. He's a good guy."

She looks at Saul.

"Isaac is in the hospital," says Saul. "You were right, Aviva. Whoever vandalized your home came back."

"In the hospital?"

"He will be all right," says Saul. "But he was badly burned."

Aviva puts her hand on her forehead and scrunches her face as though she is trying to lift something very heavy. Van pulls right up to the end of the driveway. As he steps out of the car, Saul says, "He left just before she called."

Van sits back down and grabs the mouthpiece of his radio.

"Is he armed?" asks Van.

Aviva doesn't answer.

"Aviva," says Saul, "please tell him."

"I don't know!"

"Does he own a gun?" asks Van.

She shakes her head but too quickly. The answer is yes. "Please," she says. "He is not going to hurt anyone. He wants to *help*!"

"What kind of car is he driving?"

"I know about the police in Roseville," says Aviva. "I am not going to tell you anything!"

Van's radio screams to life. *Beep beep beep* and a dispatcher's voice.

"All units all units. We have an active shooter at 67 Hillcrest in Roseville. Repeat: Active shooter. All units respond."

For a moment, we all just stare at the radio, and then Van presses a button on his mouthpiece and says he is en route.

"Stay here," says Van but we are already opening the doors on Saul's car. Aviva in the back, Saul and me in the front. Van switches on his lights and siren; he can't keep us from following. I get on my GPS and find 67 Hillcrest. We are forty miles away. Google says the address belongs to something named Toras David.

"It's called Toras David," I say.

"That's the yeshiva," says Aviva. "Sammy's yeshiva." I turn around to look at her. She is clenching her jaw. I reach over the seat and put my hand on her knee. It's going to be all right, I want to say, stupidly.

As we pass through the EZ Pass booth on the Thruway, my phone rings. It's Mike at the city desk.

"We're hearing there's an active shooter situation in Roseville," he says. "How close are you?"

"I'm on my way. Maybe half an hour. It's a yeshiva."

"We know. Photo will call you. Get everything you can from the scene. I've got a report of at least one person dead. It's usually the shooter, but it could be anything. Did you work Newtown?"

"Not the scene," I say. I was in the *Trib* office, actually, when the first reports of a shooting at Sandy Hook Elementary came in. It was a Friday and I wanted to turn in my weekly timecard before my shift. I remember everyone standing around looking at the TVs above the city desk. First it was just a teacher shot in the foot, and then a whole classroom of six-year-olds missing. I'll never forget the quiet that dropped over the newsroom when the words "at least twenty first-graders" flashed across the screens. It was just a few seconds, but everything stopped as we all began to catch glimpses in our minds of what "at least twenty first-graders" at the wrong end of a gun looked like. And then one of the women on the copy desk threw up. Her daughter was in first grade there. It wasn't until several hours later that she got word her little girl survived, kept safe by her teacher in a bathroom stall as Adam Lanza picked off his prey.

"We need a victim count. Dead and injured. Number of shooters. Weapons. This is where your girl lived, right? You know it a little?"

"Yeah," I say, thinking: what, exactly, do I know?

"School shootings are a clusterfuck. With the Jewish angle this'll be national in an hour. It's in our backyard and we need to own it, so feed everything back as soon as you get it. Cathy's lead on rewrite. Get whatever the cops on the scene will tell you, which won't be much. Take photos.

Talk to anybody you see. When did the shooting start? What did they hear? You don't speak Yiddish do you?"

"No," I say. "But I'm with someone who does."

"Great," he says. "Keep your phone by you. I'm sending Lindsay and Will. They'll be there in an hour, maybe two. Work the scene for now. Once we start getting names we'll door-knock. A lot of what you hear at first is gonna be wrong. At the Sikh Temple shooting we initially reported fifteen dead and it was only five or six. I'd like to avoid that. Makes us look bad. Usually the shooter is dead by the time we show up, but not always. This could turn into a hostage thing. What we need is a name. Once we get confirmation on a name we run with it. So: name and body count."

He's about to hang up. "Mike!"

"What?"

"I think I might be related to somebody involved in this."

"*What?* What does that mean?"

"It's a long story." I look at Saul. He nods.

"Tell it to me fast."

"The guy who I think killed Pessie, that girl I wrote about?"

"Faster."

"My uncle was dating the guy's son."

"Your uncle?"

"But I've never met him. I was . . ." Fuck! "I never knew my mom and it turns out she had a brother. That's this guy. I just found out."

"Which guy? The guy who killed the girl?"

"No, the guy who dated the guy whose dad might have killed the girl." Jesus, that sounds ridiculous. "But I don't have it on the record."

"What are you talking about? Do you have a name?"

I turn to Aviva, who is looking at me with unfocused eyes. She appears dazed, like she's concentrating so hard she's about to pass out. Is that what I look like when I'm lost in fear?

"I don't . . ."

"You never met him? You swear to God, Rebekah. If you lie to me you are fair game. If you lie to me *you* become the story. I will not protect you."

"I'm not lying. But listen. It's possible he's on the scene. With a gun."

"Your uncle might be the shooter?"

"I think the shooter might be named Conrad Hall. Call Larry, he knows him. I mean, he's covered him. He's an ex-con. Aryan Nation, that shit."

"And now he's shooting Jews in New York?" I can hear Mike typing. "Conrad Hall, you said? Traditional spelling?"

"Yes. And he has a son. Hank. Hank Hall. It could be him, too."

"Is this connected to the New Paltz thing last night?"

"Maybe," I say. "I mean, don't print these names. I'm just saying if they come up. It's a possibility."

"And what about your uncle?"

"What about him?"

"I need his name."

I hesitate. Mike was kind of a douche to me back in January when he was worried I'd make him look bad with the managing editor. But he didn't hold a grudge. And now he's asking me to trust him.

"I'm not going to print it," he says. "I'm just going to background it. If he's the shooter, we'll be ready."

I turn away from Aviva and lower my voice. "Samuel Kagan."

"I won't run it without telling you first," he says. "If he's the shooter, you're off the story. If he's not the shooter but he's connected, we need an interview."

"Okay." I'll worry about whether I can actually deliver that later.

I hang up.

"Why did you say Sammy's name?" asks Aviva. "Who were you talking to?"

"It's okay. It's my editor."

"You cannot put Sammy in the newspaper!" she shrieks, startling me. "He didn't do anything wrong! What are you doing? What do you know!"

"No," I say, stuttering, pulling back from her. "I just have to disclose . . . it's part of my job."

Aviva starts to shake. She pulls her mouth back in grimace and releases a cry.

"Please, *please*, Rebekah," she says, her face crumbling in on itself. "He did not have the advantages you did.

Please! I know he would not do this."

"They won't print it unless it's him. Unless we know for sure. I promise." But I shouldn't promise. The dread spreads through my blood like a hot shot: Mike will do whatever he wants with Sam's name.

"Then why did you give it to him?"

"Aviva," says Saul, gripping the steering wheel with both hands, still going seventy as we plow through the first intersection off the Thruway. "Can you try to call Sammy?"

Aviva wipes her face with her sleeve and puts her phone to her ear. Waits. "He is not picking up."

We can hear the horns and sirens from several streets away. People are running along the main road and up Hillcrest toward the school, lumbering and frantic like a herd. Women tripping over their long skirts. Men's hats flying off. Emergency vehicles are stopped in the middle of the street. Half a dozen men in riot gear—helmets and vests and machine guns; their black pants tucked into combat boots; twenty pounds of equipment attached to their waist—are gathered in a semicircle beside a van marked New York State Police. I see a truck from the bomb squad. I see cars marked Roseville Police and Rockland County Sheriff and Ramapo Police and Nyack Police. The local CBS affiliate is the only news van so far. Saul pulls to one side and stops, blocking in a minivan. I put my laminated *New York Tribune* ID badge around my neck and Saul opens the back door for Aviva, who is staring at her phone.

"Come with me, Aviva," says Saul. He takes her hand and we run together. People are coming from all directions, it seems, running out of apartment doors, galloping through stands of trees, their faces like masks in a horror film; too long, too wide, too red, too pale, too set, too expressive. Women's cries rise above the sirens. What do they know? What did they hear?

"I don't hear shooting," says Saul, breathing hard.

The closer we get to the school, the more people we encounter. People standing along the road, weeping, holding each other. People with cell phones pressed to their ears. They are all wearing the Haredi uniform: all in black or dark blue. I pass an hysterical middle-aged woman, waving her arms, collapsed on the concrete curb. Other women bend over her, trying to pull her up. I pass a man holding a baby, two little girls clutching his legs; one is no higher than his knees, barely able to walk. He screams into a cell phone. Saul leads us past them until we get to the place where the State Police are trying to hold a perimeter, trying to keep these panicked, desperate people from doing what nature and instinct and common sense dictate they do: find their babies.

Somehow, the chaos serves to focus my mind. I have a role here, and I know how to play it.

"Officer!" I shout, my arm up, badge in hand. "I'm from the *Tribune*. Can you tell me if any children were hurt?"

One of the four officers standing at the yellow tape looks at me for a moment, then turns his eyes back to the faces of the crowd he is trying to keep from stampeding past him.

We are being held about two hundred feet from the school entrance in a side parking lot. I move to the very edge of the yellow police tape, which allows a view of the side of the school. I see a small playground, and on the playground, bodies. I count four from where I am standing. Two have people kneeling over them. Behind us, the pop and cry of an ambulance siren and the officers shouting, *Move aside! Move aside!* The medics inch forward and the officers lift the tape. First is an ambulance with Hebrew lettering on the side; the next is marked ROCKLAND COUNTY. And the next. And the next. They move through the crowd and park in front of the playground, blocking the bodies from view. Saul and Aviva are still behind me; Saul on the telephone, Aviva allowing herself to be buoyed by the crowd. People press into her and she sways. The officers become more aggressive. *We need room!* They shout. *Clear out. We need to make room for emergency vehicles! Everybody back!* I stand my ground at the front of the pack as they use the tape to move us back farther, creating a path in and out.

"Is the shooter still alive?" I ask the officer in front of me.

"I don't have any information. You better get back."

"Can you tell me if any children were shot?"

"What did I say? I don't have anything. Now get back."

A woman beside me screams. She has just been given

some kind of news on the telephone. She begins speaking rapidly in Yiddish, telling everyone around her what she knows. A man interrupts her, they argue; everyone seems to be speaking at once, their voices getting louder and louder.

I turn to Saul and Aviva. "What are they saying?"

"The woman said her brother is inside the school and said the shooter is dead," says Saul. "She said he came out of the trees behind the building and fired on the children in the playground. She said at least five are dead. And a teacher."

"The man said ten dead," says Aviva. "And he said there were two men with guns. But he did not say any names. Did he?"

"I didn't hear one," says Saul.

The group starts arguing again and Saul and Aviva turn to listen. A younger woman appears beside me. Everyone around is talking to other people, or talking on their phones, but she is silent, clutching a pillow with a raccoon face on it.

"Do you have a child here?" I ask.

She nods. "You?"

"No," I say. "My name's Rebekah, I'm from the newspaper."

"My Avi is there."

"How old is he?" I ask.

"He is six."

Her wool coat is buttoned improperly. One side juts

against her chin and the other reveals the shirt beneath.

"Why do they not let the children go?" she asks.

"I don't know," I say. And then I think: maybe that is something I can find out. I look over her head for Saul. He is on the phone, Aviva still beside him. I catch his attention and he motions me toward him.

"What's your name?" I ask the woman.

"Henna," she says.

"Stay here, Henna. I'll be back."

I push through the crowd toward Saul and Aviva, dialing Van Keller. No answer. I try again and this time he picks up. We speak over each other: "You're okay?" I ask. "Where are you?" he asks.

"I'm here," I say. He knows what I mean. "Has the shooting stopped?"

"Yes," he says. "Connie Hall is dead. Sam is in custody. It looks like he might have shot Connie. But there's a lot to sort out."

I lower my voice "Is anyone else . . . ?"

"Dead? At least three kids, Rebekah. And two teachers. So far. There are a lot of other people shot."

The first thing I think is, *This will be on the front page tomorrow*. I don't think of it with any kind of pleasure or excitement; it is simply a fact. They'll use the word "Massacre," I imagine. And "Madman." By dinnertime, there will be hundreds of reporters in this little town. Goyim from across the globe will fill every hotel and motel room within twenty miles tomorrow night.

"Why don't they let the kids that are okay go? People are freaking out."

"They're sweeping the school. I think they're worried about timed explosives."

Dylan Klebold and Eric Harris, I remember reading, set bombs all over Columbine High—they just failed to detonate. And James Holmes—*The Dark Knight Rises* shooter—booby-trapped his apartment before he opened fire in a movie theater. What did Connie do?

"These people out here need some information," I say.

"The shooter's dead," he says. "And the kids that that got shot were the older ones. You can tell them that."

"Do you have any idea when they'll let them out?"

"No," he says.

"Can I tell my paper what you said?"

"Yeah," he says. "Don't use my name. Just . . ."

"A police source?"

"Yeah. Fine."

"I'm glad you're okay," I say. "I can't believe this is happening."

"You know what scares me, Rebekah? I can. I really fucking can."

He promises to call me if he gets more news. I elbow back to Henna and tell her what he told me. She nods, but my news about the older boys does little to comfort her. Her face has a strange expression on it, one I don't know if I've ever seen before. It's as if her features have shifted, been knocked sideways by a punch, and she's trying to recover without actually moving. She does not seem to be able to focus her eyes as she speaks. The terror, I think, has altered her appearance, perhaps forever.

Saul and Aviva have stepped back from the crowd. They are standing together, his arms around her, his head on hers. Both of them have their eyes are closed. After a moment, Saul opens his. I wave and he lifts one hand, calling me over. I tell them what Van said and Aviva grabs my hand.

"Sammy did not do this," she says. She's not pleading this time, she is telling. "I know you do not know him. I know you do not know us. But I am telling you, he did not do this."

I decide to believe her. At least for now. I will call in what Van gave me, but I will not call in what I know about Sam's role. They'll get it eventually, of course, but they won't get it from me.

CHAPTER TWENTY-FOUR

REBEKAH

The shooting at the yeshiva becomes known as "The Playground Shooting" or "Toras David" or just "Roseville," depending on the publication. Connie Hall killed seven people that day. Four students and three adults. Fewer casualties than Oklahoma City or Virginia Tech or Newtown or Aurora or Columbine, but more than Wade Michael Page slaughtered at the Sikh Temple in Oak Creek, Wisconsin, and the same number that One L. Goh gunned down at Oikos University in Oakland almost exactly a year before.

The children were, as Van initially told me, from one of the older classes. Their instructor was running late and they stayed on the playground while the other students were ushered inside for class. It was a nice morning, after all. Nearly fifty degrees and sunny. There were three acres of wooded land behind the school building, and that's where Connie hid. He came out, dressed in a t-shirt that read GOD HATES FAGS beneath green Army fatigues, shooting an AR-15. He hit thirteen-year-old Mayer Klein first. Mayer, whose bar mitzvah was to be the next weekend, was hanging from the monkey bars trying to do a third pull-up when Connie shot him in the back. The tardy instructor, twenty-six-year-old father of three, Shimon Schwartz, who had just reached the school, ran to Mayer, and was killed for it. Shot once in the stomach, once in the neck. It wasn't like Newtown, where Adam Lanza had the kids inside classrooms, like fish in a barrel. The boys of Toras David ran, and they ran fast. Four weren't recovered for more than twelve hours; they were huddled together almost a mile away behind a self-storage warehouse, their clothing torn and mud-thick. Dovid Blau, twelve, and Aaron Siegel, thirteen, made it nearly fifty feet into the trees before Connie got them. Dovid died there, after a bullet pierced his spleen; Aaron fell with a shot to his spine, and will never walk again. Twelve-year-old Joel Silverman, the boy everyone called a hero afterward, pushed four fright-frozen friends from the playground's mini suspension bridge as Connie came toward them. He paid for his selflessness with a shot to the side, which ripped through his liver and burst open his heart. Joel was an only child; his mother, Devorah, had suffered four miscarriages and a stillbirth before having him. When he was a year old, doctors discovered polyps on her ovaries and insisted on a hysterectomy. Three months after the shooting, she jumped in front of the M train at Marcy Avenue. Her husband never remarried.

Connie got just one of the boys Joel pushed before being shot: thirteen-year-old Zev Lowenstein. Zev took a bullet to the thigh and died at the hospital. He ran slower than his friends because of a birth defect that left one leg shorter than the other.

Instructor Abe Greenwald, forty, a father of six, originally thought the shooting was fireworks set off by a misbehaving boy. He came outside to investigate, and three bullets tore through his chest before he'd made four steps out the side door. The last person Connie killed was Abe's brother-in-law, Yosef Schwartz, nineteen. Yosef ran out after Abe, who was married to his sister. He saw the carnage—boys splayed over the new blue and beige playground equipment, screams coming from every direction, and a man dressed like a soldier, walking among it all—and for whatever reason could not keep himself from trying to stop it. The boys watching from inside said he went running, arms waving, shouting for the man to stop. Connie shot him six times, like he was a paper practice target.

Nechemaya also took one of Connie Hall's bullets. After getting my message the night before, he drove to the yeshiva, remembering that it had been the target of previous vandalism. He parked on the opposite side of the school from the playground, the side at the intersection of two roads. If anyone suspicious came driving up, he would see them. But Connie parked his truck a mile away and walked in through the trees. When the shooting started, Nechemaya ran toward the noise. Connie shot him in the shoulder, sending him to the ground. He hit his head on the concrete surrounding the sandbox and blacked out.

The bullet missed any major arteries and when paramedics took his pulse they realized he was still alive.

It was acknowledged almost immediately that if Sam Kagan hadn't shot Connie Hall while he reloaded his rifle, he would probably have killed a lot more people. Connie was wearing a bulletproof vest beneath his jacket. He was strapped with three hundred rounds of ammunition, and carrying two 9mm handguns in addition to the AR-15. Nechemaya called 911 as soon as he heard the shots, and three minutes later another call came in from inside the yeshiva, but it took six minutes for the first deputy to arrive—and the door to the school was unlocked.

Sam, who police found attempting to fashion a tourniquet around Zev Lowenstein's leg, was handcuffed and interviewed. Witnesses say that he, too, came out of the woods, and that he fired three shots in quick succession. Physical evidence bore this out. Sam's Smith & Wesson 9mm was originally purchased by a pharmacist at a Georgia gun store in 2004 and made its way to New York through a series of legal, and illegal, transfers. The gun had three bullets missing, and Connie had three bullets in him. Just as Aviva told me and Saul, Sam had surreptitiously installed a GPS tracking application on Connie's phone, which led him to Roseville that morning. Connie left his phone in the truck, though, and Sam lost track of him in the predawn woods. When the shooting started, he ran toward the noise.

Hank and Nan told police that Sam knew about the

plot against Roseville—although, they admitted, not the exact target—and was on board until Pessie died. Sam and Mellie denied this, however. Months later, when I finally interview her on the record, Mellie tells me that she knows she should have sounded the alarm sooner and that speaking up for Sam was her way of making up for it. Sam was arrested on gun and conspiracy charges, but with public opinion firmly on his side, in the end, prosecutors just didn't think they could convince a jury that a Jew would plot to do such a thing to his fellow Jews.

Nechemaya recovered quickly and immediately became a spokesperson for Roseville. He told Anderson Cooper and Dr. Phil and Charlie Rose and anyone who would listen—and, until the Tsarnaev brothers blew up the finish line of the Boston Marathon two weeks later, the world was listening—that the community supported Sam entirely. He said that they had hired an attorney to represent him and that the rumors he was connected to the Halls were overblown. Whenever he could, Nechemaya said Pessie's name. *Pessie Goldin was the first victim in Roseville,* he said on CNN and Fox and the BBC. *If corrupt, anti-Semitic local authorities had not ignored her death, this tragedy may never have happened.*

Chief John Gregory resigned before they could fire him, and was indicted on charges of official corruption, witness tampering, evidence tampering, and conspiracy to commit a terrorist act. The last charge didn't stick; there wasn't really evidence that Gregory knew what Connie was planning. It did stick, however, to both Hank Hall and no-legged Grandma Nan. Mellie's lawyer—a regular "contributor" on cable news—managed to convince the state that her client was terrified of Hank and his father, virtually a hostage in her home, and that she was a hero for alerting authorities "the minute she realized" what Connie had planned. She had her second baby in shackles, lost custody of Eva to the state, and, in exchange for ten years in prison, made a compelling—if occasionally hostile—witness against what was left of the Hall family. Mellie testified about how the father of her children had tried—and failed—to build a bomb that could be detonated remotely, and that Nan was routinely used as a straw purchaser for firearms. Nancy Grace called her the "terrorist tart" and excoriated prosecutors for giving her a deal. During the trial, Mellie told the court that she initially "thought they were joking" all the times Connie and Hank talked through scenarios about how to achieve the highest number of dead Jews: *Should we put the bomb on a bus? Or in a building?* For two days #Ithoughttheywerejoking trended on Twitter, with people posting pictures of Hitler and Osama bin Laden ("The guys with the box cutters said they were taking over the plane, but #Ithoughttheywerejoking"), then ever-more gruesome images of dead bodies ("The cops said not to reach into my waistband, but #Ithoughttheywerejoking"; "KKK said not to look at a white girl, but #Ithoughttheywerejoking").

Halfway through the trial, Hank changed his plea to guilty and took a life without parole sentence. He described Pessie's death to authorities, and, perhaps because his story matched Ryan's and Sam's, they believed him. Hank admitted they'd given up the plan to place an explosive device beneath the yeshiva's school bus because, just as Mellie had told me, he was a fucking idiot and couldn't make a bomb.

When prosecutors asked him why Connie targeted innocent children, Hank simply said, "He knew shooting up a playground would get a lot of attention and he wanted people to remember."

Roseville provided an angle for every journalist. Anti-Semitism, homophobia, gun control, child sex abuse, police corruption, prison gangs, the right-wing "patriot" movement; a health reporter out of Boston even did a series of articles looking at how terminal cancer diagnoses are delivered and whether dying patients should be monitored for changes in their mental health. The NRA was quick to trumpet the fact that Connie did not commit suicide or find himself in handcuffs, but rather was taken down by "a good guy with a gun." After a virtual arsenal of unregistered weapons was found at the Hall compound, activists on both sides of the gun control debate seized on the fact that an ex-con with ties to an extremist hate group was not only armed to the teeth in a state with new gun laws, but at the center of a multi-state gun trafficking organization no one in law enforcement was paying attention to. People inclined to loosen regulation saw Connie's ability to gather so many weapons as an example of the ineffectiveness of gun control laws. The other side argued that Connie's arsenal exposed loopholes that needed to be closed and an "iron pipeline" that needed to be thwarted. President Obama called the deaths "horrific" and sent his highest-ranking Jewish staffer to the funerals. New York Governor Andrew Cuomo pledged funds for a memorial. There was a lot of talk about cracking down on right-wing hate groups and the Aryan Nations. The feds made a handful of arrests, but soon both law enforcement and the media turned their attention back to the threat of domestic terror inspired by Islamic fundamentalism.

Mike pulled me off the story at noon on the day of the shooting, right after the Associated Press reported Sam's name. I passed contact information for Aviva and Isaac's New Paltz neighbors to the Albany stringer and the *Trib* got exclusives from them. Matty gave the photo desk a picture he took of the swastika the Halls spraypainted on the yellow house and it got more than five million hits.

Despite my promise in the car on the way to the scene, I did not deliver an interview with Sam. Through Aviva, I warned him and the rest of the Kagans not to say a word to the press, and they took my advice. It wasn't a tough sell; they were leveled by the shooting and their connection to it. Ashamed and guilt-sick, none seemed able to find solace in the fact that, were it not for Sam, many more people would have died. The media camped out in front of Eli and Penina's apartment for ten days, but no one came outside. Not once. Neighbors brought food and were accosted, but declined to comment. On the afternoon of the Boston Marathon bombing the reporters finally packed up and left. But the damage was done. Old Avram was dead of a stroke within a month. Diny's boys were expelled from yeshiva for fighting. A year after the shooting, Aviva was Sam's only relative still in the U.S; the rest of the Kagans made *aliyah* and try to rebuild in Israel.

Within a few days, rumors about Sam and Ryan and the "real" reason why Roseville—not Kiryas Joel or Williamsburg or Lakewood—was the target of Connie's wrath began to surface. Friends of friends told ravenous cable news producers that Sam was "in a relationship" with Connie's son—but neither gave an interview, and without confirmation and more details, the story eventually fizzled. Mike asked me about it constantly, but I shut him down. *The family won't talk,* I kept saying. I didn't tell him that I also warned Kaitlyn that the best way to help her friends was to stay away from reporters. She must have given my advice to other people who were close with Sam and Ryan because their small circle closed ranks.

People who knew Connie Hall, however, practically lined up to tell their stories. None of them had any idea Connie had a gay son, but just about everyone in the county (in a couple counties, actually) had apparently heard Connie Hall threaten to kill people. That's what he did, people told the reporters. He got drunk and spouted off about the niggers and liberals and fags he wanted to off. No one seemed surprised he'd finally made good on his threats—especially once they heard about the cancer—but the specific target, and the fact that he murdered children, came as a shock. Or so they said.

In the rest of New York, the focus became seeking forgiveness from the Jews of Roseville. Goyim throughout the state were ashamed of Connie, and even those who had been critical of the Haredi influx in the area took great pains to distance themselves from his ideas. There was a rush to show support and sympathy for the traumatized community. As the town sat shiva, religious organizations throughout the state mobilized to prepare and deliver kosher food, run errands, make phone calls, and provide rides on the Sabbath. Donations poured in: more than a quarter of a million dollars in less than a week to help bury the dead, provide counseling, and create a trust fund for the victims and their families. A month after the shooting, an interfaith group met at Nechemaya's home to discuss extending and strengthening the relationships forged in sorrow.

At just after 2:00 P.M. on the day of the shooting, police let the boys out of the yeshiva. They came out holding hands, dozens of them in one long line led by a member of the State Police. They were tiny and tall. Boys as young as four and as old as fourteen, scores of them, all dressed alike, all silent, struck mute by what they'd endured. The parents had by then been moved away from the yeshiva, down the hill and toward the parking lot of a nearby shul. At the edge of the school grounds, the Statie handed the boys off to a group of men from the community, and they all started running—as desperate to get back to their families as their families were to get to them.

I watched the reunions, trying not to gawk at the primitive, almost grotesque displays of emotion erupting all around me. I remember thinking, *My job is to approach these people.* Did you see the shooter? Do you know anyone who died? How will your community recover? But I couldn't do it. Instead, I just stood and watched, and through the crush of bodies and the confusion, I spotted Henna, her arms wrapped around a little boy clutching a raccoon pillow.

CHAPTER TWENTY-FIVE

REBEKAH

A few hours after the shooting, I text my dad to tell him I'm okay and we agree to talk later that night. When he calls, I start with Aviva. The where and when and how. I tell him what I know, which isn't much: that she lives in a house with another ex-Jew in a town about two hours north of the city; that she cleans houses for a living; that she has been estranged from her family since leaving us, and that her baby brother shot Connie Hall this morning.

"Does she have . . . other family?" he asks.

He means a husband, children, and I realize I don't know for certain. I think back to what Saul said about Isaac when Aviva was missing: *I think he's the only one she has to worry about her.*

"She seems pretty alone, Dad."

"Do you think you'll continue to see her?" he asks.

"Yeah," I say. "Though I guess I don't know how much. Do you want me to . . . tell her anything. From you?"

"Oh, I don't think so, Rebekah," he says. "But thank you for asking."

"I love you, Dad," I say.

"I love you, too."

Despite being officially off the story, I stay upstate for a week after the shooting. Almost a thousand dollars on my credit card, but at least it's tax deductible. I keep my notebook out at all times, scribbling notes about what I see and hear, engaging in conversation with anyone I can. With no pressure to call new information in to the city desk every couple hours, I actually get to absorb what people are saying—not just listen for good quotes. The rest of the news corps don't have this luxury. Roseville is a city in shock. The few Haredi who brave the media siege to do their own shopping or try to get back to work ignore the reporters entirely, and everyone is complaining that their editors and producers in Atlanta and L.A. and London don't get it.

At an ice cream parlor on Roseville's main street—which becomes a gathering spot for journalists because of its free Wi-Fi and electrical outlets—I meet a woman from a nonprofit called the Center on Culture, Crime and the Media. She tells me that she travels around the world—from Moscow to Mexico City to Roseville—providing resources and leading workshops on how to cover culturally sensitive crimes. I tell her my story and she encourages me to apply for an upcoming fellowship.

"Your connection to the story and this community could make for a really compelling piece," she says, and gives me her card.

It is at this same ice cream shop that Aviva and I finally

have an hour to spend alone together—after all the victims are in the ground, after she's been questioned and released, after she uses the last of her savings to hire a contractor to make the yellow house livable again, and after she offers her assistance to Eli and Penina, who are too broken and needy not to accept her help. I arrive first and focus my anxiety on sitting up straight so that I appear confident and nonchalant when she walks in. I want to show her what a successful, healthy woman I am. It's mid-afternoon and the sun shines in through the shop window, making it hard to see who is outside. Aviva is right on time, and as soon as I see her I realize that what I want isn't really for her to be impressed with me. What I want is for her to acknowledge me—impressive or disappointing. I want her to be forced to contend not just with the memory of me, and what she did to me, but the real live almost grown-up me. She avoided contending with me for more than twenty years, and now I've got her. Does she love me? Maybe. What does love look like on a person's face?

We embrace tentatively and she orders a coffee at the counter. I watch her, noticing everything. The faded faux-leather sack that is her purse, the way she bends over slightly to dig exact change out of a zippered pouch in her wallet. The fact that she speaks to the woman at the counter in Yiddish, and puts sugar but not milk in her mug.

"You must have so many questions," she says to me. She looks me in the eye for a moment, and then looks down. She does not wait for me to answer. "With me in your life you would never have become what you have become. You would not have had peace in your home. I am not frum but I was not like your father and his family and there would have been terrible strife."

It's such a reasonable explanation it almost makes me laugh. Isn't there always strife? Does she really not understand that her ghost, always among us, created at least as much strife as a physical body?

"But I know," she continues, her voice quieter now, "I know that what I did was a sin. I sinned against you, Rebekah. I sinned against your father. I have tried for many years to think of it as something else. Immaturity, or fear, or mental illness. And it was those. But mostly it was a sin. A grave sin. I carry it with me every day. But," and here she pauses, and looks at me, "I also carry my memories of you. Like the way you loved to point at things. Lights on the ceiling or a dog on the street, or even just me. You would point at me and open your mouth like you'd found something wonderful. And after you sneezed, you always looked happy." She giggles, thinking back. "Like you'd done something very silly and fun." She takes a deep breath and the giggles turn to tears. Her chin crumbles. She puts her hand on her heart. "If not for those bits, Rebekah, the sin would have killed me."

I reach over and put my hand on her elbow.

"I'm glad it didn't kill you," I say.

She wipes her eyes. "Are you happy with your life, Rebekah?"

Three weeks ago I was as low as I've ever been. I felt guilty and burdened and victimized and broken. And then I got back to work, and all the scary things didn't seem so scary.

"Yeah," I say. "I've got it pretty good, I think."

We stay in the ice cream shop for two hours. I tell her about Iris and Dad and my stepmom Maria, and my brother Deacon. I show her photos on my phone, and she looks at them with genuine interest. She tells me about her ex-husband, and her mother, and her cousin Gitty—the first person she told about me—who contracted HIV and died of pneumonia when she was just thirty. She tells me that she talked to me every day for twenty-three years, in her head. She says that she asked me for advice—*What do you think your mommy should do, Rebekah?*

"I know it is silly," she says. "But I think you helped me. You did not steer me wrong."

I don't ask her if she ever asked the me in her head if she should come back to us; or even just send a letter saying she was alive. I will ask her, though. Someday.

As we get up to leave, Aviva waves at the woman behind the counter.

"Excuse me," she says, handing the woman her phone. "Will you please take a picture of me and my daughter?"

By the beginning of May, I am back working shifts at the *Trib,* but I'm out on the street again, not in the office. It's better for everybody. Mike doesn't have to be reminded of my breaking-news betrayal by actually seeing my face, and I get to return to what I really like about this job: new people and new places. Iris gets promoted to assistant beauty editor and I invite Van Keller to the bar where Brice throws her a party. We've stayed in touch since Roseville. He keeps me updated on the appointment of a new police chief and stepped up efforts to engage with the Jewish community, and I "vouched" for him with Nechemaya and the rebbe. He arrives at the bar with a friend and we all have a nice time. There is an attraction, but for now, at least, neither of us acts on it.

The next afternoon, as Iris and I linger over bottomless Bloody Marys at a Park Slope brunch place, Aviva calls and invites me upstate for Shabbos dinner.

"Sammy wants to meet you," she says.

When I hang up, Iris is grinning.

"What?"

"Your face changes when you talk to her."

"No it doesn't," I say, but I know she's right. Aviva and I have been developing a kind of relationship via text message. She sent me pictures of the yellow house when the contractor finished with it, and she updates me on Sam and Ryan, who have moved in. Sam has some fairly complicated legal issues to settle. Carrying and shooting an illegal firearm—even at a man in the midst of the mass murder of children—was a violation of his parole, and although Aviva says the prosecutor appears willing to find a solution that does not involve prison time, Sam has to be extremely careful about what he says and where he goes until, as she puts it, "the ink is dry on the paper." She orders a subscription to the *Trib* and when she sees my byline, she writes. Her texts are formal, like little letters: *Dear Rebekah* . . . And she always signs her name at the end: *Aviva*. I read the messages over and over again. I find myself daydreaming about her. Replaying our talk in the ice cream shop; replaying the way it felt when she put her arms around me that first time. I've started having dreams where I run to her, and I know she'll be there. I run and she catches me, sweeping me up into her arms like I'm a child. The best part of the dreams is the sense of safety I feel, and the surprise of that safety. Like, *Look, she was here all along*. People say that parents fall in love with their children when they first set eyes on them. Could the reverse be true, too?

"I'm happy for you," Iris says. "I feel like, maybe, this is the start of you really moving on."

"Growing up," I offer.

"Yeah?"

"I guess it took actually seeing her to understand why she did what she did."

"Do you think you understand?"

"I think she got born into the wrong life. Who knows what that does to a person? I guess I can't ever *really* understand, but I think it's possible that if I was in her shoes—if I'd been raised how she was raised—I might have done the same thing."

Iris looks hard at me. "I don't think you would have, Rebekah. I don't think so for a second."

I call Saul the next day to tell him about Aviva's invitation, but he knows already.

"I'm going, too," he says. "Can you get off work a little early? I'll drive us both."

Four days later we battle Friday traffic along the West Side Highway and across the George Washington Bridge.

"Everybody going home for Shabbos," says Saul, nodding to the minivan creeping beside us. The driver is wearing sidecurls and a black hat.

"I wonder if he's going to Roseville," I say.

"Perhaps," says Saul.

"Do you ever think we could have stopped it—if we'd moved faster with Pessie?"

"Do you?"

"I think about it a lot," I say, which is kind of an understatement. I think about it all the time. I replay every interview, every phone call, every Google search. In my dreams, I see Connie and Nan at the truck and the truck is bigger than it should be. And instead of taking the wheelchair out of the back, I see Connie take out the AR-15. He laughs and I think, *But it looked like a wheelchair! How could I have missed it?* What I haven't told anyone is that I've developed a sort of—how should I say it?—*response* to pickup trucks. I have this feeling that they're coming to get me, like that demon car Stephen King wrote about. Twice since the shooting I've been sent to cover pedestrian death scenes. The first one was an eight-year-old boy on the east side of Prospect Park. Kid ran into the crosswalk after his scooter and a woman in an SUV turned without looking. His parents watched the whole thing. A couple weeks after, it was a man who worked at a fix-a-flat on Flatbush. He was opening up at 6:00 A.M. when some drunk doing sixty-five in a sports car, after a night who knows where, lost control, jumped the curb, and pinned him against the storefront. The second driver fled the scene, but the woman who killed the kid stopped. I pitched Mike a story about pedestrian fatalities, and I now know that around 130 people get killed in the city each year while "crossing the street." For whatever reason, this, plus the memory of Connie's truck, combined inside me to create an almost instant anxiety attack almost every time I see a pickup. I think: here he comes. I go hot and cold; heart stopped for a moment. A year ago, the fright would have knocked me out. I'd have thrown up, or run home. Now I'm learning to right myself, by myself. I don't know if I'm getting stronger, or just harder, but either way I have found that I can I keep working. Keep walking. Sometimes, yes, I take a pill. I went back to Anna—the student psychiatrist at Columbia—and she asked me if I thought the "he" coming to get me in the truck might be the guilt I feel about my role in Roseville. I thought that was a good question.

I don't say any of this out loud to Saul. I haven't even said it to Iris. And yet, perhaps they know.

"There is a lot of guilt to go around," he continues when I don't elaborate. "But I don't think much of it rests on your shoulders."

We ride without speaking for a while. The trees along the parkway that were still bare a month ago are popping green now. When we pass the sign announcing the exit to Roseville, Saul breaks the silence.

"We all played a role, I think. I could have found your mother years ago. It only took a few phone calls. I did not make those calls because I felt she would come to me—to us—when she was ready. But she was waiting for us." He sighs. "Perhaps if I had been in her life sooner I might have helped her with Sammy."

"Do you think you'll be in her life now?"

"I would like to be," Saul says slowly. "I think she would like me to be. But you are the most important thing to her right now. You and Sam. And if you are uncomfortable with our . . . being in each other's lives, she has made it very clear that that is her priority."

I guess I'd always sensed that Saul's relationship with Aviva might have been romantic. I didn't ask for details, though, and he didn't offer. He's still not offering, exactly, but I suppose there's time for that.

"So," I say, "I'm, like, your potential cock block?"

Saul shakes his head, smiling. "I wish you didn't talk like that, Rebekah."

"You sound like my dad," I say.

"Your dad," Saul says, "is a smart man."

Aviva answers the door and the first thing I notice is that she has cut her hair. It's not as short as mine, but instead of falling down her back like it did when we met, it now ends just above her shoulders. She sees me looking and brings her hand to it, self-consciously.

"What do you think?" she says.

"I like it." My own hair has grown through the original buzz cut and the secondary pixie cut into an awkward kind of preteen boy's 'do. It keeps wanting to part on the side, and because it's so thick it puffs out instead of falling down over my ears and neck. Iris is helping me experiment with gel, and she says that in a couple months she can get me in at a fancy salon that'll make it look better. We'll see.

"You inspired me," says Aviva, smiling.

"You could be sisters," says Saul.

Aviva waves off his compliment and opens her arms for a hug.

"I am so glad you agreed to come visit," she says. "Saul told me you are very independent. I do not want to intrude on your life. But if you don't mind, I'd like to . . . get to know you."

She looks up, but her face is angled down, like she's girding herself for a slap, and I realize that she is afraid of me in a way I have never been of her. Her abandonment made her frightening to me, a ghost that punched me in the face every time I thought of her. If she did it once she could do it again. But it didn't occur to me that as the one who was wronged, the one from whom forgiveness is sought, I have tremendous power over her. She knows what it is like to miss me, but not to be rejected by me. Some part of me still hates her, and a bigger part of me is still afraid of who she really is and how she might hurt me again, but she is no longer a monster or nightmare spirit poisoning me with the mystery of where she is and why she left. She is, just like me, only a woman trying to carve out a little space for her dreams.

"That sounds good," I say, smiling hard, pushing my mouth up as I try to control my face, which is threatening to fold and let free a lifetime's worth of sobbing. Sobbing I'd rather do alone.

Aviva ushers us into the living room where Isaac is sitting in an old leather armchair, picking at a plastic grocery store platter of cheese and crackers and fruit. White gauze is still wrapped around his arm—I imagine he'll be changing bandages for a while—but he looks otherwise healthy, and happy to see us.

We hear footsteps upstairs and down come Sam and Ryan. I didn't expect my uncle to look like the Haredi men in Borough Park or Roseville, but neither did I expect him to look so utterly different. His strawberry-blond hair is gelled into an inch-high Mohawk and he has the chest and arms of a devoted body-builder. Ryan's look is All-American—he's grown a neat goatee and his jeans look pressed—but Sam is almost punk. He has several earrings in each ear, and is wearing a leather wrist cuff and threadbare David Bowie t-shirt. His Adam's apple is prominent, straining the pale skin on his neck.

"You're my niece," he says.

"I am," I say.

Sam tries to smile, but he is clearly miserable; his shoulders hunched over and his face a blotchy, pimpled mess, red from stress and lack of sleep, I imagine.

"Thank you for not writing about us," he says.

"Of course," I say.

"Not of course. You didn't have to do that. I mean, you don't know us. It's your job."

"It's fine," I say. "You guys had enough to deal with."

Aviva and Saul smile at me. They sit next to each other on the sofa.

"Sit down, Sammy," says Aviva, patting the cushion next to her.

Sam remains standing. He looks at Ryan.

"Sam and I have something we want to tell you," says Ryan.

"You start," says Sam, his eyes on the floor.

"It's my fault," Ryan says.

"Shut up," says Sam. "You know it's not. Just tell them."

Ryan inhales. "It was back in December. Sam had only been back from prison a month or two. We went out one night and when we got back we had a really bad fight." He looks at Sam. Sam, if it's possible, looks even more unhappy. I wonder what the fight was about. "We'd taken

E, which didn't help. Sam slept on the couch and the next morning we were both just wandering around the apartment like zombies, trying to feel better. He turned on the TV and that shooting, the one in Connecticut where all the kids died? It was all over the place."

"Newtown," I say. After the copy girl had thrown up in the office, I was sent to the Upper East Side to sit on the apartment building of a man whose daughter was a teacher at the school. They sent stringers to every address of every relative they could find in the city. My guy didn't come home until after my shift was over. I heard his daughter survived.

"Right," he says. "We both kinda got sucked in."

"Me more than you," whispers Sam.

"Whatever," says Ryan. "It was nonstop. You know? The pictures of the kids running and screaming, like, all in a line. And that girl on the cell phone *the exact moment* they tell her that her sister is dead. I tried to get him to turn it off, but he kept saying we had to watch."

"I felt like, those kid are in *pain* and the least we could do was pay attention," says Sam. "I started thinking about how nobody really paid attention to me back then. I was, like, if one of those little goyish kids on the TV came home and said their teacher was making him suck his dick his parents would go to the *cops*. But in Roseville they just pretend it didn't happen so nobody who wasn't Jewish would say anything bad about the community."

"We talked about how growing up for both of us there

was this 'no snitching' thing," says Ryan. "How loyalty—like, no matter what—was the most important thing. My dad always said it was better to go to prison than be a rat."

"What I was pissed about was how adults, like, *need* to keep kids safe," Sam says. "I *needed* somebody to keep me away from him, 'Viva. Or at least to, like, *fight back*. Kill him, or at least lock him up. But nobody did. That's what I was saying. They're pussies."

"Sammy thought my family was strong. He was, like, your dad doesn't take shit from anybody."

"I was a fucking idiot," says Sam, finally sitting down next to his sister.

For a few moments there is silence. Then Sam says to Ryan, "Keep going."

"Okay, so he spent all day, like ten hours, on the couch watching the news and getting high. It was my dad's birthday and there was a party that night. I wasn't planning on going, but I felt like I had to get him out of the apartment. I'd never seen him so down. When we got there, we both started drinking. Sam went straight to the whiskey. The party broke up around two, I think. We'd gone inside my dad's place and that's when Nan started talking about the Jews. She said she'd seen some of them—the ones with the hats—at Home Depot. She was, like, I heard they're trying to take over the school board down in Rockland County . . ."

"And I just, like, went off," interrupts Sam, talking fast

now, like he wants to get to the end. "I was so drunk. I was, like, they're all on welfare and they make the women shave their heads and all the kids get molested because they're so fucked up about sex."

"And they loved it," says Ryan. "They ate it up. My family hates everybody who's not like them, but they don't really know anything about anybody else. So when he started talking they found, like, real *reasons* to hate them. To my dad, Jews were just money-grubbing rats who killed Jesus. Suddenly he's getting all this *detail*. Sam kept calling them a cult. He was, like, somebody should wipe them all out. He was drunk. But my dad and his friends *loved* it. Everybody was, like, *yeah*. And they just kept talking about it, egging each other on to come up with the most fucked up thing they could think of to strike the first blow, start their stupid race war. Nan was, like, you gotta do something people will remember. She was, like, you can't just shoot up a school because that's been done before. And my dad was, like, same thing with a church."

They both stop talking for a minute. And then Sam speaks: "So I said, a playground. Nobody's done a playground."

I open my mouth but manage not to gasp. Sam is shivering. After a moment, he looks at Aviva. She is speechless. We all are.

Sam begins to cry, and beneath his tears, he whispers, "And *Pessie*. If I had just left her alone. If I had cut her off . . . She should have gone her whole long life without ever meeting people like Connie and Hank. But because of me—because she loved me . . ." He can't finish.

Aviva wraps her arms around Sam and he wraps his arms around her. He cries and cries and she rocks him. He pulls away and bends over himself, sobbing. Aviva gets on the floor, kneeling before her baby brother, grasping his hands.

"Look at me, Sammy," she says. "You did not kill Pessie. And you did not kill all those people at the yeshiva. None of us believe this was your fault. You have had more pain in your life than anyone I know, and you will never outrun what you have seen, and what was done to you. But that is not your fault. Our family was happy until I left, Sammy. I broke our family, not you. Not Eli. Not the cook. *My* selfishness created the world you grew up in. I killed Mommy, not you. Do you understand?" Sam is still crying, but he nods. "But we have been given a second chance. *You* have been given a second chance. You can stay with me, or Isaac, wherever we go. Or you can move far away. Whatever you do, I will love you. I will know who you are inside."

"So will I," says Ryan quietly. He puts his hand on Sam's back.

Sam wipes his face and nods. "We were thinking we'd like to get out of New York, at least for a while. Go somewhere warm where nobody knows us." For the first time since he started talking, he looks at me. "We were thinking, maybe, Florida."

ACKNOWLEDGMENTS

Among the best parts of being a published author is the privilege of having very smart people weigh in on and improve your work. I am grateful every day that I can count on my agent, Stephanie Kip Rostan, and Minotaur's Kelley Ragland to tell me the truth and cheer me on.

Thank you, once again, to *48 Hours* executive producer Susan Zirinsky. I simply could not have finished this book on time had you not supported me the entire way.

Thank you to my friends and colleagues at CBSNews.com, especially the *Crimesider* team—Erin Donoghue, Branden Cobb, Barry Leibowitz, and Stephanie Slifer—for putting up with my extended absences and creating a newsroom that feels like home.

Thank you to Chuck Lewis, Wendell Cochran, Lynne Perri, and the rest of the faculty at the American University School of Communications. If I could send Rebekah to get a journalism degree from you, I would.

Thank you to Stephen Handelman, Ted Gest, and Cara Tabachnick at the Center on Media, Crime and Justice.

Working for you at *The Crime Report* was the greatest professional learning experience of my life.

Thank you to Hindy Sabel, Zelda Deutsch, Saul Friedman, and, once again, Pearl Reich, for sharing your stories and your time with me.

In the year since *Invisible City* was published, I have spent a lot of time talking and writing about my Jewish-Lutheran heritage, and sharing fairly intimate details about my upbringing and extended family. Thank you to my parents, Bill and Barbara Dahl, and my sister, Susan Sharer, for encouraging me to tell these stories. I've heard from lots of people how "special" our family must have been to sustain a happy, healthy two-religion home; I tell them, you have no idea.

Thank you to Lori, Libby, and Jerry Bukiewicz. You have loved and supported me from the moment we were introduced. I am lucky to be a part of your family.